"I wasn't suggesting that
you're not bandling this well,"

he said flatly.

"Weren't you?"

"Seeing someone die is tough. Seeing someone murdered is a hundred times worse. Fear isn't an easy thing to live with, and protective custody can be hell on a witness's nerves."

"To say nothing of a marshal's?" she asked dryly.

"Don't try to start a fight with me, Miss Marlowe. You'll lose. I don't fight fair."

Deke's formal use of "Miss Marlowe" grated. She hid behind a carefully composed mask. "Tell me something, marshal."

He had started to leave, but her coolly polite request stopped him.

"What is it about me that you dislike so much?" Her question took him by surprise— she saw it flit across his eyes, then disappear. "At first, I thought maybe you were nasty and ill-tempered with everyone, but you're not—just with me. Why?"

How could he ever tell her that he didn't *dis*like her at all?

Dear Reader,

The holidays are almost here, and with snow whipping through the air and cold winds blowing—at least in my part of the country!—I can't think of anything I'd like more than to escape to a warm climate. Let Barbara Faith help you to do just that in *Lord of the Desert*. Meet an American woman and share her adventures as she is swept into a world of robed sheikhs and sheltering desert dunes. You may not want to come home!

This month's other destinations are equally enticing. The Soviet Union is the setting of Marilyn Tracy's *Blue Ice*, and intrigue and danger are waiting there, despite the current spirit of *glasnost*. Paula Detmer Riggs returns to New Mexico's Santa Ysabel pueblo in *Forgotten Dream*, the story of a man who has forgotten much of his past and no longer has any memory of the woman he once loved—and is destined to love again. Finally, reach *Safe Haven* with Marilyn Pappano. When Tess Marlowe witnesses a murder, her only refuge is a secluded house in the Blue Ridge Mountains —and the embrace of Deputy U.S. Marshal Deke Ramsey.

In coming months, look for new books by such favorite authors as Nora Roberts, Heather Graham Pozzessere and Lee Magner, as well as a special treat in February: four brand-new authors whose debut books will leave you breathless.

Until then, happy holidays and may all your books be good ones.

Leslie J. Wainger
Senior Editor and Editorial Coordinator

MARILYN PAPPANO

Safe Haven

SILHOUETTE·INTIMATE·MOMENTS®

Published by Silhouette Books New York

America's Publisher of Contemporary Romance

SILHOUETTE BOOKS
300 East 42nd St., New York, N.Y. 10017

ISBN: 0-373-07363-1

First Silhouette Books printing December 1990

MARILYN PAPPANO

has been writing as long as she can remember, just for the fun of it, but a few years ago she decided to take her lifelong hobby seriously. She was encouraging a friend to write a romance novel and ended up writing one herself. It was accepted, and she plans to continue as an author for a long time. When she's not involved in writing, she enjoys camping, quilting, sewing and, most of all, reading. Not surprisingly, her favorite books are romance novels.

Her husband is in the navy, and in the course of her marriage, she has lived all over the U.S. Currently, she lives in Georgia with her husband and son.

Chapter 1

"Damn it, I won't do it, I swear! Come on, you've got to believe me! I'm leaving town right now. I just came back to clear out my office. I'm not going to tell them anything!"

The angry shout echoed eerily in the nearly empty building, bringing Tess Marlowe to a sudden stop. She leaned over the four-foot-high wall that separated the hallways and offices of the Bradley Building from the atrium extending to the roof, and saw three figures in the lobby two floors below.

It was one of the men, the younger one, who had shouted. Now he raked his fingers through his hair and muttered something, to which the second man, this one stout and gray-haired, responded with a rapid, obviously emotion-charged speech of his own. The third member of the group, a woman, was standing at an angle, all but a small portion of her face hidden from Tess, and her hands were clasped tightly behind her back.

Ordinarily, Tess would have been amused by the staging of such a public scene, but not tonight. The hour was too late, the building too empty, and the men below too angry. This wasn't just an argument. This exchange was so heated that she could feel the tension in the air, and there had been fear in the young man's voice. Something terrible was going on below.

She stepped back from the low wall, out of sight once more, and searched for a way to delay her departure. Those people were standing only a few feet in front of the bank of elevators and the stairs; there was no way she could leave without walking right past them, and instinct told her that wasn't a good idea—not tonight.

She was probably overreacting, she thought with an uneasy smile. It had been a long day, filled with problem after problem and topped by two hours of overtime. She was tired, frustrated, hungry and longing to be at home, warm and fed and tucked in for the night, and all those things combined were making her read more into the situation downstairs than was really there.

What she'd seen below was probably a simple disagreement between two hot-tempered people. They would yell at each other, the anger would pass, and everything would be all right again. She repeated that to herself...but she didn't believe it.

At that instant there was another shout—the same voice, but this time higher-pitched, sharper, desperate. "What the hell are you doing?" he demanded, and as Tess leaned over the wall to look again, a gunshot sounded. She stared in horror as the young man fell back half a dozen feet, landing in a careless sprawl half inside the fountain that filled the center of the lobby. A bloodstain, red and obscene, spread over his white shirt.

The woman screamed, then clamped her hands over her mouth and swiftly looked around, giving Tess a brief glimpse of her face. Then the woman turned on the older man, whose beefy hand almost enveloped the gun he held, and grabbed his arm, pulling at him. "What have you done, Tony?" she shrieked. "My God, are you crazy?"

The man shook her off, walked over to the fountain, pointed the gun at the man lying there and pulled the trigger once more. Tess spun around, sliding bonelessly to the floor, but not before she'd seen the bubbling water in the fountain turn red. Her heart was pounding, her blood was rushing in her ears, and she realized that she was going to be ill. She pressed her hands to her mouth, struggling not to make any sound that might alert the two people below to her presence, struggling not to cry out.

She didn't know how long she sat there, but finally she got to her knees, then stood up, leaning against the wall for support. There was no sign of the other two people below, just the body and the red water in the fountain. Tess found the purse she'd dropped and started back toward her office, walking faster and faster until she was running. Once inside, she locked the door behind her and made a quick dash for the bathroom.

Then she rinsed her mouth, walked to the phone and dialed 911. "There's been a murder," she whispered when the dispatcher came on the line. "In the lobby of the Bradley Building."

Deacon Ramsey glanced only briefly at the body of Walt Davis, then turned away. He'd seen a few bodies in his sixteen years with the U.S. Marshals Service, and plenty more in Vietnam with the Marine Corps, but he'd never gotten used to looking at them. This wasn't his case, anyway. He'd been invited to tag along only because he'd been playing poker with Thad McNally, one of the FBI agents who had been investigating Davis, when the call came in.

He glanced around, ignoring the agents, the Atlanta cops and the medical examiner's people, and instead studied the building. It was shaped like a triangle, with each corner blunted. The atrium extended twenty stories straight up, with three wings of offices on each floor. Low walls offered safety while still allowing a view of the lobby below, with its fountain and lush landscaping.

No doubt it was from behind one of those walls that the witness—no, witnesses; there were two, Thad had said—had watched the murder. He wondered if they'd be of any help, but he wouldn't count on it. Seeing someone violently killed, even a stranger, could be upsetting and frightening, at the least. Going into court and openly testifying about that killing was something a lot of citizens weren't willing to risk.

"Hey, Deke, I'm going to talk to one of the witnesses," Thad said. "Want to come along?"

With a shrug, he accompanied his friend to the elevators. "Who is Walt Davis that he rates two bullets in the lobby of his office building?" he asked as they stepped inside.

"He was an accountant—his office is on the eighteenth floor. We picked him up not long ago and charged him under the RICO statute. He appeared in court, posted bail and didn't show up for his trial. We've had a fugitive warrant out on him ever since. He had a passport and an airline ticket under a false name in his pocket, and they found suitcases and a large amount of cash in his car outside. Apparently he was leaving the country, but he'd come back here for something."

The elevator stopped on the third floor, and Deke, considering Thad's words, followed him out. RICO stood for Racketeering Influenced and Corrupt Organizations and covered a wide range of activities. Although recently the statute had been used against anti-abortion protesters and Wall Street inside traders, its original target had been organized crime—money laundering, gambling, prostitution, drugs and pornography. That meant Davis's murder had probably been ordered by one of the people he worked for. His plans to leave town evidently hadn't been enough to satisfy his boss ... but death had.

They went into an office on the third floor. There were several uniformed police officers inside, along with a couple of homicide detectives. In the center of the group was the witness. His first thought was that she looked fragile. His second was that it was too bad she was a woman; she would be less likely to testify than a man—more easily intimidated, more easily threatened.

She was calm, but her face was pale, her eyes still rounded with shock, and she trembled, even though the office was warm and a coat was wrapped around her. She sat behind her desk and answered each of Thad's questions in a quiet, controlled tone, although she'd already answered the same questions for the first officers to arrive and again for the detectives.

Deke found a quiet place in a corner and leaned against the wall, one arm resting on top of a filing cabinet. He already knew who Thad suspected of the murder, and the witness's mention of the name Tony confirmed it: Anthony Giamo. Every federal agency from the FBI to Drug Enforcement to the IRS, and most in between, wanted Giamo, but the old man was careful. He delegated the less-than-legal end of his business to his subordinates and kept his own hands clean. Until now. If the witness—Teresa "but I go by Tess" Marlowe—was being truthful, if the other witness backed up her story, then Anthony Giamo had made a mistake. A major one.

After hearing her story once, Deke went out into the hall and leaned against the retaining wall, gazing idly below. The fountain had been turned off and the body removed, but the gruesome red tint remained in the pool of water. He listened to the chatter that drifted up from below with half an ear while still hearing the calm, quiet voices of Thad McNally and Tess Marlowe from the office.

Thad joined him, stretching wearily. "She'll be a good witness."

"*If* she chooses to testify." Deke had seen too many people back out when they realized how powerful the defendant was—people stronger, braver and more substantial-looking than Tess Marlowe. "What about the other one?"

"I haven't seen him yet. His name is Donald Hopkins and he's a janitor. He was on the fifth floor when Davis was shot, looking over the wall, just like Marlowe."

"Are you going to request protection for them?"

"What's this? Are things so slow in your office that you're out looking for business?" Thad asked with a laugh.

Deke grinned. As it stood right now, because of the victim's ties to organized crime, the investigation would be handled by the FBI, with some assistance from the Atlanta Police Department. But because it was a federal case, if it was determined that protection for the witnesses was necessary, that would bring in the Marshals Service. Then he would be officially involved.

"I don't know," Thad went on, responding to Deke's question. "You and I both know who did it, but we've got to get an ID from the witnesses first. I'm curious about who the woman was. You know Giamo's logic—women are fine as long as they stay in their place—and that ain't in business." He considered for a moment, then shrugged. "As soon as it's all sorted out, we'll talk to Julia and see what she thinks about protection. This is the first time Giamo's ever been directly tied to a murder. I don't know what she'll want to do."

Julia Billings was the U.S. Attorney for the district that included Atlanta. She was a damn tough prosecutor and an old friend. Deke trusted her judgment implicitly. If she said Tess Marlowe and Donald Hopkins needed protection, he would help give it. If she said they'd be safe, then they would be. She was never wrong.

"But why would Giamo do it himself?" Thad asked, talking more to himself than Deke. "If he wanted Davis dead, why didn't he have one of his people do it?"

"Maybe he didn't intend to kill him. Maybe he just wanted to talk to him, only it got out of control. Giamo has a hell of a temper, you know." Deke covered a yawn with the back of his hand. "Listen, since you're going to be tied up a while, I'm going to catch a ride home."

"You can take my car, if you want."

"Nah, that's okay." He looked over Thad's shoulder into the office and met Tess Marlowe's gaze. She was tired, too, and still looked so damned fragile, as if one blow might shatter her. It was too bad she'd been caught up in this mess, he thought sympathetically. Seeing Davis die hadn't even been the worst of it. That would come later, when all the cops and agents were gone and she was alone with the darkness, alone with the memories.

Deliberately, he turned away and started toward the elevators at the far end of the hall. "See you later, Thad."

Tess sat on the sofa, staring into the distance, only vaguely aware of her mother hovering nearby. She'd spent hours at the police station waiting to look at a series of photographs. Then one of the female officers had brought her here, to her parents' home in Marietta. She hadn't wanted to return to the office to pick up her car, hadn't wanted to face going home to her empty apartment, hadn't wanted to be alone.

No one—not the FBI agents or the detectives—had been surprised that her description of the man with the gun perfectly matched one of the photographs they'd provided. She'd had the feeling that they'd been expecting the identification, that while she had been the one to actually see the killer, they had all known his identity before she had.

Her description of the woman, though, had been practically useless. Blond hair, well-dressed, tall, slim. It described thousands of women in Atlanta, and the police planned to start showing her photographs of some of them later today.

"Want something to eat, hon?"

She smiled wanly at her mother and shook her head. Her parents weren't quite able to take in what had happened. They'd been overly solicitous ever since she'd arrived in the middle of the night, hesitant to leave her alone for even a moment. Finally her father had left this morning, along with a neighbor, to retrieve her car from the office parking lot. When he returned, he would drive downtown with her to the police station for a lineup.

Her chuckle bordered on hysterical. A lineup. The whole situation sounded like something from one of the prime-time police shows her father liked to watch on TV, and felt about as real. Things like this just didn't happen to her. She was a secretary, thirty-five and divorced and perfectly happy living a quiet, unexciting life. She'd never had any dealings with the police and certainly not with the FBI. She had never seen anyone die, had never been in a police station before last night and had never seen a lineup. It wasn't real. It couldn't be.

But then she closed her eyes and recalled the image of the dead man in the fountain, and she knew it *was* real. Terrifyingly real.

"Your father will be back soon."

Tess slowly pushed herself off the couch. "I guess I'd better get ready." She didn't have any clothes here, but her mother, who was the same size, had offered Tess anything she needed from her own closet.

In the bedroom that had once been hers, she changed into a black skirt, a pearl-gray blouse and a charcoal-gray blazer. She let her hair hang loose, the curled ends brushing past her shoulders, and used the small makeup kit in her purse to apply some color to her still too-pale face. She looked better, she decided critically as her father tapped on the door. Not great, but better.

Gordon Conrad was taller than both his wife and daughter by nearly a foot. He looked as tired as she felt, Tess thought as she stood on tiptoe to give him a hug. Her parents were in their sixties, too old to be worrying so much about their daughter anymore. For their sakes as well as her own—as well as the dead man's—she regretted that any of this had happened.

"Are you ready to go?" Gordon asked gruffly.

Tess nodded. "Mom's not coming, is she?"

''She wanted to. I told her it would be better if she waited here.''

The drive to the police station passed in silence. Tess wasn't in the mood for small talk, and she didn't want to discuss last night—but she couldn't think of anything else. At the police station they were met by the detectives and the FBI agents from last night. While her father waited, she was escorted into the observation half of the lineup room. She stood near one wall, hands clasped tightly together, and waited impatiently.

Most of the men in the room were talking quietly among themselves and ignoring her. Except one. He leaned comfortably against the wall in the corner closest to her, one hand in his trousers pocket, the other holding a cup of coffee. She had noticed him last night, standing in the corner of her office, listening to the FBI agent's questions and her answers, without seeming to pay attention. He'd been wearing jeans and an emerald-green knit shirt, with only a windbreaker in spite of the chilly weather. This morning, like most of the others, he wore a dark suit, white shirt and tie.

He was watching her, his eyes expressionless, his mouth set in a thin line. He didn't seem too pleased by what he saw, she thought, and smiled humorlessly. Considering everything else that had happened, could it possibly matter that some man who wasn't even polite enough to introduce himself, as all the others had done last night, wasn't impressed with the way she looked?

But she had no complaints about the way *he* looked. He was darkly tanned, dark-haired, dark-eyed and big—about six foot, two inches of solid muscle. He was older than she was, probably in his early forties, and ruggedly handsome. He was arrogant, too, she thought, and not the slightest bit uncomfortable that he'd been caught staring.

From force of habit her gaze dropped to his left hand. The fingers wrapped around the coffee cup were long, dark and ringless. Not that it mattered. It wasn't as if she were looking for a man and saw all singles as candidates—eight years of marriage to Will had been enough to convince her that there were great advantages in spending the rest of her life alone. It was curiosity, no more.

"Miss Marlowe."

At the sound of Thad McNally's voice, she turned to face him.

"How are you doing?"

"All right. I'd like to get this over with. Are you ready?"

"Almost. I think you met everyone last night, except Deke." He gestured to the man in the corner, who was still watching her. "This is Deacon Ramsey. He's with the Marshals Service."

"Marshals?" she echoed, her gaze shifting from one man to the other. "As in U.S. Marshal? As in Matt Dillon?"

Deke finished his coffee, dropped the cup in a nearby wastebasket and straightened. "The 1990s version," he said dryly, offering her his hand.

She accepted it slowly, barely closing her fingers around his before withdrawing. "What do you do?"

"Fugitive apprehensions, some investigations." That wasn't the extent of their authority, not by any means, but he chose not to mention the rest. They also oversaw the federal witness relocation program, provided protection to judges and other officers of the court, and protected witnesses whose lives were threatened because of their decision to testify in federal court.

And, although she didn't realize it yet, Tess Marlowe was likely to become one of those witnesses. After talking to Thad earlier this morning, Deke was reasonably certain that Julia Billings would order both witnesses placed in protective custody, and he was sure to be assigned to one or the other. After several long minutes of studying her, from the top of her silky brown hair down to her feet, small and oddly delicate in black heels, he'd decided *he* would guard Donald Hopkins. Tess Marlowe was too fragile, too innocent-looking, too badly in need of watching over, and he'd felt too strong a desire to be the one watching. Maybe it was her small size—she couldn't be an inch over five foot four— or her big brown eyes, or the haunted look that slid over her features when she was remembering last night's scene. Whatever, something about her roused his protective instincts—not just marshal to witness, but man to woman— and that was a danger he wasn't willing to face. Not now, not ever.

"As soon as the assistant U.S. Attorney gets here, we'll begin," Thad said.

"I'm here now." The door swooshed shut behind a harried-looking man who held an overcoat in one hand and a thick briefcase in the other. "Is this our witness?"

Thad nodded. "Teresa—I'm sorry, Tess Marlowe."

The lawyer was about her age, Tess estimated—blond and, though not overweight, giving the appearance of softness, of harmlessness. His eyes, behind thick, tortoiseshell-framed glasses, were blue and appeared vaguely unfocused when turned on her. "Miss Marlowe, I'm Frank Harris, with the U.S. Attorney's office."

He shifted the briefcase, then stuck out his hand, and she automatically took it, hiding her dismay. Surely this wasn't the man who would prosecute this case. He reminded her of a teddy bear—a big, friendly, absentminded teddy bear. But his next words confirmed that he would, indeed, be prosecuting.

"We'll be talking quite a bit in the next few weeks, preparing our case and your testimony. Now, as soon as Thad explains the procedure to you, we'll get started here. Excuse me, will you?" He spoke politely to Deke, then joined a small group of detectives on the other side of the room.

"Don't let appearances fool you," Deke said softly, having seen Tess's dismay and found it amusing. "Frank Harris is one of the best prosecutors I've ever seen."

Arrogant, she reminded herself. Handsome or not, the man was just plain arrogant.

"He is good," Thad agreed. "Okay, Miss Marlowe, seven men matching the general description you gave us last night will be brought into the next room. Remember that they can't see you through the glass. Take your time, look at each one closely and see if you recognize any of them. Any questions?"

She shook her head and moved to stand in front of the plate glass, flanked by the FBI agent on one side, the marshal on the other.

The men around her grew quiet as seven suspects filed in a straight line into the next room. All were of average height, heavyset, gray-haired. The instant her gaze swept over them, Tess picked him out—number five—but she didn't speak. Not yet. She studied each of the others to be sure, but there was no doubt. The fifth man, a sweet grandfatherly gentleman as apparently harmless as the prosecutor, was the one who had shot and killed another man in front of her last night.

Deke, standing beside her, saw that her gaze was locked on one man. Anthony Giamo. Some part of him had hoped that last night's identification was a mistake, had hoped for her sake that the murderer was someone less dangerous, less powerful, than Anthony Giamo. But he knew that in a moment she was going to stop reliving last night's killing, open her mouth and identify number five as the murderer.

He shifted his own gaze from Tess to Giamo. The old man looked as if he didn't have a care in the world. Although he had the right to have his attorney present when the witness made the identification, he'd turned that down. He didn't need an attorney, he'd claimed. He'd done nothing wrong.

Tess felt the marshal beside her move restlessly and realized how long she'd been staring at the men. She glanced at the FBI agent on her other side and spoke quietly. "Number five."

"Are you sure?"

"Yes." She looked back at the man and shivered. Yes, she was very sure. That sweet, grandfatherly gentleman was a murderer.

The investigation had moved quickly after that, Deke thought as he fixed his dinner a few weeks later. Walt Davis's family, friends and co-workers had been interviewed, and evidence linking him with Anthony Giamo had been established. Giamo was questioned, his house, office and car searched. A handgun of the same caliber that had killed Davis was found at Giamo's home, and ballistics tests had proved it was the murder weapon. He had been arraigned, a preliminary hearing held, and had been bound over for trial. He was currently out on bail.

As for the witnesses... Deke frowned. On the recommendation of his boss, Frank Harris had chosen not to order protection for them. Thad McNally had argued with him—hell, even Deke had gotten into it. Tess Marlowe and Donald Hopkins were eyewitnesses to a mob-related murder. How could the U.S. Attorney's office *not* want them protected? But Julia Billings had been adamant. There had been no threats made against the witnesses, and there was no reason to believe there would be any. Protective custody was an expensive proposition. *If* something happened—which she clearly doubted—then they would talk about it. That was kind of like closing the barn door after the cows got out, Thad had grumbled to Deke. The FBI did have the option of going around Julia and requesting the order from a judge, but that would affect their relationship with her office. No agency wanted to do business with an antagonistic U.S. Attorney.

The microwave dinged, and Deke took his frozen dinner out, peeling the plastic liner back and getting a steam burn on his finger. He was holding his hand under cool running water in the sink when the phone rang.

It was McNally. Without any preliminary greeting, he said, "You know, I was thinking just today that this Giamo case is coming together too easily. The old man commits murder himself instead of hiring it out. There are two eyewitnesses, both willing to face him in court and testify. There's plenty of other evidence linking him to it, including the gun which he doesn't even get rid of. And there are no threats, no hassles, no dangers."

Deke waited silently for him to get to the point.

For a moment Thad was silent, too. Then he spoke quietly. "But I was wrong. Donald Hopkins was found dead at work tonight, shot twice in the back of the head at close range."

Deke's features settled into a grim expression. "What about Tess Marlowe?" His tone was calm, but as he said the words he felt a clenching in his stomach that he identified as dread. In spite of his ambivalent feelings about her, if something had happened to her, too, he didn't want to hear it.

"As far as we know, she's okay. We've been trying to reach her, but there's no answer at her house. I'm going to call Frank Harris and get a protection order for her. While I'm doing it, can you go over and pick her up?"

For a moment Deke remembered that he hadn't wanted the job of guarding Tess Marlowe, but it was logical for Thad to ask him. She had met him and wouldn't be as wary of opening her door late in the evening to him as she would with a total stranger—*if* she was home. *If* she was all right. After drying his hand, he reached for a pen and the notepad on the counter. "What's her address?"

Thad read it from the file in front of him. "Call me when you get there. I'm at the office."

Deke hung up, then placed another call. Scott Rowan, his boss, was watching *Monday Night Football*, but he immediately forgot the game when he heard Deke's voice. "What's up?"

"One of the witnesses against Giamo was killed tonight—shot twice in the head. McNally wants me to pick up the other one and take her to a safe house. He's getting an order from Frank Harris right now. Okay?''

"Yeah, go ahead. Which place?"

"On Anderson Street. Can you get a team together?"

"They'll be waiting for you."

Deke hesitated, then said, "Scott, I don't want to work this one. I'll pick her up because she knows me...but I don't want to be assigned to this."

"I'll have a full team waiting. Drop her off, and we'll sort things out tomorrow."

Relieved, Deke hung up, then went into the bedroom. He'd changed into jeans after work. Rather than take the time to thread a belt through the loops for his usual holster, he switched the gun to a waistband holster and hooked the wide metal clip in place, settling the semiautomatic pistol in the small of his back. With a jacket to cover the gun and his credentials and Tess Marlowe's address in his pocket, he left the house, locking up behind him.

It took twenty minutes to drive to Tess Marlowe's apartment complex. Once there, he followed dimly lit paths to her building, then climbed the stairs to her second floor unit. He knocked at the door, waited impatiently, then knocked again, louder. After a third knock, he paced to the end of the corridor and found an out-of-the-way place to wait.

It was chilly tonight. If he could have seen the entrance to her apartment from the parking lot, he would have waited in his car, but he couldn't. He checked his watch, noting the time—9:12—then began pacing again. Where was she? He knew there were logical, safe explanations for her absence—shopping, dinner, a date. But he also knew there was another explanation: she could be in trouble. Like Donald Hopkins, Giamo's people could have found her. Like Hopkins, she could be dead.

The shiver that raced through him had nothing to do with the cold.

He had reached the shadows at the end once more and was turning when he heard footsteps on the stairs. He stopped where he was, motionless except for the slow movement of his hand sliding under his jacket, flipping up the strap that secured the pistol in the holster.

The steps came closer, slowing as they approached the top. Deke tensed, his fingers curling around the textured grips of the gun. It was half out of the holster when Tess Marlowe rounded the corner, a bag of groceries in one arm, her keys dangling from her free hand.

With a sigh of relief, Deke slid the gun back into place and fastened the snap to hold it, then stepped out of the shadows. "Miss Marlowe?"

She gave a startled cry and fell back a few steps. Then she recognized him, and the fear in her eyes was replaced by wariness. "Mr. Ramsey. Or should I call you 'Marshal'?"

He shrugged. He wasn't going to spend enough time in her company for names or titles to matter. "Can we go inside?"

For a long moment she looked at him; then she turned to unlock the door. Inside, she turned on lights as she walked, moving through the entryway, the living room, the kitchen. There she set down the bag and calmly unpacked and put away her groceries before facing him across the wide counter that divided the living room and kitchen. "Mr. McNally told me last week that part of your job is protecting witnesses when a threat exists." She paused, and her voice grew softer, wistful. "I'd hoped I would never have to see you again."

He didn't tell her that he had shared the same hope, for personal as well as professional reasons.

"So... is Anthony Giamo making threats?"

He came to stand across the counter from her. "No." No, Giamo had skipped making threats and gone straight to carrying them out.

"Then what—"

Before she could finish, he interrupted. "We're placing you in protective custody, Miss Marlowe. Pack whatever you need for the next few weeks, and do it quickly." He didn't want her in the apartment one minute longer than necessary. If Giamo's people didn't already have her address, getting it would be a simple matter of picking up the phone book.

But she didn't make any move to do as he'd said. "What does that mean—protective custody?"

"It means I'm taking you to a safe house, and you're going to stay there under twenty-four-hour guard until the trial is over."

"It doesn't even start for more than three weeks," she protested. "You can't do that."

"I certainly can."

"And if I refuse to go?"

He rested his hands on the countertop. "You don't have a choice, Miss Marlowe. I'm taking you with me when I leave, whether you want to go or not."

She stared at him, the soft brown of her eyes edged now with dread. "What happened?" she asked in a whisper. "Mr. Hopkins..."

Deke shifted uneasily and took a few steps back. He wasn't looking at her, and his voice when he spoke was flat and emotionless. "He's dead. He was killed tonight."

"Oh, God." Tess clutched the rounded edge of the counter for support. She had never met Donald Hopkins before the murder—his workday didn't start until 5:00 p.m., when hers usually ended, and she rarely worked late—and Frank Harris had warned them not to seek each other out afterward. Still, because of their mutual connection to the case, she'd felt a certain kinship with the man, and the news of his death filled her with sorrow. "How did he die? Was it an accident?"

Placing his weight on his hands, Deke leaned over the counter close to her. "No," he said softly. "Two bullets in the brain usually qualifies as deliberate."

He immediately regretted his bluntness when she turned so pale and shaky that he thought she was going to faint. He circled the counter and grasped her arms, giving her a gentle shake. "Look, Miss Marlowe, I'm sorry. I'm not handling this well." Something about her got on his nerves and under his skin. Maybe the fact that she was even smaller, more helpless-looking, than he'd remembered, that her eyes were even bigger and more expressive than he'd recalled, that she was unquestionably as beautiful as he'd remembered.

He made an effort to soften his voice, to soften the effect of what he'd said and what he was about to say. "Donald Hopkins was murdered tonight in your office building. There's nothing so far to tie his death to Anthony Giamo, but he's the main suspect. As soon as you get your bags packed, I'm going to take you to a safe house, and it's just that—*safe*. No one will know where you are. No one will be able to get to you. Do you understand?"

Numbly, she nodded. "I'll get my things."

But she didn't move. She couldn't, Deke realized, until he let go of her. Slowly his fingers slid away, still warm from contact with her skin, and he backed up until he hit the opposite counter. "Go."

Feeling unbalanced, Tess left the kitchen for her bedroom at the end of the short hallway. There she pulled a big suitcase from the closet and began packing: jeans and sweaters; sweatpants and T-shirts; lingerie; slippers; nightgowns and a robe. Toiletries and makeup, along with an extra pair of shoes, went into a matching shoulder bag.

For one dazed moment, she sank down on the bed, her trembling hands clasped together in her lap. If she concentrated, she could still feel the pressure of the marshal's fingers around her wrists. Long fingers. Strong, but gentle, too. She could still hear his slow drawl, native to Georgia but tempered by time spent elsewhere. She could close her eyes and still see the hard, muscular length of his body.

Suddenly she shuddered. Donald Hopkins was dead, murdered, and here she sat thinking about the good-looking marshal waiting in her kitchen. God, what was wrong with her?

It just didn't seem real. In spite of the grim man waiting for her and the sobering phrases that sprinkled his conversation—protective custody, safe house, bullets in the brain—she couldn't quite accept the reality of the situation. She was afraid—she'd lived with fear since seeing Walt Davis killed. But she didn't feel threatened. She didn't sense any danger. If her life was imperiled, wouldn't she somehow know it?

Down the hall, Deke was on the phone, talking quietly to Thad McNally.

"How did she react to the news?"

"She was pretty shaken." Though it was debatable, he acknowledged darkly, whether she was more shaken by the shock of Hopkins's murder or by the thoroughly unprofessional way he'd told her about it. "Did you get the protection order?"

"Yeah. When will you have her settled?"

"As soon as she's packed. Rowan is supposed to get a team together and have them waiting when we get there."

"Give me a call, will you?"

Deke agreed and hung up, then looked around the apartment. It was like thousands of others in Atlanta—boxy rooms, limited space and an unimpressive layout. From a security standpoint, it was a cop's nightmare: an inexpensive single-key deadbolt lock that could be easily jimmied, a lightweight wooden front door that would collapse under one strong kick and a sliding glass door leading to a small balcony that could be lifted off its track in a matter of seconds. Even the second-story location wouldn't keep a determined burglar—or someone worse—out. Any reasonably agile person could swing up from the ground floor patio railing to the second-floor balcony and be inside in no time.

Those problems aside, it was a homey place. The walls were painted a soft buttery yellow, setting off the sand-colored carpet. The furniture was wood, the cushions covered in soft desert hues. The fireplace mantel displayed a collection of Indian pottery. Bronze figures and cacti in heavy clay pots competed for space on the tables, and a grouping of framed prints of round-cheeked Indian children shared a wall with a quilted turquoise, rust and black wall hanging.

As he picked up a small black pot to study the symbols etched into it, Tess came into the room and set her shoulder bag on the floor. "That's Cherokee," she said, sounding almost normal. "From the reservation in North Carolina. Have you ever been there?"

He shook his head and replaced the pot. "Are you ready?"

"Almost."

She went back to the bedroom, returning a moment later with the suitcase. She carried it the way a child would, Deke thought, in front of her, with both hands wrapped around the handle and a tilted gait to balance its weight. He met her halfway and easily lifted it. "Is this all?"

She hadn't removed her coat, and her purse was on the counter where she'd left it. "Yes."

"You bought cat food," he reminded her, having seen her stack the cans neatly in a kitchen cabinet. "Do you have a cat?"

Eyes wide, she hurried back to the bedroom, dropping to the floor and coaxing a reluctant fluffy white cat out from under the bed. She returned, cuddling him in her arms. "Can I take him with me?"

He shook his head. "If we have to move in a hurry, we can't worry about a cat. Can someone keep him for you?"

She considered a moment.

"If it's a problem, I can find someone at the office to take care of him," he offered.

"I'd rather take him to my parents' house. They live in Marietta. It won't take me long. You could follow—"

Deke shook his head again. "I thought you understood. You're not going anywhere without me, Miss Marlowe. We'll drop him off on the way. Where are your keys?"

"Beside my purse."

He found them, then picked up the two bags. "I'll put these in the car, then come back for you and the cat. While I'm gone, get together everything the cat needs. And *don't* open the door for anyone. I'll let myself in. Okay?"

She nodded and watched him leave, listening to the click of the lock, then went into the kitchen to pack the cat food. "He certainly is bossy, isn't he, Omar?" she muttered. "And overbearing. He doesn't have much patience, either, and he's a bit too fond of giving orders."

But he was capable, too. Efficient. Strong. Big enough to give her a sense of security, but not so big that she felt like a small child beside him. Of all the law-enforcement people she'd met in the last few weeks, if she had to depend on one to keep her safe, in spite of his less than sparkling personality, Deacon Ramsey was the one she would choose.

When he returned, he took the bag of catfood, handed Tess her purse and began turning out lights. Outside, they paused while he locked the door; then he took her arm and led the way to his car.

Tess released the cat long enough to fasten her seat belt. Omar stretched and jumped onto the back seat, where he made himself comfortable on Deke's suit coat. Looking over his shoulder, Deke thought of long white cat hair on the black fabric and, grimacing, started the engine.

"Will they question Anthony Giamo about Mr. Hopkins's death?" she asked, shivering in the cold.

Deke glanced at her, then turned the heat to high. "Yeah, but he'll have an alibi. They won't be able to prove anything."

"Maybe he didn't do it. Maybe Donald Hopkins had other enemies."

He looked at her again, his eyes as dark as the night. "Maybe."

But he didn't think so—Tess heard the doubt in that single word. He believed that Anthony Giamo had had Donald Hopkins murdered, and that she was next on the list. But she didn't want to believe it. Maybe she was being naive, maybe she was indulging in wishful thinking, but she didn't want to believe that some man she'd never met wanted her dead. She couldn't believe it, because if she did, she would be overwhelmed by terror.

"A few weeks ago you people said we would be safe. You said we didn't need protective custody, because nothing was going to happen."

"We were wrong."

She turned from the window to look at him. As Thad McNally had explained, that determination had been strictly based on the opinion of the U.S. Attorney's office, not the FBI or anyone else. Certainly not the Marshals Service. Yet, rather than pointing fingers at those responsible, Deacon Ramsey was willing to accept the blame for a bad decision he'd had no part in making. She liked such loyalty and dedication.

"What exit do I take?"

Tess realized they were approaching Marietta, one of Atlanta's sprawling suburbs, and gave him directions to her parents' home. Fifteen minutes later they were back on the interstate to Atlanta.

Her parents had been concerned by the late-night visit, and worried even more by the marshal's presence. Tess had tried to reassure them, to convince them that this was more a precaution than a necessity, but she didn't think they'd believed her. They seemed to have aged years during the brief visit.

"You know I'm going to miss Thanksgiving with my parents," she remarked to her silent companion.

He glanced at her, then back at the road.

"I *always* spend Thanksgiving with my parents and my grandparents."

He looked at her again. "And the marshals who will be guarding you always spend it with their families. But not this time."

His response effectively quieted her. What about him? she wondered. Did he have a family? In spite of the absence of a wedding ring, did he have a wife and children waiting for him at home, or was he, like her, divorced? She didn't consider the possibility that he'd never married, not a man as handsome as he was. Then again, as unpleasant as he could be, she thought with a faint smile, she wouldn't be surprised if he'd never found a woman who could tolerate living with him. Well, it looked as if she would find out for herself how tolerable he was in the next three weeks.

More to break the silence than because she cared, she asked, "So...how many of you people will be guarding me?"

"There will be two inside at all times, and four outside watching the street and the alley in the evenings and at night."

"What do we do to pass the time?"

"You can do anything you want as long as it doesn't involve using the phone or going outside. They'll be standing watch."

"And what does that involve—standing watch?"

His jaw tightened. "It involves keeping you alive, Miss Marlowe," he said curtly. Glancing over his shoulder, he changed lanes, then exited the freeway. After a couple of miles, he turned off the well-traveled Atlanta street and into a quiet neighborhood.

It was middle-class, block after block of red brick houses interspersed with single-story, wood-frame homes painted white. The backyards, all fenced, opened onto alleys, and the front yards edged right down to the street, with no sidewalks or curbs. Few of the houses had garages, and cars filled the driveways and both sides of the street, making it seem narrower than it was.

Tess had never been in this neighborhood before, but she'd grown up in one just like it. It was family oriented—a nice quiet place to raise kids. It seemed an odd location for a safe house. A seedy, rent-by-the-week motel or an isolated house surrounded by acres of nothing seemed more logical, more in keeping with her television-inspired image of safe houses, than a middle-class-surrounded-by-kids-skate-boards-and-bikes neighborhood.

Their destination was a house in the middle of the block. It was part brick, part wood, and identical to a dozen other houses in the neighborhood, with a narrow porch, a carport on one side and a gate leading into the fenced backyard. Like most of the other houses on the street, the grass in front grew in scraggly patches, because the tall live oaks, pines and dogwoods prevented much of the sunlight from reaching the ground. Also like most of the other houses, red-tip shrubs and azaleas were planted along the front of the house and in clumps around the base of each tree. It looked like a typical home. There was nothing on the outside to give away the fact that it was owned by the Marshals Service, or that it was being temporarily occupied for the sole purpose of keeping Tess Marlowe alive.

There was a car already under the carport, and lights were on inside. Deke pulled off the driveway onto the tire-tracked patch of grass beside the carport and shut off the engine. He hurried Tess around the other car and through the door tucked into the corner of the carport.

The door led into a dimly lit kitchen. Before Tess had a chance to look around, they were joined by two men, one middle-aged with graying hair and the other in his late twenties. Deke introduced them as Al Meyers and Ross Boren, then gave his keys to Ross and asked him to get her bags from the car.

"The rules are simple," he said, his gaze locked on hers. "You're not expected to do anything—no cooking or cleaning. You can't go outside. You can't use the phone, and even though they're bulletproof glass, stay away from the windows. Do you understand?"

She tilted her head back to see him better. "I'm really quite intelligent, Mr. Ramsey, and those are very simple rules. I understand them perfectly."

Behind her, Al Meyers stifled a chuckle, and she looked at him. In contrast to Deacon Ramsey, the older marshal seemed friendly, warm. Approachable. She knew instinctively she would get along with him and become friends, while she couldn't begin to imagine friendship with Deacon Ramsey. He was too distant, too disapproving. He'd tried to hide it, but something about her annoyed him and made him dislike her. She felt a moment's brief regret for that.

"Come on," Deke said, speaking through clenched teeth. "I'll show you your room." Then he could leave. Then he would never have to see Tess Marlowe again.

He led the way down the narrow hall. "This is the bathroom." He touched the first door on the right, then gestured to the door down the hall on the left and the one at the end of the hallway. "And those rooms are where Al and Ross will sleep. They'll work in shifts. One of them will always be awake and on watch." He pushed open the second door on the right and stepped inside. "This is yours."

Tess slipped past him and surveyed the small square room. It smelled musty and unused, as if the single window, with its heavy drapes drawn tight, was never opened. An overhead light shone pitilessly on the plain and sparse furnishings: a double bed with a faded blue spread, a dresser and a nightstand that held a lamp. The door to the tiny closet was open, revealing a bare shelf and a clothes rod empty but for a tangle of wire hangers.

"If you don't have any questions, I'll be going—"

Tess whirled to face him. "Going where?"

"Home."

"You're not staying here?"

He shifted uncomfortably. "No. I told you, you'd have four men outside and two in—Al and Ross. That's all you need."

"But...I thought..." The dismay Tess felt was profound. She had thought *Deke* was going to protect her. She had liked that idea because, whether he liked her or not, she felt safe with him. She trusted him. She *knew* him—better, at least, than she knew either of the other men.

"McNally asked me to pick you up because I was the only one from our office you'd met," he explained. "He thought you'd feel more comfortable finding me on your doorstep than a stranger. But I'm not assigned to this. Al and Ross will take care of you. They know what they're doing."

She was sure they did. She was also sure that she would feel better with Deacon Ramsey in the house—and equally sure that he didn't *want* to be here. Shoving her hands into her pockets, she rocked back on her heels. "Of course they do. By all means, go on home. Don't let us keep you any longer."

He was glad to do just that. Without so much as a good-bye, he left her alone in the little bedroom.

Tess went into the hallway, leaning one shoulder against the wall, and watched him. He stopped in the kitchen to talk to the two men. Though his voice was low, she could make out his words.

"Take care of this one. She's important," he said, and she smiled a bit, thinking of all the various meanings that could be attached to that last statement. His next one, though, made the smile fade. "Without her, we've got nothing against Giamo."

Grimly she went back into the bedroom, closing the door quietly behind her. She was foolish to let the words sting. To Deacon Ramsey, Thad McNally, Frank Harris and everyone else involved in this case, she was simply business—a means to an end. There was nothing personal involved. Deacon Ramsey didn't like her or *dis*like her.

Beyond the fact that she was a witness in one of their cases, he didn't give a damn about her.

Chapter 2

Deke slumped in one of two chairs that fronted Scott Rowan's desk, one ankle resting over the other knee, a ceramic coffee mug in one hand and his head hung forward, eyes closed. God, he was tired. Instead of calling Thad on the radio last night, he'd driven by the FBI office. It had been past two in the morning when he left, and he had come into the office before seven, so he'd managed just barely three hours sleep.

The summons to Scott's office had come nearly half an hour ago, but his boss had been tied up with other matters. Deke had passed the time in this chair with his eyes shut and his mind wandering. Unfortunately, this morning it had a tendency to wander in the wrong direction, to a small brick house on Anderson Street and the petite brunette staying there.

"How is Tess Marlowe?"

Slowly Deke blinked, wondering how someone could have read his thoughts, then raised his head. His boss and Julia Billings, the U.S. Attorney, were standing outside the open door of the office. It was Julia who had asked the question and Rowan who answered it.

"According to Ross, last night was quiet. She seems to be all right. Here, talk to Deke. He's the one who picked her up and told her about Hopkins."

Coming into the office, she read the fatigue on Deke's face and smiled sympathetically. "Tough night, huh?"

"Not one I'd like to repeat anytime soon." He knew the night had been tougher for her. They had been friends a long time, associates even longer, and, for a short while, something more. He knew the signs of tension and where they appeared, not in her face—for she looked as lovely as ever—but in the taut lines of her body and the stressed tone of her voice.

"You picked up Marlowe?"

"Yeah. Thad called and asked me to."

"Why you?"

"I met her the day of the lineup."

"And you told her about Hopkins."

"Yeah. She seemed sorry he was dead, shocked that he'd been murdered." He quickly replayed last night's events in his mind, then said, "I'm not sure she really understood the significance of it as far as how it concerns her. She didn't seem particularly frightened for herself."

Julia shrugged. "People handle fear in different ways. Maybe Miss Marlowe deals with it by refusing to acknowledge it. That might be good. I'd rather have her denying it—as long as she continues to cooperate with us—than have a terrified or hysterical witness on our hands."

"She'll cooperate," Scott put in. "Now that she's at the safe haven, she'll have no choice."

"Who's with her?" Julia asked, then nodded approvingly as Scott ran down the list of names. "That sounds fine. Frank will be in touch with you soon. I know he'll want regular reports on his witness."

She started to leave, then came back, laying her hand on Deke's shoulder. "I'm really sorry about Donald Hopkins,

Deke. I should have listened to you and Thad. If I had, he would still be alive.'' Her smile was sad and heavily laced with guilt. "From now on, on matters of protection, I'll bow to the advice of the experts.''

Deke simply nodded. There was nothing he could say. He wouldn't add to her guilt by agreeing that she'd made a fatal mistake, and he wouldn't insult her by lying and saying that it wasn't her fault.

"I'll see you two around.''

When she left the office, Scott closed the door behind her, then seated himself at the desk. "I want to talk to you about Tess Marlowe.''

"Okay.'' Deke finished his now-cold coffee and sat straighter in the chair.

"I want you to take over the protection detail.''

The coffee—or was it his boss's announcement?—set off an unpleasant churning in the pit of his stomach. "I don't want to do that, Scott,'' he said, his voice cautiously neutral.

"I want you to.''

"Why?''

"For a variety of reasons. This is the government's best chance ever to get Anthony Giamo. We started out with two unimpeachable witnesses, and now one of them is dead. We can't afford to lose the other.''

"You've got some good men over there with her. You don't need me.''

"They *are* good—but you're better. You've worked more protection assignments than anyone else in this office. You're the best we've got.''

An ache in his jaw made Deke realize that he'd clenched it too tightly. He forced himself to relax enough to respond. "She's in a *safe house*, Scott. No one can touch her there, not even Giamo. You don't need me.''

"But maybe *she* does. Why did Thad call you last night instead of me or Al or Ross, or anyone else?''

"You just heard me. Because I'd met Tess at the lineup. I was the only one from this office who she knew."

"Because you were familiar to her." Scott shrugged. "That's what she needs right now—familiarity. Through no fault of her own, Tess Marlowe's life has been thrown into turmoil. She saw a man brutally murdered. Another man whom she had ties to has also been murdered, and now her own life is in danger. Last night you were the only familiar thing in a suddenly dangerous and frightening world. If she feels safer with you around, then you'll be around."

"But she doesn't feel..." Remembering her dismay when he'd told her that he was going home last night, he let his protest fade away unfinished. For a moment she had looked frightened, abandoned; then she had covered it up with that carelessly airy command to "go on home."

But he didn't want to protect a woman. Not a pretty woman with eyes as big and soft as Tess Marlowe's. Not a fragile, delicate woman who looked as if she needed protection not just from criminals but from the harsh realities of life. God, certainly not a woman who could tie him in knots and make the next three weeks of his life a living hell.

"Look, Scott," he began, his voice tautly controlled, his desperation carefully hidden, "you know about my connection to Giamo. If he finds out that I'm on the protection team, he's going to go to his lawyer, and they'll use me to discredit the government. You can't risk compromising the case."

"You're right," Scott said stubbornly. "I know about you and Giamo. And not even that is going to distract the jury from the story Tess Marlowe is going to tell them. So what's the real reason you don't want to work this case?"

Deke's scowl deepened, and Scott went on. "You know, I haven't seen Tess Marlowe yet, but I understand she reminds a man of Angela Wright."

Deke's head jerked up, and his eyes, dark with anger, locked with his boss's. "Leave Angela out of this," he growled. "It doesn't concern her."

"You're right—it doesn't. It concerns the U.S. Marshals Service, of which you are a member, and a witness. It's business, Deke. Don't let your personal life interfere with business. We're protecting Tess Marlowe, and you're heading the detail. Clear your desk, go home and pack a bag, and get over to that safe house. Keep whichever man you want and send the other back to me. Understand?''

"I understand." Keeping a tight rein on his temper, Deke stalked out of the office and into his own down the hall. He had expected some measure of consideration from his boss, who knew all about Angela Wright, yet he'd gotten nothing but an admonition to keep his personal life separate from business—as if he'd had any choice with Angela. Was Scott foolish enough to think he'd *wanted* to fall in love with the witness he'd been protecting?

It damn well wouldn't happen again, he swore. Not with Tess Marlowe. So he was slightly attracted to her. Probably every man who knew her was attracted to her. But attractions didn't have to be acted on, didn't even have to be acknowledged. He could ignore it, ignore *her*, and still do his job.

As he shrugged into the coat he'd left hanging on the back of his chair, he grimly hoped he was right. Tess Marlowe's life—and his—might very well depend on it.

Tess sat at the small kitchen table, her fingers laced around her third cup of coffee. Ordinarily one cup was enough to keep her going all day, but there was nothing ordinary about this day. She hadn't slept at all last night. The unfamiliar bed, the strange surroundings, the presence of the others in the house and the fear—oh, yes, she couldn't forget the fear—had all combined to keep her awake, tossing restlessly from one side of the bed to the other. At four o'clock she'd given up, gotten dressed and joined Al Meyers in the living room.

He'd been watching a twenty-four-hour news channel, but he had obligingly turned down the volume and talked with her instead. Although he couldn't be more than fifteen years older than she was, he reminded Tess of her father—authoritative, but also warm, friendly, caring. She hadn't been surprised to learn that he had three daughters of his own. He'd told her more—that Ross Boren had been with the Marshals Service only two years, that Ross's wife had recently had a baby and that Tess was the first person he'd known besides their boss to stand up to Deacon Ramsey in a bad mood.

He'd also told her that Deacon wasn't married. That tidbit interested her, although for the life of her, she couldn't say why. He'd made it clear last night that he wouldn't be working this assignment. She would probably never see him again.

Al was asleep now, replaced by Ross Boren. The younger man was in the living room, stretched out in a recliner reading the morning paper. On the table beside him were a cup of coffee, the remains of a stale doughnut, a hand-held two-way radio and a .357 magnum revolver.

Donald Hopkins and Anthony Giamo were front-page news this morning. Tess could see it from where she sat. Giamo Witness Murdered read the inch-high headline, and underneath it were photographs of both men. She didn't want to see more.

With a sigh, she emptied her coffee cup, rinsed it and left it in the sink, then went into the living room. The drapes on the big picture window were open, the miniblinds raised to the top. She stopped in front of the window and touched her hand to the glass. It was cold outside, in spite of the bright sunshine that filtered through the trees. For mid-November it was unusually cold.

"What the hell are you doing?"

Before Tess could react to the angry voice coming from the kitchen doorway, Deke had crossed the room in two strides, grasped her arm and yanked her away from the window. She lost her balance and fell hard against him, then righted herself as he continued to drag her back.

"It's a simple rule, Miss Marlowe. *Stay away from the windows.* Do you want to get yourself killed?"

She twisted until he was forced to let go or risk hurting her. When her arm was free, she rubbed it gingerly. "They're made of bulletproof glass—you said so last night."

"So you actually listened to part of what I said." He was practically sneering. "I said *even though* they're bulletproof glass, *stay away from them.*"

Ross had dropped the paper and gotten to his feet. Now he hesitantly approached them. "Hey, come on, Deke..."

Deke never took his eyes off Tess. "You never should have let her get close to the window, Boren. Next time, pay more attention to your protectee and forget about the newspaper. I'm taking over here. Get your stuff and go back to the office."

"But, Deke..." When Deke slowly shifted his gaze and Ross saw the fury in his eyes, he swallowed back the rest of his complaint. Cautiously he squeezed past them and went to the bedroom down the hall to pack.

"Well, you certainly intimidated him, didn't you?" Folding her arms over her chest, Tess took a step back and tried to calm her jumpy nerves with a few deep breaths.

He moved forward, and she moved back again. Too soon the wall was against her back and the marshal was scant inches in front of her. He rested his hands on the wall above her and leaned menacingly closer. She had to tilt her head back to see his face when he spoke.

"Lady, I don't care if you approve of my tactics. Try to understand this. The purpose of taking you into protective custody is to keep you under wraps so no one can find you to kill you. We want you out of sight. Hidden. Now, if you stand in front of that window over there, bulletproof glass or not, someone's going to see you—someone who might be able to identify you. And if that someone wants to give or sell that information to certain interested parties, that would make it pretty damn easy for said interested parties to kill you.''

''But—''

''Bulletproof glass has one function, Miss Marlowe—to stop bullets that are fired at that window. It won't do a damn thing about bullets fired through the door or the wall, and those can kill you just as easily.''

She looked down, her gaze settling on the knit shirt stretched across his chest. She wanted to argue, to defend herself, but there was nothing she could say. He was right, and she'd been wrong. ''I'm sorry.''

Her tone, soft and remorseful, defused his anger quicker than anything else could have. He had overreacted, he realized. A simple explanation of why she had to avoid the windows would have been sufficient. But seeing her there and knowing that such an innocent mistake could result in her death had fanned his already smoldering temper into full-fledged fury.

Slowly he became aware of the intimacy of their positions. They were as close as two people could get without actually touching—close enough for him to feel the faint tremors of her body, to see the weariness etched into her face and the shadows beneath her eyes, close enough to smell the fragrance of her perfume.

He straightened and moved away. ''Don't let it happen again.'' He sounded brusque, and he didn't try to soften it. He wouldn't let himself feel sympathy for her. Damn it, he wouldn't let himself feel anything gentle for her.

At the window he stopped, pulling the cord that would lower the blinds, then using another cord to tilt them to a forty-five degree angle. That allowed light to enter, but anyone standing outside would have difficulty seeing in.

Moving cautiously, as if to avoid more of his wrath, Tess sat sideways on the sofa and drew her knees to her chest. Part of her was still shaken from the incident, while part of her was ridiculously glad to see him. In spite of his temper,

Deke made her feel safer than Ross Boren or Al Meyers ever could.

Deacon Ramsey. The name was strong, masculine. It suited him. So did Deke—the nickname the men at the lineup and Ross Boren had used.

She watched silently as Ross Boren returned, suitcase in hand, and collected his radio and revolver from the end table. Deke turned from adjusting the blinds on the smaller window at the end of the room. "Don't worry about it, Ross," he said quietly. "You're not being pulled because you did anything wrong. Rowan was determined to stick me in here, and he told me to send either you or Al back."

"I could have handled this," the younger man said with conviction.

"I know it, and you'll get another chance. Look, be grateful. There's not a person in the office who wouldn't be happy to get pulled off a three-week assignment." He didn't look in Tess's direction as he said it. "Go on back to the office and check in with Scott. We'll see you sometime next month."

When the back door closed, Tess stretched and yawned. "So you can be human, after all."

Ignoring her, Deke stalked into the kitchen and pulled the refrigerator door open. Al had stopped at the grocery store last night and stocked up on enough food to last a week, but nothing there appealed to him. He decided on an apple and a glass of milk, taking them into the living room with him.

There he removed his leather jacket, hanging it on the closet doorknob, then—as Ross had done—he removed his pistol and radio from his belt and laid them on the table. He settled into the chair, picked up the paper and bit into the crunchy apple.

He was wearing jeans again, old and faded, that fit superbly. As nice as he'd looked in the suit at the police station that day, Tess decided she liked him better this way. The knit shirt, this time bright red, was tucked into the jeans and stretched taut over his broad chest. His leather tennis shoes had once been white but were now scuffed to a shade some-where between that and gray. He looked casual and relaxed in the comfortable clothes, but he'd told her before not to let appearances fool her. He was just as alert, just as ill-tempered and just as formidable as ever.

Even though he seemed absorbed in the paper, he was watching her. If she moved, he saw it. If she sighed, he heard it. It made her feel uncomfortably like a specimen on display.

When he finished with the front section and laid it on the table, she went to get it. She still wasn't certain she wanted to know any more about Donald Hopkins's murder than she'd already been told, but at least it would give her some-thing to do other than stare at Deke Ramsey all day.

She padded in her socks across the room and grasped the corner of the paper. As soon as she started to pull, though, he caught the opposite corner and held it. He looked at her over the Metro and State news section. "You don't want to read that."

Tess hesitated. He was probably right—she was begin-ning to suspect that he always was. Still, she tugged. "Con-sidering my involvement in this, I think I have a right to know what's going on."

This time it was Deke who hesitated. "Knowing more details about how Donald Hopkins died isn't going to make it any easier for you."

"Nothing is going to make it easier, Mr. Ramsey." But that wasn't quite true. Having him here made it easier, even though he annoyed, angered and frightened the hell out of her. "May I please have the paper?"

He gave it up with a shrug, then watched her settle on the couch and begin reading. She wore baggy gray sweatpants and an oversize white T-shirt. Without makeup, with her hair pulled back into a careless ponytail, she looked like a little girl in Mommy's clothes pretending to read Mommy's paper. If he could only continue to think of her that way, he thought grimly, he wouldn't have a problem.

But he knew she wasn't a little girl. He knew she was thirty-five years old, divorced, independent, mature. He knew that underneath the baggy clothes was a woman's body, slim, with soft curves and small breasts and gorgeous legs.

Before the vague stirrings of desire deep in his belly could grow stronger, he forced his attention back to her face, reading her emotions as easily as she read the newspaper. He knew when the color drained from her face that she was reading the details of the shooting, knew when she bit hard on her lower lip that she'd come across her own name and the common ground that had connected her to Donald Hopkins.

She looked up at him, her eyes big, her voice small. "They wrote about me."

"Yes, they did. You're lucky they didn't publish your picture right beside Hopkins's. That would have made it real easy for the neighbors around here to identify you this morning."

But she didn't respond to the sarcasm in his voice. She carefully folded the paper and laid it on the coffee table, then slid down until she was lying on the sofa and turned her face away from him.

Her parents had already read that story, she was sure. They shared the morning paper over breakfast every day. The reporter had stressed that she was the only other witness, that with Hopkins dead, only *she* could send Giamo to prison. He had all but written that she would be the next target. She had tried, in the little time Deke had given her last night, to reassure her parents, but all the assurances in the world would mean nothing to them now. Every minute of the next three weeks and longer, they would worry about her.

Deke knew the exact moment she fell asleep. He laid the paper aside and, for a moment, indulged himself in watching her. The tension slowly drained from her body, and the color returned to her face with the slow, steady rise and fall of her breasts. She looked even more innocent, even more fragile, in sleep. Not for the first time, he wondered if she could hold up under the stress the next few weeks and the trial were sure to bring. Would she testify, or would the pressure and fear be more than she could bear?

He admired her. He admired anyone with the courage to put his or her life on the line in the name of justice. Although he and Al and the others did it, too, that was different. It was their job, something they'd been trained to do. Nothing in Tess Marlowe's background could have prepared her for this—for the threat, the danger, the risk. Yet she was willing to go ahead anyway.

Angela had done it, too. She had given up everything to testify—*everything*. It had cost him a lot, as well. He had lost her.

He thought about Scott's remark this morning that Tess Marlowe might remind a man of Angela and smiled faintly. There was no physical resemblance beyond the fact that they were both beautiful women. Tess was short and slim; Angela had been tall, with generous curves. Tess's hair was long, brown, silky and straight; Angela's had been blond, waist-length, wild and heavy with curls. Tess's eyes were a solemn brown; Angela's had been a sparkling, lively blue.

But there were similarities, too—the innocence, the delicacy, the helplessness. They both gave the impression that they desperately needed to be cared for, that life was too hard for such gentle souls as theirs—an impression that he was beginning to suspect was a hundred and eighty degrees wrong in Tess's case, just as it had been in Angela's.

There was one other disturbing similarity: like Angela, Tess was a witness under his care. And like Angela, almost instantly he'd felt something for her. Lust? Desire? Need? He didn't label it. He didn't want to know. All that mattered was ignoring it. Denying it.

Destroying it.

* * *

Tess slept for a few hours, then awakened to the savory aromas of food being cooked. For a long moment she lay where she was, trying to remember why she was asleep on a couch in the middle of the day, why she wasn't at work. When she opened her eyes and saw Deke Ramsey standing at the foot of the sofa, everything came back—Donald Hopkins's murder, her own danger, the safe house.

"You want some lunch?"

Slowly she sat up, running her fingers through her hair. The band that had secured her ponytail slid out, and her hair fell, mussed and soft, to her shoulders. She combed her fingers through it and tried to remember the last time she'd eaten. It must have been lunchtime yesterday, she decided, considering the emptiness of her stomach.

"Yes, I do."

Her voice was husky with sleep, and her eyes were soft and barely focused. She should have looked unappealing, Deke thought, or at the very most cute, but not sexy. Not make-his-gut-clench-and-his-body-go-hard sexy. Gritting his teeth on a curse, Deke spun on his heel and returned to the kitchen.

Lunch was ham sandwiches heated in the microwave and dripping with melted cheese, and a big bag of spicy potato chips. Tess tried to tell him that it was good, but he wasn't in the mood for accepting compliments. When they finished, she tried to help him clear the dishes and put away the leftovers, but he wasn't in the mood for accepting help, either. After he growled at her that cleaning up was *his* job, she withdrew in a huff to the safety of the doorway. "I thought my taking a nap and leaving you alone would improve your mood," she said sarcastically, "but obviously I was wrong."

He dropped the dishes into the sink with a force that should have broken them.

"I understand that you don't want to be here, that you came because your boss ordered you to. I just want to ask one question." She paused. "Is that going to make a difference in the effort you expend on the job?"

He stood frozen at the sink, his hands gripping the counter. She swore she could see the anger spreading through the taut muscles of his back and the stiff line of his neck. Slowly he turned, and she decided that anger was perhaps too mild a word for the emotion that was darkening his eyes and spreading its thunder across his face. "What did you say?"

She shifted and wet her lips nervously, but didn't back down. "I want to know if the fact that you were ordered here against your will is going to affect how well you guard me."

For a long time he stared at her, the struggle to control his temper evident in the compressed line of his mouth. When he finally responded, his voice vibrated with barely leashed violence. "You're way out of line, lady. I don't have to like you to protect you. The only way Giamo's going to get to you is if he kills me first." His voice changed then, becoming derisive and mocking. "If your feelings are hurt because I haven't been nice to you, that's your problem. But don't *ever* question the way I do my job again."

Tess withstood the heat of his glare as long as she could, then beat a hasty retreat down the hall and into the safety of her bedroom. As small and musty smelling as it was, she could tolerate it for a while until Al Meyers woke up and Deke Ramsey went to bed—where, if luck was with her, he would sleep through the entire next three weeks.

By nine o'clock that evening Tess had a new understanding of the concept of cabin fever. She had eaten dinner, read the paper, watched television, chatted with Al Meyers and played half a dozen games of solitaire, and she was ready to climb the walls. She had never realized how much she depended on her usual routine—work, shopping, phone conversations with her mother, contact with other people—to maintain her sanity. She missed the familiar surroundings of her own apartment, the comforting sameness of her job, the freedom to go out for a walk, to stand on the balcony, even to look out the window. She didn't like having every move she made scrutinized, didn't like having two pairs of eyes—one friendly, the other not—watching her every time she so much as changed position on the couch. She especially didn't like the lack of privacy.

She could find privacy in her bedroom, she mused. Unless a danger existed, neither marshal would follow her there—Al, because it wasn't proper and Deke because... She smiled faintly. Having to stand guard over her was clearly bad enough for him; he would probably find being alone with her in the intimacy of her bedroom intolerable.

The crackle of the two-way radio on the coffee table interrupted her thoughts and drew her attention. The marshals outside checked in on a regular basis, letting them know that all was quiet in their little world. She wondered what the neighbors thought of the men who sat in their cars at night and discreetly watched the house and the streets. Did they suspect that the men were U.S. marshals on a stakeout? Did they wonder what was going on in this plain little brick and wood house? Did they even care?

Deke responded to the radio call, then got to his feet. "I'm going to bed, Al. Which room is mine?"

"The first one."

The one almost directly across from Tess's, he thought with a scowl. That was just what he needed for a good night's rest—to know that she was sleeping only twenty feet away. Balancing his pistol and radio in one hand, he picked up the heavy nylon bag he'd left near the kitchen door in the other. "If I oversleep, wake me at seven."

"Will do." Al watched him go down the hall, then turned to Tess. "You must be tired, too. I know you were up most of the night."

She smiled faintly. "I took a nap this morning." But he was right: she *was* tired. Just not tired enough to face the still darkness of her room. Not tired enough to risk the memories, still brutally vivid, of Walt Davis's death. And definitely not tired enough to allow her subconscious mind to contemplate the possibility of her own death.

She lasted through a television movie and the first few minutes of the eleven o'clock news. When the anchor began to lead into a report on Donald Hopkins's murder, she quietly said good-night and went to her room.

She undressed by lamplight and put on a pink cotton nightgown, then slid into bed. She wouldn't think bad thoughts, she cautioned herself as she snuggled deeper under the covers. She would concentrate only on good things, only on pleasure.

Her suggestion must have worked, because the last thing on her mind as she fell asleep a short while later was definitely a pleasure: a dark-eyed, dark-haired man who made her feel so much more than just safe....

Unlike most people, Deke came awake easily, instantly alert, with never a doubt as to where he was or what he was doing there. That little quirk was a definite advantage when he was working protection assignments, when even the slightest out of place sound, like the one that had just awakened him, could signal danger.

Swiftly he stepped into the jeans he'd left on the floor only a few hours ago, then reached unerringly in the darkness for his pistol. Chances were nothing was wrong—after all, the safe house was as secure as it could be—but he didn't take chances, not with a witness's life at stake.

The door swung open silently. From down the hall he could hear the television, tuned to a late-night talk show, and beyond that Al searching for a snack in the kitchen. So Al hadn't heard anything, or he would be down here with his own gun drawn.

For a long moment he stood motionless in the doorway, listening. The rest of the house was silent. Then the noise came again from across the hall. From Tess's room. A sob.

He considered calling Al and letting him check it out while he sneaked like a coward back into the safety of his own room, because he knew in his gut what he was going to find when he opened that door: Tess in a T-shirt or nightgown or nothing at all, vulnerable and frightened and badly in need of comfort. And he couldn't give it. He couldn't offer even the mildest, most impersonal of reassurances, because if he did, God help him, he would give everything. There was no middle ground with her. He couldn't be distantly polite or coolly professional. Hell, "cool" and "professional" had disappeared from his vocabulary since meeting Tess Marlowe.

There was another sound—breath caught in a swift intake—and he crossed the hall. Like his, her door swung silently inward. He took two steps inside and came to a sudden halt. The lamp was on, and it shone on Tess sitting in bed, her head bowed, her hands over her face. She was wearing a plain pink nightgown that left her arms bare, and she shivered in the cool night air.

As he watched her, a tightness began in his chest and slowly spiraled downward, making his nerves tingle and his muscles clench. He reminded himself that she was a witness. It was wrong to want her this way, so badly that he ached with it. He was here to protect her, his conscience insisted, not seduce her. Hadn't he learned anything with Angela?

But the reminders were pointless. All he could think of was that he *did* want her. Right or wrong, professional or not, he wanted Tess Marlowe with a ferocity that was frightening.

Satisfied that physically she was all right, and unable to do anything about her emotional state, Deke started to back out, intending to retreat to the cool, dark safety of his own room. There he would lie awake for a very long time, he thought with a touch of self-mockery, and wait for his hunger to ease enough so he could sleep again.

Tess couldn't say what made her look up at that moment. She hadn't heard the door open, hadn't heard him come in, hadn't heard him start to slip out again, but some-

how she had felt him. Perhaps it had been the fierce strength
of the glare that seemed permanently etched into the handsome lines of his face. Or maybe it had been the puzzling
sense of security he gave her even when he was at his most
hostile.

Or maybe, she acknowledged solemnly, it was something
simpler, something as basic as the desire he stirred in her, the
long-forgotten quivering deep in her belly, the sweetly uncomfortable fullness in her breasts, the dampness between
her thighs. With no more than a glower, he made her feel
those things. He made her think of the long, long months of
celibacy since her divorce . . . and of ending them. He made
her think of passion as hot as his anger, but gentle, too, and
fiery and loving. He made her want—in vain, she knew, because nothing would ever come of it. But the simple act of
wanting a man was something she'd thought Will had destroyed in her forever.

And Deke Ramsey was definitely a man worth wanting.
She'd known he was unfairly handsome since the first time
she'd really looked at him, and she had suspected that underneath the clothes was an equally unfairly nice body. As
he stood there now, wearing nothing but a pair of tight
faded jeans that rode low on his hips and clung to his thighs,
she knew "nice" was a gross understatement. His chest was
broad, hard-muscled, with a light scattering of hair, his belly
flat, his hips slim. Beneath the soft denim his thighs were
long, lean, muscular. His arms were powerfully shaped, too.
A nice body? She snorted silently. This was probably the
most gorgeous body she had ever seen.

But wanting was all she would have. Deke Ramsey could
barely stand the sight of her. She was his job, just as an-
swering the phone, typing letters and filing was her job, and
she meant no more to him than her job meant to her.

Deke realized how long they'd been staring at each other
and uncomfortably shifted his weight from one foot to the
other. Part of him wanted to forget the haunted fear that
had been in her eyes when she'd first looked up, to ignore

the soft, faint regret that had replaced it. That part of him wanted to walk out of the room without so much as a word and pretend tomorrow morning that these last few minutes had never happened—that he hadn't seen her in her soft pink gown, that he hadn't noticed how achingly beautiful she was. That, damn the consequences, he hadn't wanted more than anything to crawl inside those covers with her, to crawl inside *her*.

But he couldn't. He couldn't leave her looking so sad and lost. "Are you all right?"

His harsh tone effectively veiled the natural softening of his Georgia drawl and made Tess shiver once more. Not trusting her voice to be any steadier than she was, she simply nodded.

"You were crying."

She edged the covers up to her shoulders, huddling underneath them. "I was dreaming."

"About what?"

Her shrug was eloquent. "Dying."

Deke shifted again, moving his pistol to his left hand, leaning his right shoulder against the doorjamb. "If you want to talk to a psychologist, it can be arranged."

Before she could respond, there was a soft shuffling in the hall and Al appeared behind Deke. "Is everything okay?"

Tess drew strength from the kindly concern evident in the older man's face. "I had a bad dream," she said, leaning back against the headboard. "Mr. Ramsey was just suggesting that maybe I should see a psychologist. Apparently he thinks I'm not dealing with this as well as I should, especially since my dream disturbed his sleep."

Deke's eyes narrowed and cooled a few degrees. He didn't like her interpretation of his suggestion or the breezy, offhanded way she had dismissed it. And as for her disturbing his sleep...all the mind doctors in the world couldn't do a damn thing about that.

"It's not a bad idea, Tess," Al said. "You've been through some pretty traumatic experiences in the last couple of weeks. Just talking it over with someone who's trained to listen might help.''

"And what about the trial? When Anthony Giamo's lawyer finds out the government's only witness has been seeing a shrink? It wouldn't take a brilliant attorney to make the most of that. He would say I was so traumatized by seeing that man murdered that my testimony was undependable.'' She gave a shake of her head. "I'm not going through all this just to be judged unreliable in court.''

"We're probably talking a couple of hours, Tess, no more,'' Al argued. "No one would ever know, I promise.''

"Maybe, maybe not.'' She glanced from him to Deke, then back again. "I'm sorry, Al. It's nothing against you personally. I'm just learning to be a little bit skeptical when the government makes promises.''

He shrugged, acknowledging her right to skepticism. "Are you okay now? Will you be able to sleep again?''

"I think so.''

"Then good night, Tess. I'll see you tomorrow afternoon.''

He left, returning to the living room, but Deke remained where he was. "I wasn't suggesting that you're not handling this well,'' he said flatly.

"Weren't you?''

"Seeing someone die is tough. Seeing someone murdered is a hundred times worse. Fear isn't an easy thing to live with, and protective custody can be hell on a witness's nerves.''

"To say nothing of a marshal's?'' she asked dryly.

"Don't try to start a fight with me, Miss Marlowe. You'll lose. I don't fight fair.''

After Al's casual use of her first name, Deke's more formal "Miss Marlowe'' grated. She hid it behind a carefully composed mask. "Tell me something, Marshal.''

He had started to leave again, but her coolly polite request stopped him. He turned to her once more.

"What is it about me that you dislike so much?" Her question took him by surprise; she saw it flit across his eyes, then disappear. "At first I thought maybe you were nasty and ill-tempered with everyone, but you're not—just with me. You know nothing about me, so just what is it you dislike so much?"

"I know everything about you," he countered with a slow, lazy, arrogant smile. "I know where you were born, where you grew up, where you went to school. I know the date you got married and the date your husband filed for divorce. I know who you work for, who your friends are, who you date. I know your hobbies, your habits, your routines."

She stiffened, both angered and embarrassed that a group of people who'd never met her could have access to all the personal details of her life. "How?"

"Do you think the government's going to put a witness on the stand in a murder trial without knowing all her secrets?" The smile grew more arrogant. "The U.S. Attorney doesn't like unpleasant surprises."

"Donald Hopkins's murder—does the U.S. Attorney consider that an unpleasant surprise?"

His smile faded as quickly as she'd suspected it would. "No one regrets that more than Julia does."

"I beg to differ with you." Her voice was husky, and clearing her throat didn't help. "I think Mr. Hopkins's wife and children and grandchildren regret it far more than Julia ever could. I also think it's safe to say that *I* regret it more than she could." And since one of the results of the murder was forcing Deke to spend twenty-four hours a day with her, she thought it was also safe to say that even *he* regretted it more than Julia Billings.

"So..." She settled more comfortably in the bed. "You didn't answer my question. Why do you dislike me?"

He let his gaze linger on her for a long time, hiding his desire underneath a sharp edge of antagonism. "I don't have to like you to do my job, Miss Marlowe."

"I'm sure you don't. I'm sure if the tables were turned and Anthony Giamo was testifying for the government, you would treat him the same way you treat me. There's just one difference, Marshal. Anthony Giamo is a murderer and God knows what else. I'm just a woman who was unlucky enough to be in the wrong place at the wrong time."

Just a woman. Deke shook his head. She was wrong there. There was no way in this lifetime that Tess Marlowe could be "just a woman." No other woman but Angela had ever affected him this way, not even the one he'd married more than eighteen years ago. No other woman could make him forget his job, his duty, his obligations, with no more than a look. And no other woman could make him instantly, achingly hard without even a touch.

She was waiting for an answer, and he didn't have one to give. He wouldn't lie and make up some flaw in her to excuse his behavior, and he wouldn't give her the satisfaction of knowing what she did to him. So he settled on the same reply that had put her off so completely after lunch.

"If you have a complaint about the way I'm doing my job, Miss Marlowe, we'll discuss it, and we'll resolve it. But as I told you earlier, if your feelings are hurt because I'm not nice to you...that's your problem." He waited a moment for a response, then silently walked out, closing the door behind him.

Chapter 3

It was chilly again Wednesday morning, but the temperature outside was no colder than the reception Deke got inside. Tess was already awake and dressed, sharing a breakfast of eggs, bacon and toast with Al at the kitchen table. Her easy, warm conversation faded away when Deke walked into the room, and by the time he'd poured himself a cup of coffee and taken a seat at the small table, she sat in frigid silence, deliberately ignoring him.

It was just the response he needed to cool his desire for her, he kept telling himself. How could he think of steamy, passionate lovemaking with a woman who so closely resembled an ice sculpture?

But her wintry response didn't cool him off one degree. Instead, his mind conjured up tantalizing images of melting that ice, of unlocking the fiery nature he knew was inside—images that made him feel overly warm in spite of the morning's chill. Images that had already caused an uncomfortable swelling that pulled his jeans tight.

"Well, I'm going to bed," Al said around a yawn. "See you guys for dinner."

Tess and Deke sat alone in uncomfortable silence for a moment; then she asked hostilely, "Do you want some breakfast?"

"I can scramble my own eggs," he replied with just as much hostility, then silently clarified that: when it was safe to get up from the table. Considering the way he was feeling, that might take quite a while.

Tess scooted her chair back and went to the stove, using a pot holder to remove a dish towel-covered plate from the warm oven. She set it down with a thunk in front of Deke, then sat down and turned her attention to her own food.

Underneath the towel were a healthy portion of scrambled eggs, half a dozen strips of bacon and several warm slices of toast. He was searching for the generosity to thank her when she spoke again.

"Al cooked it, and Al saved it for you." She didn't want him to think that *she* cared whether he ever ate again. After last night, she was going to be just as cool and cutting as he was. She wasn't going to care a damn about him.

But that wasn't really possible. Honesty forced her to admit that, silly as it seemed, her feelings were hurt. She wasn't used to being around someone who actively disliked her. She was an easygoing, good-natured woman. The last person she'd been unable to get along with had been her ex-husband, and God knows she had certainly tried with him.

Not everyone had to like her; not everyone had to be nice to her. She wasn't naive enough to expect that. But it would have been nice, she thought regretfully, if the first man in years who made her remember what it was like to be a woman could at least tolerate her presence.

"Did you get any more sleep last night?"

Startled by his question, she set her fork down and linked her fingers together. There was no animosity in his voice this time—but no warmth, either. Just a flat, emotionless politeness. "I slept a couple of hours," she replied cautiously.

"It shows."

The implied insult set her teeth on edge. "Listen, Marshal—"

Cradling his coffee mug in both hands, he interrupted her. "My name is Deke."

She closed her mouth and warily watched him.

"I wasn't trying to insult you."

"Trying?" she asked snidely.

Frustration forced out each word. "It wasn't an insult. Al said you were up almost all of Monday night, and you only slept a few hours last night. You can't keep this up for three more weeks."

"So what would you suggest?" she demanded recklessly. "Sleeping pills? No, of course not, they're too dangerous. I know—why don't I talk to a psychologist? I can tell him all the things that bother me, and poof! Everything will be okay. No more nightmares, no more fear, no more wondering what kind of mess I've gotten myself into and whether or not I'm going to come out of it alive."

"Why don't you talk to *me*?" he asked quietly.

She stared at him for a long moment, then shoved her chair back and carried her dishes to the sink. After rinsing them, she leaned back against the counter, arms folded over her chest, and sarcastically asked, "What good would that do? What do *you* know about being afraid?"

"I've been a marshal for sixteen years. Before that I was in school, but the four years before *that*, I spent in the Marine Corps, part of it in Vietnam. I've seen people killed, I've had them trying to kill me, and I've killed my share. I know more about fear than you'll ever have to learn, Miss Marlowe."

Again she stared at him. Deciding if she could trust him? he wondered, and hoped she did. Even if he had been nasty and ill-tempered with her, he wanted her to trust him.

Suddenly her shoulders sagged as the bravado drained away. "I don't want to talk. I just want to go home. I want to forget that any of this ever happened. I want my life to go back to the way it was before Walt Davis died. I want to be left alone."

Deke twisted his chair around to face her. "But you can't have any of that. You can't go home. You can't forget. You can't, for a while at least, be left alone. And nothing's ever going to be quite the same again." He paused. "Those are facts, Tess, and you have to deal with them."

It was the first time he'd used her name, she thought numbly as she slid down to sit on the floor. "I'm not usually like this," she murmured, drawing her knees to her chest. "I'm usually a very even-tempered person."

"Usually, so am I." He saw her quick, disbelieving glance and was tempted to smile. "But under the circumstances, you can't expect things to be normal."

"I hate this. I hate spending twenty-four hours a day with people I don't know. I hate not being able to call my mom or sleep in my own bed or go to my job. I hate not even being able to take a walk around the block."

"Like I said, protective custody can be hell on your nerves."

She smiled bittersweetly. "*You're* hell on my nerves."

Well, lady, you aren't doing wonders for mine, either, he thought grimly. "I can ask my boss to send someone else in." For a long moment he was still, barely breathing, hoping she would accept the offer—and praying that she wouldn't.

Tess ran her fingers through her hair. Did she want Ross Boren or someone equally as pleasant and nice and harmless to take Deke Ramsey's place? Would she feel as safe with someone like that as she did with Deke Ramsey?

The answer, she thought with a rueful smile, was no. If he was this ill-tempered and mean with her, when they were on the same side, she could only imagine how much worse he would be with anyone who wanted to harm her. He was obviously dedicated to his job and, most likely, very good at it, since his boss had insisted on assigning him to this case. More importantly, he made her feel secure. If anything

happened, he would protect her. She couldn't make that
statement with as much conviction about anyone else.

"No," she said at last, pushing herself to her feet. "You
don't get off that easily."

Deke was aware of a mild disappointment, over-
shadowed by an overwhelming relief. If she'd said yes, he
would have contacted Scott on the two-way and told him
that his presence was doing the witness more harm than
good, and Scott would have replaced him. Then he wouldn't
have been around her—looking at her, talking to her, arguing with her, wanting her. No, then he would have spent
the next three-plus weeks worrying if his replacement was
good enough, cautious enough, conscientious enough, to
keep Tess alive.

She went into the living room, leaving him alone to finish his breakfast. From his seat, he could see most of the
room. Like a child who had learned a painful lesson, he
noticed that she stayed a more-than-adequate distance from
the windows before she settled on the couch with a news-
magazine open on her lap.

She moved often as she read—drawing first one leg beneath her, then the other, then propping both feet on the
coffee table or turning onto her side with one leg stretched
out and the other bent at the knee—and Deke watched every
motion. She wore jeans this morning, their rich dark color
attesting to their newness. Unlike the baggy sweatpants
she'd worn yesterday, which had hidden everything, the
jeans concealed nothing, molding her slim hips, shapely
bottom and gorgeous legs. As she shifted once again, sliding down farther onto the couch, the ivory sweater she wore
slid up, revealing a narrow line of skin above her jeans, still
showing the summer's tan. It looked smooth, soft, warm,
and all he had to do to confirm it, he thought, his mouth
suddenly dry, was walk ten feet and touch her.

Swallowing hard, he looked away, then closed his eyes,
concentrating on ignoring the hunger that wasn't going
away. What had he done to deserve this? He'd been a good

marshal. His sixteen years on the job had been distinguished ones. So why was he being punished, first with Angela, and now with Tess? Why, with his desire for her so strong, did Tess have to be a witness? Why couldn't he have met her the way men and women normally met—on a blind date, at a club, through mutual friends?

It had been six years since Angela. The first year had been tough. He'd been haunted by what-ifs and might-have-beens. Even a transfer from Jacksonville back to his old hometown of Atlanta hadn't helped much. But gradually he'd dealt with his feelings for Angela, had acknowledged that he'd loved her and lost her, and he'd gotten on with his life. There had been other women since then, though only a few. He was long past the age where a different woman every week, or even every month, was acceptable. The relationships had been mild—mildly lustful, mildly passionate, mildly affectionate, even mildly sad when they'd ended. That was the way he liked it. Invest as little of yourself in a relationship as possible, and come out intact when it ended.

But there was nothing mild about what he was feeling for Tess Marlowe. From the first moment he'd seen her, surrounded by cops in her office, she'd touched the part of him he'd kept safely hidden for six years, and he'd been fighting his feelings ever since. It had been the same with Angela; only he had foolishly given in to his need for her, and it had almost destroyed him. He wouldn't make the same mistake with Tess. No matter what the cost—and he was beginning to suspect it might be high—he wouldn't take the risk and lose again.

Although the food on his plate was cold and tasteless, he finished it anyway, stacked his dishes in the sink, then refilled his coffee mug. He had delayed as long as he could. It was time to go into the living room, time to face a long, endless day of watching Tess Marlowe.

Time to face a long, endless day of wanting her... and knowing he couldn't have her.

* * *

It was hard to say who was more relieved by Al's reappearance at about five that afternoon, her or Deke, Tess thought. The older man was so friendly and easygoing. If she wanted conversation, he would talk, but if she wanted silence, that was fine. He was a hell of a poker player, too, she admitted, remembering the early-morning games they'd played, and not bad with a crossword puzzle. And on top of all that, he didn't scowl every time he looked at her, the way Deke did.

She had thought, after their talk at breakfast this morning, that Deke would relax a bit, maybe quit looking at her as if she were the enemy instead of one of the good guys. But she'd been wrong. While he hadn't been quite as antagonistic as before, he hadn't been friendly, either, or welcomed the casual conversation that she indulged in with Al to keep her mind off her fears. His responses to her few conversational attempts had been short, clipped, abrupt, and the glare had never, when he was looking at her, left his face.

"Think you can stomach meat loaf for dinner?" Al asked from the kitchen doorway, drawing Tess's thoughts away from his partner.

She smiled. "Sure. My mother used to fix it every Thursday night when I was growing up."

"Didn't everyone's?" Al replied with a laugh. "But it was Tuesday night for my family. What about you, Deke?"

He didn't look up from the magazine he was reading. "My mother worked nights," he said in a flat voice. And after his father had died, she'd worked days, too. It hadn't been easy keeping a family of five boys together on what she could make as a nurse's aide at one of the local hospitals, so she'd gotten a day job working the breakfast and lunch shifts at a nearby restaurant.

When he realized that his answer had caused a brief silence, he looked up and saw they were both looking at him.

With a shrug, he smiled faintly. "I did most of the cooking, and I never made meat loaf."

"You can't cook," Al reminded him.

"But I make a hell of a sandwich. We all survived."

"You certainly did." Al directed his next remarks to Tess. "You should see his brothers. They're all bigger than he is."

Tess imagined an entire family of men who looked like Deke—dark and handsome, but bigger. It was a very appealing picture. How many should be in it? she wondered. Three? Four? Five? But she couldn't ask him. She knew that Al had three daughters—the oldest twenty-five and married, the middle one twenty-two and a senior at Georgia Tech and the youngest eighteen and in her last year of high school. She knew his wife was an interior designer and that they'd been married straight out of college nearly thirty years ago.

But all she knew about Deke Ramsey was that he had some brothers and that he wasn't married. Oh, yes, she added wryly, and he didn't much like her.

She rose easily from the couch and followed Al into the kitchen. "Can I help you with dinner?"

"You don't have to do that."

"I know. But if I sit around doing nothing one more day, I'm probably going to start pulling my hair out. So...can I help?"

"You can chop that onion. I thought we'd have mashed potatoes and green beans, too, so if you want to peel the potatoes..."

She took the paring knife he offered and began peeling away thin layers of onion skin. When she started dicing the onion, Deke came into the kitchen, his radio and pistol in hand, and took a seat at the table with his back to the wall, so he could watch. And what he mostly watched was her. She could feel his gaze, somber and unwavering, on her. The longer he stared, the clumsier she got, until she sliced neatly through the last chunk of onion and into the tip of her finger.

The knife had gone deep enough for a moment's pain, but not deep enough for the cut to bleed more than a drop. As Tess slowly turned to look at Deke, she lifted her finger to her mouth. When her lips closed around the tip, he swallowed but didn't look away. The action wasn't meant to be sensual, he told himself, because the look in her eyes was reproving, silently chastising him for deliberately making her uncomfortable. But that didn't stop the heat pumping through his body. It didn't stop the flush that crept into his face, or the hoarseness that would be in his voice if he tried to speak, or the fullness taking shape in his lower body.

Just as slowly as she'd faced him, she turned away, speaking to Al, giving him the onions and beginning work on the potatoes. *She* was perfectly normal, totally unaffected, he thought with a scowl, while *he* needed a long walk in the cool night air to lower the fever that had taken over his body.

In need of a release for the excessive physical energy she'd created in him, he left the kitchen and went to the living room windows, closing the blinds. Opening the blinds each morning was partly for security, to give them a clear view of the street during the day when there was no outside surveillance, and partly a concession to the neighborhood. They roused enough curiosity by suddenly moving into an empty house and never going out. If they kept the blinds and curtains closed up tight, people would begin to wonder what they were doing in here. The more they blended in and appeared like all the other families on the block, the better.

In front of the picture window, he paused, tilting one plastic slat so he could see out. At the end of the block on the left, parked behind a battered old Volkswagen, was a Grand Prix, four or five years old, painted an unremarkable brown. Well used, with a dent here and there, and badly in need of a wash and wax, the car fit in nicely with the other cars in the neighborhood. The only thing that set it apart was the engine, modified for pursuit. Looking at the body, though, no one would ever suspect the power under its hood.

A similar car, this one a ten-year-old Mustang, was parked on the cross street to the right. There, an empty lot provided a clear view of the house and the street while allowing the marshal inside to stay as far away as possible.

It would be a long, chilly night for the men assigned to those cars and for the two parked in the alley out back, Deke acknowledged as he stepped away from the window. But not as long as it would be for *him*. He would gladly trade places with any of them.

Dinner was ready by seven o'clock and finished by seven-thirty, but they lingered at the table. Al and Tess shared a pot of coffee—stimulation that she didn't need, Deke thought sourly, considering the state of her nerves and how little sleep she'd had the past two nights. But, certain she would take any suggestions he made as criticism and respond with a flare of anger, he didn't say anything. He just sat quietly and drank his milk.

Tess refilled her cup and stirred in sugar and cream. She knew the caffeine would probably make sleep hard to come by tonight, but that was what she was hoping for. If she could just stay awake until she was so exhausted that she *had* to sleep, then maybe she would sleep soundly, without dreams or fear. Without nightmares.

She heard the crackle of static on the radio, then a voice, but paid it no attention. Another routine check-in from the men in the street, she thought, watching the coffee in her cup swirl lazily as she stirred it. Just like the old town crier: seven-thirty and all's well.

But all wasn't well this time. Before the words on the radio—"...observed a late-model tan Buick with three occupants, just turned west on Anderson with no headlights..."—were finished, the first gunshots rang out. Al dropped to the floor, taking both his radio and revolver with him. Deke didn't bother with either of those items but grabbed Tess as he rose from his chair and, with the weight of his body, carried her down to the floor, rolling to the protection of the kitchen cabinets and settling on top of her.

His nearly two hundred pounds pushed her down to the linoleum with a thud, forcing the breath from her lungs, causing her to catch her lip between her teeth. For an instant, tasting blood, she was dazed, confused. Before she could recover, before she could even breathe, the gunfire increased, loud and rapid, splintering wood, shattering glass, destroying the walls and the furniture around them. It seemed to go on forever, making her ears ring, setting every nerve in her body to quivering, filling her with the need to cry, to scream hysterically until it stopped. She tried to raise her hands to cover her ears, to block out whatever sound she could, but the weight of Deke's body held her trapped, and she gave up the struggle when she heard his curses, soft and vicious, in her ear.

The silence, when it came seconds later, was as deafening as the shots had been. Tess felt her heart start beating again, thudding painfully in her chest, and she filled her lungs with sweet air, her breath catching on a sob.

Her entire body was trembling badly. Deke could feel it even in her feet, trapped beneath his. He knew she couldn't have been hit—he had shielded her with his own body—but she must have been terrified. Hell, *he* was. He was frightened beyond anything he'd ever felt before. And he was furious. He was so furious that he thought he might explode.

The radio began squawking again, and he heard Al answer. Slowly he shifted off Tess, rising to his knees, gently laying his hands on her shoulders. "Tess? Are you all right?"

She didn't respond. Her forehead was pressed to the cool linoleum, her eyes squeezed shut, and she was shaking with silent sobs.

"Is she okay?" Al asked, slowly getting to his feet.

Deke forcefully lifted her, maneuvering her to sit with her back against the cabinet, then lifted her face so he could see her. "Tess, answer me, damn it," he said sharply. "Are you hurt?"

Eyes still closed, she shook her head. Her cheeks were wet with tears, but she had them under control now. It was the trembling she couldn't stop.

"She's okay," Deke said. "Just scared senseless."

"Who isn't?" Al muttered before passing along the information.

Deke stood up and strode to the table. Some of the dishes were broken, and the chairs were shot up. The coffeepot was shattered, the milk carton full of holes, and the liquids had mixed and were dribbling to the floor. On the unoccupied side of the table lay his radio, also broken, and his pistol, dry and unharmed. He slid it into the holster threaded through his belt and secured it, then went to the back door to unlock it. The cars on the west side of the house were gone, in pursuit of the shooters, but the other two would be here any time now, probably as bewildered and outraged as *he* was.

This was a *safe house*, he thought, tasting the anger, the sense of violation. No one made a hit on a safe house! This location was closely guarded, given only to those with a valid need to know in the Marshals Service, the FBI field office and the U.S. Attorney's office—only to people he knew, people he trusted.

And one of them was dirty. One of them had sold them out.

There was a pounding on the back door. Although he knew it would be the other marshals, he and Al drew their guns anyway. The two marshals had their guns drawn, too, when he opened the door, and they both wore the same shocked, disbelieving expression. "My God, Deke, what happened?" one of them demanded, leaning against the doorjamb to catch his breath.

"Your guess is as good as mine." Deke looked over the man's shoulder and saw neighbors beginning to come out of their houses. In the distance and drawing nearer were the wails of sirens, quite a few of them, he judged. A drive-by shooting in a nice, quiet neighborhood like this was sure to draw plenty of attention. "We're okay in here. Keep all those people back until the cops arrive. We don't want anyone getting close enough to see our witness."

When they left again, he closed the door and turned to Tess. She was sitting where he'd left her, staring sightlessly at her unsteady hands. He bent, brushing his hand over her hair. Even at a time like this, he thought with disgust, he couldn't help noticing that it was as soft and silky as it looked. "Why don't you come into the living room and sit down?" he suggested, trying, for his sake, not to be gentle but unable to completely resist the urge. The result was an unaccustomed huskiness in his voice.

She shook her head without looking at him. "I'll stay here," she whispered.

Within minutes the street out front was blocked with cars, both marked and unmarked police cars, and unmarked units belonging to the Marshals Service and the FBI. Their blue lights cast an eery glow in the darkness, the static and crackle of their radios disturbing the quiet that should have been found on such a street at night.

Scott Rowan took a look around the living room, then joined Deke, Al and Thad McNally in the dining area. "What do you think they were using?"

"AK-47s," Deke replied. He'd heard enough of them to recognize their distinctive report, and it fit the rapid rate of fire. In the few seconds the car had been out front, the shooters had gotten off several hundred rounds.

Scott gestured toward Tess, who was still sitting on the floor, and lowered his voice. "What about her? Is she going to be all right?"

"She'll be okay," Al replied at the same time Deke said, "She's just shaken."

Their boss looked at her again. She was staring at nothing, knees drawn to her chest, hands clasped tightly together, face drained of all color. Then he looked skeptically at his men. "Shaken?"

It was Deke who responded, his voice hard and cold. "You would be, too, if someone had just come after you with an AK. She'll be fine."

"Well, keep an eye on her. We don't want her falling apart on us now." Scott returned to the living room, taking Al with him.

Thad drew Deke away from the doorway, then echoed the question the first marshal to arrive on the scene had asked. "My God, Deke, what happened? This is a *safe house*."

"You *know* what happened." He glanced at Tess and saw that she was paying no attention to them, but he dropped his voice to a whisper anyway. "Someone sold us out." He saw that Thad wanted to deny the possibility, and saw, too, that he couldn't.

"You don't think it's possible that someone followed one of the men stationed outside?" Even as he asked, Thad knew the answer.

"No. I know those men. They're too good, too careful. The only way Giamo could have found Tess here was if someone told him. Someone gave him this address."

The implications of that were enough to keep both men silent for a moment. Finally Thad turned to watch Tess. "Is she going to hold up?"

"Yes."

"You sound awfully sure."

"I am. She's a lot stronger than she looks."

"Is that respect I hear in your voice?" Thad smiled faintly. "And coming from a man who had to be ordered here in the first place."

Deke didn't smile. He looked fiercer than ever. "Are you hinting that maybe I had something to do with this?"

His question stunned the FBI agent. For a long moment they stared at each other; then Thad responded coolly, "If I thought you had anything to do with it, pal, I'd take you out and shoot you myself."

Stepping around Deke, Thad walked into the kitchen and nelt beside Tess. "Miss Marlowe, do you remember me? 'm Special Agent McNally, with the FBI."

She glanced at him only briefly. "I think I've changed my nind, Mr. McNally," she said, her voice oddly calm. "I hink I want to go home."

"I'm afraid we can't let you do that. Someone tried to kill ou."

She smiled then, a taut, humorless gesture. "I know. I vas here." Suddenly, uncontrollably, she shivered. "I guess t's time for another of your you'll-be-safe-and-nothing's-;oing-to-happen-to-you speeches, right?" She paused, but either man spoke. "Well, save your breath. I've heard it rom the U.S. Attorney's office, from the FBI and from the narshals, and I don't believe it anymore. As long as I'm villing to testify against Anthony Giamo, I'm *not* going to e safe."

Deke crouched beside her. "But you'll be alive," he said aarshly. He grasped her chin, forcing her to look at him. "If we hadn't taken you into custody, you would be dead right aow. Giamo's men were probably looking for you the night I picked you up. These people aren't stupid. They knew that as soon as we found out about Donald Hopkins's murder, we would take you in. Ideally, they needed to kill you then. The only reason they didn't was because *we* got to you first."

She jerked away from him. "So they tried here!"

"*Tried*, Tess. They *tried*, but they failed. Listen to me. If you refuse to testify, we can no longer offer you protection, and then they *will* kill you. As long as you live, as long as you can identify Anthony Giamo as the man who murdered Walt Davis, you're a danger to him, whether you testify or not. From the moment you saw him shoot Davis, you've had only two choices—to cooperate with us, or to die." He paused. "You've got to trust us, Tess."

"Trust you?" she whispered, her voice unsteady. "You can't even trust each other! You people told me how safe I

was here because you were the only ones who knew where
was! Well, somebody told Giamo.''

Deke exchanged grim looks with Thad, then spok
quietly. ''Then trust *me*.''

She held his gaze for endless seconds, searching for as
surance, for reasons why she *should* trust him. She foun
revulsion and anger—no, more than that. Fury. Fury tha
someone he'd worked with had almost gotten them killed
that someone he'd trusted had betrayed them. It could b
someone who was in the house right now. For all she knew
it could be Thad McNally or Al Meyers. Or the outrag
could be an act. It could be Deke himself.

Slowly she turned away to hide the path her thoughts were
taking, and her eyes settled on the cabinets across from her.
They were badly damaged by an uneven row of bullet hole
that stretched from one end to the other. Curiously sh
turned to study the cabinets she was leaning against an
found a matching row. The bullets had exited these cabi
nets bare inches above Deke's body when he'd shoved he
down, then entered the others. *The only way Giamo's going
to get to you*, he'd told her yesterday, *is if he kills me first*
She had been terrified during the shooting, but *he* had beer
in more danger.

With an uneven sigh, she ran her fingers through her hair
and dislodged particles of plaster and wood. ''All right.''

He had to lean forward to make out her whisper. Quickly
he got to his feet. ''Scott, come in here, would you?'' he
called. ''Al, get her stuff together.''

When Scott Rowan came in, he, Deke and Thad huddled
together, talking in low tones, as they'd done earlier. This
time, though, Tess was listening.

''We don't have any options left,'' Scott said wearily.
''She goes to jail.''

''No.''

He looked annoyed by Deke's flat refusal. ''Be reasonable, Ramsey. Whoever knew about this place probably

knows about the other safe houses, too. She'll be virtually untouchable in jail.''

"Yeah, and after being locked up for the next three weeks in a place not much bigger than this kitchen, she'll be virtually nuts by the time the case goes to trial," Deke retorted. Protective confinement in the federal correctional center wasn't even open for consideration as far as he was concerned.

"You want to try another safe house? You want to risk this again?" Scott shook his head. "You might not be so lucky next time. They might get all of you."

Deke looked at Tess. Her eyes had widened at the mention of jail. They were so big that they dominated her face, and they were filled with dread and fear. "No," he quietly agreed. "Not another safe house."

"Then it's the correctional center, unless you can come up with a better idea."

"Yeah, I have a better idea." It damn sure wasn't better for him, but it was the only solution. It would keep her safe. It would keep her alive. As for what it would do to him, he could deal with that later, when the trial was over. He swung his gaze back to Scott and Thad. "Let me take her out of the city—just me. No team."

There was a heavy silence; then Scott made the obvious objection. "To move her safely, you need at least six, maybe eight, men."

"One woman traveling with six or eight men is going to draw attention. One woman, one man—nobody will look twice."

"Where would you take her?"

Deke hesitated. He knew his boss was already skeptical; this part of his proposition would probably prompt an adamant, unyielding refusal. "That would be between you and me. No one else would need to know—not Thad, not Frank Harris, not even Julia Billings."

Scott walked to the doorway leading into the wrecked living room, surveying the damage while talking to the man

behind him. "You expect me to let you take off to parts unknown with Tess Marlowe and to tell the United States
Attorney that she has no need to know where the only witness in a major murder case has gone?" He gave a dis-
mayed chuckle. "She'd have my head on a platter."

"Protecting the witness is *your* job, not Julia's," Thad
pointed out. "You don't owe her anything beyond produc-
ing Miss Marlowe in court on December eighth."

Scott looked at him over his shoulder. "You think this is
a good idea?"

Thad shrugged. "*I* don't want to know where she's being
held. I think, under the circumstances, the fewer people who
do, the better. Someone's dirty, Scott, and we don't know
who it is. We don't know who to trust. Let Deke take her
away. She'll be a hell of a lot safer away from Atlanta with
him than she will be here."

"All right." Scott came back. "Julia and Frank are going
to scream their heads off, but...take her away. What do you
need?"

"A different car—something with four-wheel drive." It
was only mid-November, but it wasn't unusual for the place
Deke had in mind to get sleet and occasionally snow this
early in the winter. "Get me another two-way, too. Mine
took a couple of hits. And some cash." The twenty dollars
in his pocket wouldn't take them far, and the use of credit
cards was definitely out of the question. That would leave a
paper trail that any idiot could follow.

"All right," Scott repeated. "I'll take care of it now.
Where do you want to meet?"

They agreed on a location in the parking lot of a mall not
far away, then Scott left. Deke went to his room to pack,
leaving Tess alone with Thad, who smiled reassuringly at
her. "The plan's a little unorthodox, but it'll work. You'll
be safe with Deke."

"Maybe."

The doubt in her voice made him focus more clearly on her. "You don't think he was involved in what happened here, do you?"

"No, he wasn't." She believed that. For a moment back there, she'd been forced to consider the possibility that he *was* involved. But in ways she couldn't explain, even to herself, she knew it wasn't so. It wasn't that she wanted to believe in his innocence because she was attracted to him; it was something more basic than that. She just *knew* that he would never betray himself or his responsibility like that, the same way she knew that *she* could never do such a thing.

"But, like you said, Mr. McNally," she continued, "you don't know who to trust. If you don't know, how can I?"

"You trust Deke."

She nodded.

"And he trusts Scott Rowan."

Her nod this time was more reluctant. With a weary sigh, she moved away from the counter and got her first real look at the damage done to the rest of the house. She shuddered violently. "I wished to God none of this had ever happened."

Thad McNally smiled regretfully. "So do I, Miss Marlowe."

Deke and Al returned with their bags. While the older marshal loaded them in the car outside, Deke got their jackets from the closet and shrugged into his while Thad helped Tess with hers. "Are you ready?" Deke asked. When she nodded, he turned to Thad. "Do you have to hang around here?"

Thad shook his head. "We've got plenty of people here."

"Follow us for a while, will you?" There was always the possibility, one he didn't want to mention in front of Tess, that the purpose of the drive-by shooting hadn't been to kill her but rather to flush them out of the house and onto the streets, where an ambush would offer the shooters a much better chance of success.

The FBI agent agreed, called to one of his men that he was leaving, then led the way outside. He opened the door of Deke's car for Tess, then bent down. "Take care," he said solemnly. After pushing the lock down, he closed the door, then went to his own car, which was parked in the street.

Tess fastened her seat belt, then huddled deep in her coat. She felt the marshal watching her while he let the engine warm, but she didn't look at him. As he backed out of the driveway, she saw signs of the exterior damage to the house and choked back a half laugh, half sob. "It's getting to the point where being awake is as big a nightmare as the dreams when I sleep."

"After spending the next three weeks alone with me, you'll think getting shot at was a piece of cake." His teasing effort fell flat. In one sentence he'd managed to touch on two very disturbing thoughts. His anger over tonight's attack was based on more than an associate's betrayal. That betrayal alone was enough to make him angry, but the fact that it was directed toward Tess—delicate, helpless, innocent Tess—was the true cause of his fury.

As for spending the next three weeks alone with her... His jaw set in a taut line. He must have been out of his mind to even suggest it when the need for her had already burned its way into his soul. But he hadn't been able to face the idea of her locked up like a criminal, and he hadn't been willing to turn the responsibility for her safety over to someone else— someone who might betray her again. She had to come out of this safe and whole, and if that meant he had to spend the next three weeks in hell, that was what he would do.

Routinely, he checked the rearview mirror as he drove. Traffic was light, and the only car that stayed with them was Thad's. He'd known the possibility of an ambush was remote, but he wasn't taking any chances.

When they turned into the mall parking lot, Thad drove on. Deke found the meeting place, backed the car into a space and shut the headlights off. He kept the engine running.

"Where are we going?" Tess asked. Her voice sounded small, heavy, lifeless.

"The northeastern part of the state."

"And nobody will know where we are except your boss?"

"That's right."

"You're sure he won't tell anyone?"

He was looking to the left, the right, straight ahead—everywhere but at her. When he answered, there was dry sarcasm in his voice. "I assure you, he won't. He recognizes the seriousness of the situation."

"'The seriousness of the situation.'" Her laugh was thinly controlled. "We almost got killed tonight! I'm glad someone realizes it was serious."

Finally he turned his head to look at her. Her nerves were stretched to the breaking point—he could see it in her eyes, in her face, in the stiff, unyielding lines of her body. The tight rein she was keeping on her emotions was costing her dearly. She needed to release them, to react as hysterically as anyone else would in her place, but for some reason, she wouldn't. Because she thought it would annoy him? Had he somehow made her feel that she had to keep whatever she was feeling under rigid control? "Why don't you cry?" he asked bluntly.

"What?"

"Why don't you cry or yell or stamp your feet or hit something? Why do you have to pretend to be so brave and strong?"

She sat silent for a long time, blinking back the tears that stung her eyes. Finally, in a quavering, husky voice, she replied, "I'm not brave or strong. It's just that if I start crying... I'm never going to stop." It was the plain, simple truth. If she gave in to the fear, it would destroy her.

Deke looked away. Julia had suggested on Tuesday—God, was that only yesterday?—that perhaps Tess dealt with fear by refusing to acknowledge it. Denial was better than hysteria, she'd said. At the time he'd agreed, but right now he thought a little hysteria would go a long way toward easing the stress that Tess was under.

Maybe this change of scene would help. She would still be stuck twenty-four hours a day with a near stranger, but the confinement wouldn't be so strict. Whenever he went out—for food, supplies or to contact Scott—she would go with him. And if she had to be a prisoner, the area where they would be staying, the foothills of the Blue Ridge Mountains, was a beautiful place to be held.

He saw the truck turn into the parking lot and head toward them before Tess did. Warily he slid his hand behind him to his gun, then relaxed when he recognized Scott behind the wheel. Scott parked on Tess's side, so that her move from the car to the Bronco would be a simple matter of a few steps. While she settled in, tossing her purse and coat into the back seat and fastening her seat belt, the two men transferred the luggage.

Deke climbed in and rolled the window down to get final instructions from his boss.

"Call me as soon as you find a place tonight. And check in with me at the office every other day between ten and noon, even on weekends. If you have to move for any reason, let me know as soon as possible." He removed a thick envelope from inside his jacket and handed it to Deke. "If you need more money, let me know and we'll arrange something."

Deke pocketed the envelope. "If anyone seems unduly concerned about where I've taken her..."

"This leak is going to be a joint FBI-Marshals Service investigation. We'll find out who's responsible."

Deke glanced at Tess, then lowered his voice a shade. "I know they're going to look at me along with everyone else. If that connection comes up between me and Giamo..." He broke off, trusting his boss to understand.

"I'll handle it." Scott stepped back, ran his fingers through his graying hair, then looked from Tess to Deke. He seemed to want to say something, but couldn't find the words. Finally he muttered, "For God's sake, be careful."

With a grim smile, Deke backed out of the parking space, rolling the window up as he did. He shifted positions, settled his seat belt more comfortably, then glanced at Tess. "From now on, it's just you and me."

She gave him a sickly smile, then turned to lean her head against the cool window glass. His words brought an old song to mind, the one about two people alone against the world. She wasn't sure she liked the odds.

Chapter 4

They took Interstate 85 northeast out of Atlanta, then switched to a short divided highway, then a state road. The farther they got from the city, the fewer the towns and the thinner the traffic became. Deke drove below the speed limit and kept a vigilant watch in his mirror, tracking the cars behind them. Few followed them for long, and none was interested enough to drive at the slower pace he'd chosen. Every car that came up behind them eventually passed and disappeared ahead.

He liked the response of the Bronco. Like all their undercover vehicles, it had a powerful engine and responded to the lightest touch. It was relatively small, easily maneuverable and would stand them in good stead if they ran into bad weather. Scott had chosen well.

Restlessly, he shifted, then glanced at Tess. "Take the wheel, will you?"

Without hesitation she leaned over and grasped the steering wheel with one hand. While she steered, he wriggled out of his leather jacket, tossed it in the back, then took over again. "Why don't you climb in back and get some rest?"

"No, thank you." She winced when she heard the prim formality of her response. "I don't think I'll ever sleep again."

"Sleep deprivation is an effective form of duress," he remarked conversationally. "Keep someone awake long enough, and eventually he'll tell you everything you want to know."

The look she gave him was long, silent and wry; then she shrugged. "I've already told you everything I know. If you'll tell me where we're going, I can drive, and you can climb in back and get some rest."

"No thanks. You're in no condition to be driving."

"And you are?"

"Sure." He offered a half grin. It felt rusty. "Getting shot at doesn't faze me."

"Yeah, sure," she agreed dryly. "Back there on the floor in that kitchen, when I was trying my best not to scream hysterically, I believe you were the one swearing violently."

The unaccustomed grin faded under a renewed surge of fury as he remembered the soundless sobs that had wracked her body. "I'm not ashamed to admit I was afraid back there. Anyone who can sit through the two hundred-some rounds of fully automatic fire from an AK-47 without being terrified is a fool or a liar, and I'm not either."

"Why did he do it?" she asked suddenly, the quiver back in her voice.

"Who?"

"Whoever gave Giamo the location of that house."

His voice when it came was hard and cold, and the fierce scowl was back in place on his face. "I don't know. Money. Blackmail. We'll find out eventually."

She turned to face him as far as the seat belt would allow. "Knowing that someone with connections to the Mafia wants me dead *should* be the most frightening thing in my life. But it doesn't begin to compare to knowing that someone with connections to the *government*—an FBI agent, a marshal, someone in the federal prosecutor's office—wants me dead. You people are supposed to be above suspicion. You're supposed to be honest and loyal and trustworthy.''

He didn't respond. He couldn't tell her she was wrong, and she didn't need to be told she was right. They *were* supposed to be above suspicion, and honest and loyal and trustworthy. They were supposed to be the good guys, the ones she could count on, the ones she could entrust her life to, and one of them had almost gotten her killed. Deliberately.

She sounded bleak as she turned back to lean against the locked door. "I don't know. I guess money will buy anything these days. Even an FBI agent." She sighed deeply. "Even a marshal."

She lost interest in the conversation after that, and Deke let it end. He didn't resent her bitter disillusionment—hell, he shared it, perhaps felt it even more deeply. She had been betrayed by a stranger whose authority she had inherently trusted, while he had been betrayed by someone he worked with and socialized with, by someone he called friend. No matter what level—city, county, state or federal—there was nothing as bad as a dirty cop. No one deserved prison, or worse, more than a cop who used the law to commit his own crimes.

It was nearly eleven o'clock when they drove into Altus, a small town about ten miles south of the North Carolina state line and a few miles west of the South Carolina border. He pulled into the first motel he saw, a reasonably clean-looking place with a garish pink neon vacancy sign shimmering in the night air. He stopped in front of the office and switched the engine off, then pulled the envelope of money from his coat pocket, counting out five twenties and sliding them into his jeans pocket. There was no need to flash a lot of cash.

"I'm going to get a room. Keep the doors locked." He looked at her, spoke her name and realized that she was asleep. Taking the keys with him, he climbed out, pulled his jacket on to cover his gun, closed the door as quietly as he could and went inside.

The desk clerk, a potbellied gray-haired man in overalls, slid a registration form across the counter to Deke without taking his attention from the small color television on his desk. "We got double beds and king-size beds, and only one to a room. You want two beds, you have to get two rooms. The doubles are twenty-four dollars a night for one person, and the kings are thirty-four. There's five bucks extra for the second person. Plus tax."

Deke didn't look up from the card he was filling out. If he had, the old man would have seen the frustration in his eyes. Connecting rooms were out of the question—there was no way he could provide security for two rooms. But if he had to share a bed with her, it would damn sure be the biggest one he could find, so she wouldn't crowd him—or tempt him. As if simply being in the same room wasn't tempting enough. "We'll take a king."

"Just you and your wife, Mr. . . . ?" The clerk picked up the three by five card and squinted to read it. "Mr. Marshall?"

"Yes, just the two of us."

"That'll be thirty-nine dollars plus tax. Room one-eighteen. Near the end of the row."

Deke gave him three twenties, pocketed his change and the room key, and started to leave.

"Checkout's at 11:00 a.m. Not 11:30 and not noon," the old man called after him. "Eleven a.m. sharp."

Deke climbed into the truck and drove toward the end of the building. One-eighteen was three rooms from the end, and, judging from the dark interiors and open drapes, those rooms were all empty. So were one-seventeen, one-sixteen and one-fifteen. Business was not booming at the Altus Motel tonight.

Between the last two rooms were a soda machine, an ice machine and a pay phone. He could call Scott from there, he decided, and avoid charging the call to the room or calling collect. It was just one more precaution to keep their location a secret.

Tess didn't stir when he got out of the Bronco again and set the luggage inside the door. If he weren't so tired himself, he would sit here and let her sleep. God knows, she needed it. But he *was* tired, and out in the open wasn't the best place for her to be. He propped the door open with her suitcase, turned back the covers on the wide bed and returned to the Bronco, carefully opening the passenger door, bracing her with one hand so she didn't fall as her support swung away.

She was incredibly light in his arms. If she weighed even a hundred pounds, he would be surprised. He pushed the door lock down with his elbow, shoved the door shut with his shoulder and carried her inside, kicking the suitcase away as he passed so the door could swing shut. He laid her on the bed, removed her tennis shoes and pulled the covers over her, and through it all, she never stirred.

He wanted to stand beside the bed for a few hours and just look at her, but business came first. He locked the door and closed the drapes, blocking the faint rays of the street lamps. Next he checked the bathroom. There was a window in there, its lock flimsy and easily jimmied, but it was a tiny window. Only someone very small—like Tess—could squeeze through it. Still, he found a can of hair spray in her bag and wedged it in place so the window couldn't be raised.

Suddenly weariness swept over him like a wave, causing him to lean back against the door and close his eyes. He'd been alert and energetic up until now because he'd *had* to be. Now all he wanted—needed—was sleep, but there was one last thing he had to do.

The cold penetrated his jacket as he walked the fifty feet to the pay phone. He placed his call, then made a precautionary survey of the area while waiting for Scott to answer. There was no activity in the parking lot. The few guests at the motel seemed to be in for the night. Through the plate glass windows of the office, he could see the night clerk still watching television and laughing heartily.

When Scott picked up the phone, Deke turned to lean against the wall, watching their room. "We're in Altus at the Altus Motel," he said in clipped tones. "Room one-eighteen. We're only staying for the night. Tomorrow I want to look for someplace nicer, a little more secure."

"Did you have any problems?"

He yawned. "Nah. How are things going at your end? Anything on the shooters?" He knew two members of the surveillance team had gone in pursuit of the Buick, but he'd figured they wouldn't catch it. Scott confirmed it for him.

"Tompkins was in an accident that disabled his car. You know how panicked some people get when they see a blue light. They don't know what to do, and as often as not, we're the ones who pay the price. Velez stayed with the shooters for another four or five miles, then lost them in traffic. The car they were driving was found abandoned downtown about an hour ago. It was wiped clean."

"Of course. And it was probably reported stolen a couple of hours earlier, wasn't it?"

"You guessed it. Are you calling from a pay phone?"

"Yeah. I'm about fifty feet from the room." He yawned. "Listen, I'm beat. When we find a new place, I'll let you know."

Back in the room, he locked the door, fastened the security chain and propped the only chair beneath the doorknob. None of the measures actually made the room safe, but at least someone trying to break in would make enough noise to awaken him. Then he removed his jacket and shoes, laid his pistol on the nightstand, turned out the light and climbed into bed.

Unused to sleeping fully dressed, he tossed fitfully for a few minutes, then got up again and removed his shirt, belt and socks. It would be inappropriate to take off anything else, he drowsily reminded himself as he settled in again. Totally inappropriate.

Tess awoke with a start, her eyes squeezed shut, her hands over her ears amplifying the sound of her ragged breathing. Another dream, she thought, still hearing the echoes of the gunfire in her head.

She sat up in bed, shivering in the cold room, and realized she was still dressed. An instant later she realized that she wasn't alone. Deke was coming out of the bathroom, where a dim light shone, looking as haggard as she felt, carrying a plastic cup of water and wearing nothing but faded jeans. He thrust the cup into her hand. "Here, drink this," he growled as he slid under the covers on the opposite side of the bed.

"I—I'm not thirsty," she said numbly.

"With all the noise you've been making, you should be." He rubbed both hands over his face, then yawned, not bothering to cover it.

Noise? Tess raised her free hand to her face. Her cheeks were wet, and her eyes felt puffy—and not, she realized, from lack of sleep. She had been crying in her sleep, because of the dream, and just like last night, she had awakened him, since they were sleeping in the same bed. Swiftly, her head snapped around to look at him. "What are you doing in my bed?"

"We got double beds and king-size beds, one to a room. You want two beds, you have to get two rooms," he parroted the clerk. "We're not sharing a double, you're not getting a room by yourself, and I'm not sleeping on the floor."

"This must be against the rules," she protested in a small voice. "Surely you people have rules when you do things like this, and this must be breaking them."

"In case you didn't notice, lady, the game changed last night. There aren't any more rules. Someone's trying to kill you, and I'm going to keep you alive."

"We could get connecting rooms and leave the door open. It would be better that way. I have bad dreams—they disturb your sleep."

He turned onto his stomach, cradled his pillow in both arms and opened one eye to look at her. "It isn't your dreams that disturb me," he muttered, then took a deep breath. "You may have noticed that I'm not in a very good mood. I am exhausted. I couldn't compromise your virtue, if that's what you're worried about, if my life depended on it."

When she blushed, he closed his eye and turned his face into the pillow. Earlier he'd told her that he wasn't a fool or a liar, but even then he'd lied. He *was* a fool when it came to her, wanting what he couldn't have, needing what wasn't his. And just now he had lied again. He wasn't lying facedown because it was comfortable. As jumpy as she was about sharing a bed with him, she would be unmanageable if she had even the vaguest idea how aroused he was.

He hadn't been. He'd been fine all night, even when her tears had awakened him from a badly needed sleep, until the moment he'd come out of the bathroom and seen her sitting there, looking vulnerable and soft and more beautiful than any woman had the right to be. Instantly, with a fierceness that had left him breathless, he'd grown achy and hard, and the condition showed no signs of abating anytime soon.

Tess's cheeks were burning. She wasn't concerned about what *he* might do. Deke Ramsey was a professional. She would bet he never lost control. She, on the other hand, had little control left to lose. God only knew what she might ask of him if she lost it. "I…uh…" She sipped the water. "I'm sorry."

"For what?"

"Waking you. Snapping at you."

"Forget it," came the muffled response.

"I—I don't like sleeping in my clothes. Could I put on my nightgown?" she asked hesitantly. It was long and full and at least as modest as the jeans and sweater she wore.

He remembered the small portion of the gown he'd seen last night—pink, soft, very feminine—and choked back a groan. "No, not if—" He broke off. Not if you want me to stay on my side of the bed, he'd started to say. What if, just what if, she said no, she didn't want that? He could tell himself not to touch her, but God help him, if she showed even the slightest sexual interest in him, how would he find the strength to stay away? "No," he finished abruptly. "You'd better not."

She nodded once and slid down beneath the covers again.

"By the way, if anyone around here asks, you're my wife, and our name is Marshall." He saw her look at him again and could have sworn there was amusement in her eyes.

"Marshall?" she repeated, beginning to sound normal again, the fear and hesitation fading away. "You don't show much imagination, Marshal."

"It's the one name besides my own that I *know* I'll answer to," he defended himself.

"What first name did you use? Something equally inspired?"

"Just the initials D.A."

"Are those your initials?" Her voice sounded softer, sleepier, and she wasn't looking at him anymore.

"Yeah."

"What does the A stand for? Adam? Alan? Alexander?"

"Andrew," he murmured, watching her.

She turned onto her side, tucking one hand under her pillow, the other beneath her cheek. "Andrew?" she whispered.

Her breathing had deepened and slowed, and her eyes fluttered shut. Another few seconds, he thought with an ache in his chest, and she would be asleep again. "Yeah." He was whispering, too. "The A stands for Andrew."

Waking up to find a man in her bed was a rare experience for Tess, and not an entirely pleasant one. Maybe it would have been, she mused, if Deke hadn't carried her to bed like an overtired child, or if they'd spent the night doing something a bit more intimate than talking and sleeping. Or even if he weren't sleeping so darned soundly, as if he were totally unaffected by her.

Which, of course, he was. She wasn't a woman to him, certainly not a desirable one. She was part of his job. This trip, this sharing a bed—it was all business. She had to keep reminding herself of that, because she found it so easy to forget.

He lay on his back, sprawled across his half of the bed. The exhaustion that had etched his face in the middle of the night was gone, leaving easy, peaceful rest in its place. He was a handsome man, she admitted, but there was more to him than a pretty face. He was strong in body and also in character. He wouldn't compromise his morals or his ethics for any reason. He couldn't be anything less than the man he was: honest, trustworthy, principled.

It would certainly be easier, she thought grumpily as she got up, to remember that the only thing between them was business if she could just quit finding so much to admire about him.

She went to the climate control unit built in beneath the window and turned the heat on, then lifted one flap of the rubber-backed curtain to peek outside. Except for the Bronco, the parking lot was empty. Across the lot was a doughnut shop, a flashing sign advertising Hot Donuts Now. The thought of a chocolate-glazed doughnut made her stomach rumble. Idly, she glanced back at the bed where Deke was still sleeping. The shop was only a hundred yards away. She could walk over, buy coffee and a box of doughnuts and be back in a matter of minutes. He wouldn't know she was gone until she was safely back.

She awkwardly put her shoes on while standing up, then searched for her purse and jacket. He must have left them in the truck, she finally decided, because there was no sign of them in the small room. She would have to borrow his jacket and some of his money, and she needed the room key, too.

She felt silly tiptoeing around the bed to his side, where he'd left his jacket and the rest of his clothes draped across her suitcase. The room key, slipped onto his key ring for safekeeping, was on the nightstand beside his pistol, and there was money, an entire thick envelope of it, underneath his jacket. She put the jacket on, pocketed the keys, then opened the envelope.

Just as she withdrew the stack of money, Deke's hand shot out, grabbing her wrist. He pulled her down on the bed and rolled with her until she was on her back and he was leaning over her. The money scattered around them—twenty-, fifty- and hundred-dollar bills drifting down to rest on the pillows and sheets. "What the hell are you doing?" he demanded through gritted teeth.

"Let go of me!" She tried to wriggle free, twisting and bucking beneath him. When her knee came perilously close to his groin, he straddled her, using the powerful muscles of his legs to clamp hers together. Tess took a deep breath, closed her eyes and silently counted to ten, then said in the calmest voice she could muster, "Please get off me *now*."

Deke released her arms and sat back on his heels, trapping her with his body. He brushed away a few bills that had landed on her stomach, then quickly patted her down. The pockets of her jeans were empty, but in his jacket he found the room key, along with the keys to the truck. "What were you going to do, Tess? Take off on your own? Leave me here without money, without a car, without even a jacket? What about my gun? Weren't you planning to steal that, too?"

The sarcasm and derision in his voice shattered her composure, and she began to struggle again. "I wasn't stealing anything!"

"That's not what it looks like to me. You had my keys, my jacket, and the money was in your hands." One of her blows landed harmlessly on his chest, and he leaned forward again, forcing her arms to her sides and locking them there with his hands on her wrists. "So try again."

"I wasn't stealing anything," she repeated coldly. "I was going to walk across the parking lot and get some coffee and doughnuts for breakfast and bring them back here."

He stared at her disbelievingly for so long that she defensively continued, "I needed your jacket and some money because you left my coat and purse in the truck last night. I was going to come right back. It's the truth, I swear."

"I'm sure it is." He made a disgusted sound, then leaned closer, close enough to see the delicate shadings of brown in her eyes. "Tell me something, Miss Marlowe. How can a seemingly intelligent woman be so damn stupid?"

"I'm not stupid!"

"Lady, you set new records for it! Little more than twelve hours ago, someone tried to kill you! It wasn't some impersonal attack. They wanted *you*, and they wanted you badly enough that they didn't care who else got killed in the process! And this morning you think you can just waltz off to some damn doughnut shop by yourself as if you don't have a care in the world?"

"But . . . no one followed us," she whispered. "You were careful. You watched."

"How careful I am doesn't matter a damn when you pull idiotic stunts like this! You might as well wear a target painted across your chest!" He drew in a deep breath, then noisily exhaled. "Anthony Giamo is a very powerful man, and that power extends a long way. You're right. No one followed us here, but that doesn't guarantee that they won't find us. It doesn't mean you're out of danger. *Think* about it, Tess. He's already tried once to kill you, and he failed. Do you think he's going to give up that easily?"

"Maybe," she said hopefully, and Deke deliberately, brutally, destroyed that hope.

"Never. He'll try again and again. He won't stop until you send him to prison—or until his men succeed in killing you. You're too young to die, Tess." He released his grip on her wrists and slid his hands down to clasp her hands, small and cold. "I'll do the best I can to protect you, but you have to help. You don't set foot outside without me, and sure as hell not while I'm asleep. You stay away from the windows, and you don't answer the phone or open the door. When we go out, you stay by my side. Don't leave me for any reason. Don't be friendly with the people we meet. Don't encourage conversation. Let me answer any questions they have. Do you understand?''

She nodded meekly, and the tension drained from his body, to be quickly replaced by tension of a different sort. In the heat of anger, he had been aware only of the need to restrain her, but now that his anger had cooled, he was swiftly becoming aware of the intimacy of their position. His thighs were open, straddling hers, his legs pressed tightly against hers. Leaning forward the way he was brought his hips into intimate contact with hers, softness to cradle his hardness, and allowed her breasts, as small as they were, to brush his bare chest with every deep breath she took—and she was taking them regularly.

God, she was soft and sweet smelling, he thought, stifling a groan. He ached to take her right now, to strip off their clothes, open her legs and sink mindlessly inside her, filling her, feeling her glove him.

Abruptly he moved away, but not before she felt him growing harder, longer, against her belly. She lay there stunned, surprised that she could elicit such a response from him. Then she chastened herself. His physical response was perfectly natural under the circumstances. After all, even though Deke Ramsey was a complete and thorough professional, he was still a man—very much so, she thought admiringly.

Slowly she sat up and began gathering the money she'd dropped earlier. Deke was standing with his back to her. He'd put his shirt on and carelessly tucked it in without unzipping his jeans. Now he was sliding his belt through the loops, replacing the holster he'd removed last night, reaching behind him for the pistol and snapping it in place. Was he as surprised by the incident as she was? she wondered.

Embarrassed because he'd demonstrated he could be human? Or more likely, simply worried that she might think it meant something?

"We've got to be out of here in half an hour," he said curtly, rummaging through his bag for an electric razor, toothbrush and toothpaste. In the bathroom he brushed his teeth, plugged in the razor, then stared for a moment at his reflection in the mirror.

His face was so familiar to him that he rarely bothered to look at it, to *really* look, to see himself the way others saw him. He was forty-two years old, and even though he didn't have any gray hair yet, he could see every one of those years in the lines of his face. He didn't think it was a particularly handsome face; rather it was tough, hard. Yet most women didn't seem to mind.

Did Tess?

He'd known the instant she'd become aware of the changes in his body. Her big eyes had gotten even bigger, round with shock. She'd certainly never expected *that* from him. Had she been offended? he wondered, beginning the task of shaving. Unaffected, unconcerned . . . or maybe interested? He hadn't found the courage to look at her once her shock had passed, to find out.

As long as it didn't affect her trust—that was the important thing. Displaying all the maturity and restraint of a horny teenager when he was around her wasn't doing much for the professional image he needed to project, but as long as she still trusted him, he could deal with the rest.

When he finished shaving, he returned to the bedroom while Tess took over the bathroom. She looked at the tub longingly, thinking how much a long, hot shower could improve her temperament this morning. As soon as they settled in at the next place, she'd take one, she promised herself.

"Are we going to move every night?" she asked when she came out again.

"No. We're looking for a place that's a little more private, more secure. Hopefully with a kitchen and two bedrooms. When we find it, we'll stay there as long as it's safe."

The carefully empty tone of his voice made it clear that he didn't want a repeat of last night . . . or this morning. Tess smiled tautly. Well, neither did she. She slept alone by choice. If she wanted a man in her bed, it would be for a whole lot more than sleeping or talking or arguing or being yelled at, and it would be someone a whole lot less difficult than Deke Ramsey. "That's a lot to ask for."

He moved the chair away from the door and undid the locks. "Give me my jacket, will you?" He watched her start to shrug out of it, then looked away. A moment later, she draped it across his outstretched hand, and he put it on. In spite of the short time she'd been wearing it, it smelled faintly of her. "There's a place near the state park north of here that rents cabins. We should find what we need there."

"How do you know that?"

"I saw a brochure for it once."

"And you just happened to remember it."

He shrugged as he opened the door and scanned the parking lot.

"You seem awfully familiar with this part of the state. You didn't need a map to get here last night, and you remembered those cabins. Is it wise to hide out someplace where people know you go?"

"I've never *been* to this part of the state. Sometimes I go skiing at Sapphire Valley, or camping in the Great Smoky Mountains National Park. I pass through here when I do." He glanced over his shoulder at her. "Wait here until I get the bags in the car. I'll bring your jacket to you."

She pulled the chair away from the door and waited as he'd ordered. When he brought her coat back, she slipped it on, shivering when the quilted flannel lining came in contact with her bare forearms.

Skiing and camping, she thought with a wry smile as he left with her heavy bag. It figured that his hobbies would be outdoor things. She'd bet he liked football and baseball, too, and, being a native Southerner, fishing and stock-car racing. She, on the other hand, hated sports, would probably break her neck skiing, didn't like any fish too big to go in an aquarium and would enjoy camping only if her tent came with electric lights, a thick soft bed at least two feet above the ground and modern toilet facilities.

Not that it mattered. Incompatible interests would be a problem only if their relationship were permanent, or even personal. Professionally, it wasn't important that they shared absolutely nothing in common besides an interest in her well-being.

Deke returned, tossed the room key on the built-in dresser and gestured for Tess to follow him. The door locked automatically behind them. By the time it clicked, she was already in the Bronco and he was circling to the driver's side.

"Can we get some breakfast?" she asked as he settled in. "No."

She waited for a reason, but he didn't offer one. "We are planning to eat in the next few weeks, aren't we?"

He stopped at the street, waiting for a chance to turn out of the parking lot. "The idea of finding a place with a kitchen is to keep you out of restaurants. As soon as we get checked in at the cabin, we'll come back into town and get groceries. Then you can eat." He pulled onto the street, then scowled at her. "I know I told you earlier that you didn't have to help out, but that was because Al's a pretty good cook. *I* don't cook. We can have sandwiches and frozen dinners for the next three weeks, or you can take responsibility for our meals."

He didn't seem to care one way or the other what she decided, Tess thought sourly. He would probably be as happy with sandwiches and frozen dinners, even on Thanksgiving, as he would be with her home-cooked meals.

Thanksgiving. The thought of next week's holiday made her sad. This would be the first time she'd ever spent it away from her family. Even during the eight years she and Will were married, they had always spent the holidays with her parents. Her only consolation, she thought with a sigh, was that up here in the mountains she was making only one marshal miss the holiday, as opposed to the two or possibly more who would have been with her at the safe house.

"Do you usually spend Thanksgiving with your family?" she asked softly, gazing out the side window.

He hesitated. He didn't want to discuss anything personal with her. He wanted to keep the distance of not knowing each other between them. The only time he'd ever opened up about himself to a witness was with Angela, and look what that had brought him—nothing but heartache. But with a grudging shrug, he answered anyway. "Yes, I do."

"Do they live in Atlanta?"

"Yes."

"At least your parents will have your brothers and their families there." But she was an only child. Her parents wouldn't have anyone else but her grandparents, and they would have little to be thankful for. Instead they would spend the day as she knew they'd spent the last three, worrying about her, wondering if she were all right, hoping that she stayed alive, praying. . . .

Abruptly, she frowned at her reflection in the window. That was enough self-pity for one morning. If she kept it up, she would end up shedding those tears she'd sworn not to cry. "How many brothers do you have?"

He gave her a sharp look that said she was prying. "My father is dead. I have four brothers, all of them younger than me. The two oldest are married and have six kids between them, and the younger two are wisely still single. Is there anything else you'd like to know?"

She ignored his sarcasm, ignored *him*, and considered what he'd said. *Wisely still single*. Was it just a phrase, or did it describe his own feelings about marriage? Probably the latter, she decided. To be forty-something, handsome as sin and single hinted—in spite of his ill-tempered arrogance—at a romance gone bad, a relationship that had caused too much pain or bitterness to risk repeating. Maybe he no longer trusted women with his love, his heart or any part of his life. He certainly hadn't shown much faith in *her* this morning when he'd accused her of planning to steal the money and the truck and run away.

Dismissing her thoughts, she realized that Deke was slowing to turn off the highway. Ahead on the right was a narrow road, bordered by a sign pointing down it and advising that the Mountain Lake Cabin Resort was located one-half mile northeast.

Exactly one-half mile later, they came upon a small cluster of buildings. The office was in front, an A-frame constructed of logs and chinking and vast expanses of glass. Behind it was another log structure, resembling a small, two-story motel, and to the side stood a third building with soda and candy machines on the porch and the word Laundry burned into a wooden sign out front.

"I'll wait out here," Tess said as Deke brought the truck to a halt.

"You'll come inside where I can keep an eye on you."

"Are we registering as husband and wife again?"

He nodded.

"Then unless you want them believing that we came here to hammer out a divorce settlement, I'd better wait here. The way you look at me, there's no way you're going to convince anyone that we're here together willingly."

Oh, he could correct that, he thought. He could look at her in such a way that no one would have any doubt as to exactly what they'd come here to do. He could look at her as if she were the single most important thing in his life— and it wouldn't all be pretense.

He climbed out of the truck and slammed the door. Tess was starting to relax when her door was pulled open. "Don't argue with me, lady. I have a pair of handcuffs, and I'm not above using them," he warned. "Come inside, stand beside me, smile and keep your mouth shut."

She unfastened her seat belt and slid to the ground, helped along by the tug of his hand on her wrist. They climbed the steps side by side, and he held the door for her, then followed her into the office. It was warm inside, and smelled of coffee and cinnamon and apples. The aromas made Tess more aware than ever of her hunger.

"Good morning," came a booming greeting from the man behind the counter. He stood up as they approached and wiped his hands on an old dish towel. "What can I do for you?"

He was probably in his early fifties, Deke estimated, and several inches taller than him and about thirty pounds lighter. A blue-and-gold plaid flannel shirt hung loosely from his shoulders and was tucked unevenly into khaki work trousers. He was cleaning a hunting rifle, the parts scattered around him on the desk.

"Do you have a cabin available?"

"We certainly do. The color's all gone from the leaves, and most of the tourists disappeared with it." He looked at his hands, wiped away one last spot of lubricating oil, then tossed the rag on the desk. "We have efficiencies with a microwave and refrigerator in the building behind the office here, and two- and three-bedroom cabins with fully equipped kitchens scattered back through the woods. How long will you be staying?"

"We're not sure yet. A couple of weeks, maybe three." Deke pulled Tess a little closer to his side, and she tried hard not to look uncomfortable. "We're just looking for a quiet, peaceful place where we can relax."

"It *is* quiet and peaceful here," the manager agreed. "Especially now that we're just about empty. You want a room or a cabin?"

"A cabin would be fine—the most remote one you have." He turned a warm, measuring gaze on Tess that made heat spread from her face down her throat and lower still. "We like our privacy."

Laughing, the manager reached for a pad of registration slips. "I'm sure you do. Just fill this out, and I'll see which cabin I can give you."

Deke had to release her to fill out the slip. Tess leaned on the counter and watched as he scrawled in the information: name, address, phone number; make, model and tag number of the truck. He used the same name, D.A. Marshall, and gave a Jacksonville, Florida, address and phone number. The Bronco had Florida tags, she realized, a small fact that she'd overlooked.

She moved away from his side and went to stare out the plate glass window that faced east. Over here the scents of apple and cinnamon were stronger. Apple pie, she thought, closing her eyes and breathing deeply. If Deke deigned to go grocery shopping before she starved to death, she would ask him to get the makings for apple pie and a half gallon of vanilla ice cream. Comfort food, she thought with a smile. Just what she needed.

"Just follow this road all the way to the end," the manager said, handing Deke a key. "Number eight's on the right. Your closest neighbors right now are in cabins two and three, so you and your wife should have plenty of privacy."

"Thanks. Let's go, sweetheart."

Tess stiffened. She'd grown used to "Miss Marlowe," to "lady" and, gradually, to "Tess." But "sweetheart"? Then she remembered their charade and forced a smile as she turned. He was waiting for her at the door, one hand outstretched. She smiled a goodbye to the manager, placed her hand in Deke's and went outside with him.

As soon as the door closed behind them, she let her fingers go limp, but he continued to hold on until they reached the truck and he'd helped her inside. Tess sat motionless while he went around to the driver's side. Her right hand was tucked inside her left, and she could still feel the heat, the tingling, that his touch had generated.

The road they followed wound through the trees, over one hill and around another. On the far side of the second hill, they found cabin eight. It sat about a hundred feet off the road at the end of a narrow gravel drive, completely out of sight of the office and the other cabins. Except for the Bronco, there wasn't a sign of the modern world anywhere.

"Isn't this lovely?" Tess asked as she looked around the small clearing. "It looks so isolated and rustic."

Deke surveyed it, too, but with other purposes in mind. The cabin seemed sturdy, foot-thick logs separated by buff-colored chinking. A porch extended across the front, with the door in the center and two big windows on each side. The foundation and fireplace were both built of fieldstone, and he could see more windows on the side. The cabin sat in the center of a meadow, with the nearest cover for any-one who wanted to watch them more than a hundred yards away.

He got their bags out of the truck and started for the porch. "Let's get inside," he said shortly.

Tess was as pleased by the interior as she'd been by the exterior. It was small—a living room and kitchen on one side, two bedrooms and a connecting bath on the other. The floors were pine, the furniture oak, the fireplace massive and stone. Oval rugs, braided in earthy tones of brown, rust and moss-green, were scattered across the floor, and pil-lows in the same colors covered the green sofa. The bed-spreads were machine-quilted and thick, white and rust in one room, beige and green in the other, and the matching curtains hung by wide loops from dull brass rods.

Deke set Tess's bags in the back bedroom, then closed the curtains on both windows. She shivered as gloom settled over the room. "Do I have to keep those closed?"

He barely glanced at her. "Yes."

The kitchen was small, too, but efficiently organized. In-expensive plastic dishes were stacked in one cabinet, along with a set of aluminum cookware and half a dozen heavy iced tea glasses. One drawer yielded a butcher knife, a paring knife and service for six in battered stainless, and another held dish towels and oven mitts.

"All the comforts of home," she murmured to herself, opening the oven, then the refrigerator.

"Look, it's only for a few weeks. You can stand it that long, can't you?"

She turned to look at Deke, who was leaning against the doorjamb with his arms folded over his chest. "I wasn't complaining," she informed him. "I like the place. I'll like it even more after I've had lunch, so why don't you go on to the store while I clean up?"

"You're going with me." He saw her protest forming and raised one hand to forestall it. "Those rules you agreed to this morning work both ways. You can't go out alone, and you can't stay in alone. You can't leave me, and I can't leave you."

Thoughts of a soothing hot bath slipped away, leaving an unintentionally sharp edge to her voice. "I thought the purpose of protective custody was to keep me under wraps, out of sight, hidden. *Not* going shopping in the local grocery store."

Slowly he straightened and started toward her, moving with menacing grace. "So you remember me telling you that," he said sarcastically. "Do you also remember that I wasn't in a real good mood at the time?"

"Are you ever?" she muttered.

Deke took a deep breath, but it did nothing to bank his mounting frustration. "Damn it, I *know* you hear what I say. I *know* it gets through that thick skull of yours, where you file it away to throw up at me at some later time. So listen to me now, Tess, and pay attention. This is not a safe house. You don't have a half-dozen marshals watching every move both inside and outside this cabin. It's a different situation now. All you've got is me, and you have to let me give the orders. You have to go where I go. You have to do what I tell you to do."

With a scowl, she protested, "I already agreed to that. I'll do whatever you ask."

"No, Tess," he corrected with exaggerated patience, "you'll do whatever I *say*. There's a big difference. You're in a tough situation—I understand that. It's boring as hell most of the time, but it has the potential to become a matter of life and death. Because of that, I can't *ask* for everything I need from you, and you can't argue every minor point with me. I need to know that when I tell you to do something, you'll do it—without hesitation. Without discussion. Without debate." He paused and shook his head in dismay. "I know that in your head you understand these things, so why are you being so damn difficult?"

"Difficult?" she echoed, her voice rising several notes between syllables. "*Me?* You are the bossiest, most arrogant, most domineering and ill-tempered man I've ever known, and *you* call *me* difficult?"

He leaned closer. "I should have let Scott put you in jail," he said softly, threateningly. "Then you wouldn't be my problem anymore."

Tess stared stonily at him, masking her hurt feelings. "You can fix that little mistake quite easily. One phone call to Anthony Giamo and I won't be *anyone's* 'problem' anymore."

Her barb struck home just as surely as his had. The color drained from his face, and his icy dark eyes narrowed. "Don't joke about that, Tess," he warned, turning the anger inward, controlling it. "You know I would never do anything to endanger your life. You *know* that."

Yes, she did, she silently, ashamedly admitted. She was depending on him to die for her if necessary, and yet, with her suggestion, she had insulted his honor and his integrity. "I'm sorry."

Deke walked to the back door next to the refrigerator and stared for a long moment at its locks. The knob lock was basically worthless, he thought idly, but the double-key deadbolt was a good one. An intruder would have an easier

time kicking in the solid wood door than picking or jim-
mying the deadbolt.

At last, hands in his hip pockets, he turned to Tess. She
gave him a sickly smile. "We seem to bring out the worst in
each other."

"No, we don't. It's the circumstances. You're afraid of
dying. You're even afraid of the fear. You won't express it
by crying or panicking or getting hysterical, and you can't
ignore it any longer, so you argue with me."

That was his excuse, too, he silently admitted. *He* was also
afraid. Afraid that he had already lost this battle. Afraid
that he wouldn't come out of it unscathed. Afraid that he
couldn't continue being hostile to her while sharing such
close quarters, and afraid that if he gave up the hostility, his
passion would express itself in other more pleasurable, more
physical, more damning ways.

And he, too, was afraid of dying. But he was more afraid
of her death—of losing Tess in a way that was more brutal,
more violent, more permanent, than losing Angela had ever
been.

"Let's go get groceries," he said quietly. "Then, when we
get back, you can eat and do whatever it is you want to do."

She nodded once. "Give me a minute, and I'll be ready
to go."

Deke continued to gaze at the place where she had stood
long after the bedroom door had closed behind her. For one
fanciful moment, he could still feel the shimmering of their
argument in the air: tension, anger, passion, heat. Two
people who fought so passionately would love the same
way—with savage tenderness and tender violence; with a
fiery need that burned, consumed, destroyed and created
anew; with a painfully pleasurable hunger that found satisfaction only in their souls.

All the more reason, he thought grimly, squeezing his eyes
shut on the images his thoughts conjured, to keep his dis-

tance from Tess Marlowe. Desire that fiery, that strong, was dangerous. One time—that was all it would take. If he gave in to the need just once, he would get burned.

And he might not survive.

Chapter 5

The drive back into town passed in total silence. Deke told himself he should be grateful. He didn't want to chat with Tess, didn't want to learn anything more about her. He didn't want to find out how much he might like her, didn't want to be forced into giving up the defenses he'd built around himself.

But he wasn't grateful, because total silence gave him too much time to think. It gave him too many opportunities to look at her, sitting primly, hands folded in her lap, on the other side of the truck. It gave him too many chances to imagine her in his bed, not prim but passionate, not silent but moaning with pleasure.

He wondered curiously what she thought of him, beyond the fact that he was bossy, arrogant, domineering and ill-tempered. If she thought of him as anything other than a less-than-pleasant source of protection. If she thought of him as a man.

Their first stop in town was the hardware store. Tess followed him down the aisles as he picked out a screwdriver and a dozen small window locks. She didn't ask what they were for, since she already knew he wouldn't tell her, not now. He didn't seem to think she needed to know much about his plans for her security beyond the rules he expected her to follow. He was great with rules, she thought with a scowl. He probably even had one against marshals being friendly with witnesses.

From the hardware store they went to the grocery store down the street. "What are we going to get?" she asked as he pulled a shopping cart from the long line.

He shrugged. "You agreed to cook."

"Am I supposed to stick to some sort of a budget?"

"We're not eating lobster every night for three weeks at the taxpayers' expense," he said impatiently, "but we don't have a budget. Buy enough food for the two of us for two weeks or so."

She turned toward the produce section, considering menus in her head. "What do you like?" she asked as she began filling plastic bags with vegetables.

"I can eat sandwiches and frozen dinners for three weeks. I'm not picky. I'll eat whatever you fix."

The strain in his voice made her glance at him, then murmur too softly for him to hear, "Definitely ill-tempered."

She bought fresh fruits and vegetables, eggs, milk and cheese, beef, chicken and pork, sandwich makings and everything necessary for a small Thanksgiving dinner. She also bought fresh apples, cinnamon and sugar, frozen pie crusts and vanilla ice cream. Comfort food, she reminded herself. Living with Deke Ramsey, she was going to need it.

As he'd said, he wasn't picky. He showed no preferences for anything the few times she bothered to ask his opinion. The only items he picked out himself were a stack of paperback bestsellers from the magazine rack and a bag of fruit—big awkward shaped items with dirty yellow and green skin. Uglifruit, according to the label, Tess noticed. The name was appropriate.

As soon as the groceries were paid for and bagged in the back of the truck, they drove, once again in silence, to a gas station on the edge of town. It took Deke only a few minutes to pump the gas and pay; then he walked to the pay phone a few yards away. When Scott came on the line, Deke gave him the name, location and phone number of the cabins, and the name he'd registered under.

His boss's response was the same as Tess's. "Marshall? Real original, Deke."

"That number is for the office," Deke continued, scowling at the jibe and certain that Scott knew he was scowling. "There's no phone in the cabin."

"Does the place seem pretty secure?"

"I wouldn't keep her there if it didn't," he snapped.

For a moment Scott was silent. "You don't seem to be in a very good mood this afternoon. Regretting your idea to take Miss Marlowe out of town?"

Deke silently considered his boss's suggestion. He would rather be anywhere in the world than holed up in a tiny isolated log cabin with Tess Marlowe. He would rather do anything in the world for three weeks than spend them with her. But he didn't regret his decision. He had believed last night that this was the only way to keep her safe and that he was the only man to do it. After spending the night with her, watching her, arguing with her and wanting her, he still believed that. "No, I'm not. She would have hated it in jail."

Again Scott paused, then asked cautiously, "And you care how she feels?"

"Look, she could have avoided this mess easily enough by refusing to come forward as a witness, by refusing to testify at the preliminary hearing, or by making a deal with Giamo. People do it all the time. But instead she chose to be a good citizen and do her civic duty by testifying, thereby setting herself up as a target. We have a responsibility to keep her safe and to do it as painlessly as possible. That doesn't mean locking her up in jail while Giamo goes free."

"Are you two getting along okay?"

Deke considered all their arguments and sharp words, the incident in bed this morning and his growing need for her, still under control but threatening, and replied in an easy drawl, "Yeah, we're getting along fine. What's happening at your end?"

"It's slow going. We've made up a list of everyone who knew Tess Marlowe was at that particular safe house. Counting you and me, it numbers twenty-two. We have another list of people who knew that we use that house as a safe haven—other witnesses who were kept there, the marshals, FBI agents and prosecutors connected with those cases. We haven't even counted everyone on *that* one. Checking out every single name is going to take some time."

"When are you going to get to me?" It would take a very thorough investigation to turn up his long-ago ties to Anthony Giamo, but considering the circumstances, this one would be thorough. With the pride, reputation and reliability of both the Marshals Service and the FBI field office at stake, it would be *very* thorough.

"You're the first on the list, pal. After all, *you've* got our witness."

Deke shifted positions so he could see Tess more easily. "Who's handling this on the FBI side?"

"McNally."

"If he wants me pulled off, make sure you send the best you've got to replace me. Al would be good."

"If he checks out." Scott made a bitter, frustrated sound. "God, I hate having to investigate people I work with and like and trust. We're even running a check on Thad while his people do one on me."

"It's better to trust no one than to trust the wrong person. Listen, I've got to go. I'll check in with you Saturday morning."

"Yeah. Be careful."

Scott hung up, then withdrew his credentials case from inside his suit coat. He neatly folded the piece of paper with

Deke's location on it and slid it behind the photo identification card. He had just returned the case to his pocket when a knock sounded at his closed door.

At his invitation, Julia Billings walked in. She closed the door, set her briefcase on the floor and sat down, crossing her legs and folding her hands in her lap. For a moment she coolly studied him, then asked in a voice frigid with anger yet tautly controlled, "Where the hell is our witness?"

Scott sighed softly. He had been expecting this visit all day, had in fact been preparing for it until he'd found out that Julia would be in court most of the day. "She's safe."

"Where?"

He said nothing.

"Where?"

The softer her voice got, he knew, the angrier she was. He had expected this. He had told Deke that Julia would have his head for this stunt. She was an aggressive prosecutor who liked to win, and she was very protective of the witnesses who helped her do that. After the mistake she'd made in not ordering protection for Donald Hopkins, Scott had known she would be livid at being cut out of their plans for protecting Tess Marlowe. "That information isn't being made available, Julia."

The color drained from her face, and she clasped her hands tighter. "What?" It was a gasp, sharpened by anger and colored by shock. She had never found herself in this situation, Scott thought regretfully, had never been denied access to one of her own office's witnesses. Well, it was new for him, too, knowing that one of his people, or one of hers or Thad's, had betrayed them.

"Only two people know her location—the marshal with her and me. If the information leaks this time, we'll know who it was."

"'The marshal'? You have only *one* man guarding her? For God's sake, Scott, someone tried to kill her! And you have only *one* man with her?"

"If it's done right, one is all it takes—and we're doing it right."

"One man." Julia shook her head in amazement. "Do you know how important this case is? Do you know how long we've waited to put Anthony Giamo away?" She didn't wait for a response. "My God, if we can get to him, we have a real chance at bringing down organized crime in Atlanta. He's at the top. There's no one more powerful than him."

Scott silently watched her. Although she sat practically motionless, energy seemed to flow through her. That dynamism and vibrancy were powerful tools, and she used them well. They drew people to her, swayed juries to her side, got her just about anything she wanted. Except Tess Marlowe's location. "I understand the importance of this trial and this witness," he said calmly.

"Good. Then you'll listen to what I have to say. I want a net around her that no one can breach—eight, ten, twelve of your best men. I want security around her as tight as if she were the President of the United States. I want—"

"No."

She stopped in midsentence, eyes wide and round, mouth still open. After a moment she closed her mouth, blinked, then spoke very quietly. "What do you mean, *no*?"

"I mean that Tess Marlowe is safe where she is, and she's staying there. Two days ago, Julia, you stood in this office with Deke and me and said that from then on, on matters of protection, you would bow to the advice of the experts. That's us. We don't have to tell you what we're doing or how we're doing it. All we owe you is your witness, alive and well, in court on the eighth." He stood up and walked around his desk, leaning against the corner closest to her. "Under other circumstances, I would probably handle it just as you suggested. But right now, I don't know if I have eight or ten or twelve men I can trust. I *do* know I have one, and he's with her now."

"Can you at least tell me who that is?" When he didn't answer, she nodded knowingly. "It's Deke, isn't it?"

He still gave no response.

"Well, if anyone can keep her alive, he can. All right. I'll leave this to you." She managed to be gracious in spite of the fact that she had no other choice, because he was right: the Marshals Service owed her nothing but a healthy witness in court. "If anything happens..."

"We'll let you know."

Back at the cabin, Tess put the groceries away while Deke installed the window locks. She occasionally glanced at him as he worked on the two windows in the dining area and the small window over the sink. "Why are you doing that? Those windows already have locks."

He inserted one of the narrow metal clamps on the window frame, then tightened the screw that held it in place. Without damaging the frame, it secured the window in the closed position. "Those locks might keep your average two-bit punk out, but they're not going to stand up to someone who knows his business."

"And you think Giamo would hire someone who knows his business?"

He gave her a derisive look. "The man's freedom, if not his life, depends on silencing you permanently. You can bet he's not going to send a couple of good ol' boys named Bubba and Earl after you." With the last lock in place, he leaned against the cabinets, his hands resting on the edge of the counter. "Do you really understand who Anthony Giamo is?"

"Sure. Do you want stuffed pork chops or baked chicken for dinner tonight?" When he shrugged, she laid the package of chicken breasts on the counter and put the pork chops in the freezer, then continued. "He's a gangster. A mobster. A Mafioso." She grinned over her shoulder at him. "A wiseguy."

Her banter didn't lessen his scowl one bit. "Anthony Giamo controls a major share of the illegal activity in the city of Atlanta and the surrounding area. Prostitution, pornography, drugs, gambling, protection, money laundering—you name it, he's involved. It's made him a rich man, and he uses that money wisely. He hires no one but the best.''

''Then why didn't they kill us last night?''

''Pure luck. They came after dark to lessen the chances of being seen or identified, and we had four men on the street, watching for unusual activity. If they'd made that drive-by in the afternoon, when we had no outside surveillance, chances are real good that we all would have been killed.'' He opened the drawer that held the silverware and dropped the screwdriver inside. ''I'm going to unpack now.''

Tess nodded as she reached for the last bag of groceries. The refrigerator and freezer were nearly full, along with one small cabinet. She put away the remaining items, then stood for a moment in the center of the room, her hands on her hips. Lunch came next on her list of priorities, followed by a long hot bath and clean clothes. Then she would ask the marshal to build a fire in that big stone fireplace, filch one of the paperbacks he'd bought and curl up on the sofa until it was time to fix dinner.

Deke slowly sat up in bed and swung his legs to the side, resting his feet on the cold wood floor. He'd come to bed at eleven last night and had fallen asleep as soon as Tess had settled into the back room. He had managed only three hours of sleep before the noises from her room had awakened him—the protest of the bedsprings, the creak of the door, the shuffle of slippered feet—and he was tired, so tired.

Now he waited for the quick return to her room that would signify that she was up for something no more important than a trip to the bathroom or maybe to the kitchen for a drink. But when a strip of light appeared beneath his door from the living room, he admitted that he had to get up, get dressed and find out what was wrong.

He couldn't handle many more of these late-night encounters, he thought, stifling a groan. Those were the times when she was the softest, the most vulnerable, the most in need of comfort. Hell, those were the times when *he* was most vulnerable.

Stepping over the jeans on the floor, he pulled a pair of sweatpants from a hanger and slipped into them. He didn't bother with a shirt but headed instead for the door.

Tess was sitting on the braided rug in front of the fireplace, a pink-and-white robe wrapped tightly around her. She had opened the fire screen and rebuilt the fire he had banked only a few hours earlier. It was burning brightly now, sending the smoky, fragrant scent of pine through the cabin. Its glow touched her hair and played over her skin, turning it gold and soft and warm. He wanted to touch her, to find out just how soft, how warm, but he forced his hands to remain unclenched at his sides as he went over and sat on the opposite end of the rug.

"Did you have another dream?"

She gave him only a brief glance and shook her head. "I haven't been to sleep yet. I tried to be quiet. I know how easily you awaken."

"Don't worry about it. I'm supposed to be awake when you are." He leaned against the stone hearth, his back absorbing the heat from the fire, and combed his fingers through his hair, then covered a yawn. "I know you're tired. Considering how little sleep you've had in the last four nights, you've got to be. Are you afraid to sleep?"

She smiled faintly. "You can't have bad dreams if you don't sleep."

"You can't do a lot of things if you don't sleep—like function."

She drew her knees to her chest and rested her chin on them. The action tugged her robe up, exposing her feet in thick pink booties. "Don't fuss, Marshal. If I stay awake all night, maybe I'll sleep all day tomorrow. That would make this enforced confinement easier for both of us."

"No, that would mean I'd have to start staying awake nights and sleeping days, too." He shifted away from the fire a bit, resettled, then quietly asked, "Are you afraid that I can't protect you?"

She considered and rejected his suggestion. She felt completely safe with him, safer than ever before. "No," she said simply. "I trust you."

The soft, sincere tone of her voice warmed him inside. It wasn't really important—her faith in him would make it easier to do his job, but lack of faith on her part wouldn't stop him from protecting her. Still, for reasons he wouldn't think about right now, it mattered to him.

"I'm not even sure it's the dreams that I dread so much," she said, gazing into the fire. "Maybe it's the loss of control. Ever since my divorce, I've had total control over my life—where I go, what I do, how I live. Now...you control my waking hours, and the dreams control my sleep. There's nothing left for me."

"But it's only for three weeks," he reminded her. "You can endure anything for three weeks."

"What about during the trial? Do I get to go back home then?"

He shook his head.

"So it'll be more than three weeks. And what about after the trial? Even if Giamo's convicted, he'll appeal. Even if he goes to prison, he'll still have the power to destroy me."

"We have ways of protecting you even afterward."

"What ways?"

He shook his head again, this time uneasily. No one had discussed the witness relocation program with her yet, although it was always one of their options. Telling her that, if circumstances demanded it, she might have to accept a new home, a new life, a new identity, that she might be forced to give up all contact with the parents she loved so much, would probably accomplish what almost getting killed hadn't: it would convince her not to testify.

"Don't go looking for trouble," he warned her. "If you do, you'll probably find plenty of it. Take it a day at a time. Get through the next three weeks, then worry about the trial."

"That's easy enough for you to say. After the trial, you go back home to your family and friends, and it's as if nothing ever happened. You don't care what happens to the witnesses once you're finished protecting them. Hey, it's just your job." She paused, and her voice grew husky. "But it's *my* life, and I'm not sure I can get through the next three weeks, and then the trial, and then whatever happens afterward."

She made it sound so cut-and-dried. *It's just your job.* As if protecting her was no more important to him than ringing up groceries was to a checker, or dishing out dinner was to a waiter. He wanted to tell her that she was wrong, that he cared—far more than he should, damn it—about what happened to her. He wanted to make her see that whatever happened to her would happen to him, too, that they were in this together.

But it wasn't true. After the trial, just as she'd said, he would go back to his home, his family and friends and another assignment. Whether she took her chances in Atlanta or entered the relocation program, he wouldn't be with her. He wouldn't be a part of her life anymore.

"You'll do what has to be done," he said, his voice harsher than he'd intended. "You'll get through this because you have no other choice, and you'll get through what follows for the same reason. Watching someone die is never easy. Knowing someone wants you dead is even tougher, and it's too damn bad that you got caught up in it, but you'll survive."

She reached out and laid her hand on his knee. "I'm sorry *you* got caught up in it. I'm sorry someone tried to kill you because of me."

For a long time he stared at her hand, so small and delicate, and felt heat from it spreading through him. He'd never considered the knee an erogenous zone, but there was definitely something erotic about her touch there. Of course, he admitted grimly, there would be something erotic about her touch anywhere.

He lifted her hand, held it for a second too long, then laid it on her own leg. "Don't worry about it," he said quietly. "Like you said, it's my job."

He got easily to his feet and extended one hand to her. As soon as she was on her feet, he released her and turned his attention to the fireplace, settling the screen in place. "Try to get some sleep," he advised, walking to the bedroom with her. "Don't worry about the dreams. If they come, at least you'll have had some rest. If they don't . . ."

She watched the muscles across his chest ripple as he shrugged, and she smiled faintly. If the nightmares didn't come, maybe she would dream of something more pleasant.

Maybe she would dream of him.

The last few days had been quiet, Tess thought as they drove into town Monday morning, and peaceful in an odd sort of way. She had been bored—after all, she could read only so many hours a day, and the cabin, along with not having a telephone, had no television or radio, either, and Deke, while excellent protection, wasn't much on idle conversation.

Still, she had needed the quiet, the lack of demands and the freedom of doing absolutely nothing she didn't want to do. The time had been soothing, healing. The fear that was always present in the back of her mind was under control, and she was sleeping better at night. The dreams still came, but she'd found that as soon as she woke up and realized that she was safe in the cabin with Deke within calling range, she could go back to sleep almost immediately.

As it always did when she thought about him, her gaze shifted to him, covertly studying him. She had thought he might relax his guard a little after he got used to spending time alone with her, but it hadn't happened yet. He still didn't welcome small talk; he'd shown no interest in talking about himself or listening to chatter about her. He was distant, aloof, talking to her when he had to and simply watching her when he didn't.

He was fascinating, though. From what little he did say, she knew he was intelligent and sharp-witted, with a little wisdom, a lot of common sense, and a dose of hardheadedness thrown in for good measure. And of course, she added dryly, he was handsome, sexy and did funny things to her heart rate without even trying.

He stopped at a pay phone in a small shopping center. There were six stores—a barber shop, a fabric shop and a hair salon and, on the other side of a small open plaza, an insurance office, a dentist's office and a grocery store. Tess idly watched the few shoppers, noticing that Deke did, too, even while he spoke with his boss.

In the barber shop directly in front of the Bronco, a small boy played at the plate glass window. When he saw Tess watching him, he ducked behind a chair, then slowly peeked over the back. She smiled and waved, and he ducked again, but when he came up this time, he waved, too.

"You're not supposed to be drawing attention to yourself," Deke said as he got into the truck and fastened his seat belt.

"Oh, yes, excuse me. Why, that little boy must be all of four years old, a real threat to my life."

His expression was harsher than usual when he looked at her, but he didn't speak; he simply started the engine and drove back to the cabin. There he waited until Tess had removed her jacket and hung it up on the brass hooks next to the door, then gestured for her to sit down. "We need to talk."

Curious, she glanced at him, then went to sit on the end of the sofa. He chose to remain standing, his jacket still on, his hands in his back pockets. "Someone broke into your apartment last week."

Her expression was blank for a moment, as if her brain had difficulty processing his announcement; then the blankness abruptly changed to shock. "Wh—what?"

"One of your neighbors noticed that your sliding glass door was open a few inches for several days. When he couldn't get hold of you, he called the manager. She let herself in, discovered that someone had broken in and called your parents. Eventually the information got to our office."

"Was anything stolen?" The question sounded stupid in her ears; she had insurance to cover any losses, and why in the world would she worry about property when someone wanted to kill her?

"They weren't burglars," he said, impatience straining his voice. "They were there for you. It probably happened Monday night—your neighbor first noticed the door on Tuesday. They discovered you weren't home and broke in to wait, to surprise you when you did arrive."

Tess began shaking her head, slowly at first, then vehemently. "How do you know that? People get robbed all the time. It happened just last month to a woman in the next building, and the month before that to a guy on the other side. What makes you so sure it was Giamo's people?"

"Because nothing was stolen. The television, the stereo, the VCR, the microwave, that portable computer you keep in your desk drawer—not touched."

"Maybe they got scared away." Her voice had dropped to a whisper now, soft and quavery with fear.

"They were there long enough to go through your desk, your dresser and your closet." He shook his head. "They weren't scared away."

"Why? What interest could they possibly have in my things?"

He stared straight ahead, seeing Tess only as an indistinct blur, all soft and hazy. "I don't know. Maybe they were just nosy. Maybe they were checking to make sure all your clothes were there. Maybe they suspected that you might go somewhere and were searching for clues as to where.''

Tess felt a chill pass through her. A total stranger could have looked in her closet and known that most of her clothes were gone; there had been bunches of empty hangers when she'd finished packing. The toiletries that normally spilled out of the medicine chest and across the bathroom counter were all gone, too, and only a few pieces of lingerie and a few pairs of socks had been left in their respective drawers.

So Giamo's men had known she wasn't coming back, and they had gone to the small desk in the corner of her bedroom to find a clue to her whereabouts. To the desk with her address book clearly visible beside the phone. The address book where her parents' current address was stupidly listed under M for Mom and Dad instead of C for Conrad. ''My God, my parents!''

Deke paced to the fireplace, leaning one arm on the mantel, staring sightlessly at the stones. He wasn't going to tell her that part—about the address book open to the M's, about the notepad next to it, the top page ripped off, from which the lab had been able to lift off the impressions of Gordon and Rose Conrad's address and phone number. Tess had enough to worry about without adding the fear that she'd put her parents' lives in danger, too. ''Your parents are fine.''

Tess jumped to her feet and joined him at the fireplace, tugging at his arm. ''How do you know that?'' she demanded tearfully. ''How do you know they're fine, that they'll stay fine? Anthony Giamo could have my parents' address! He could know where they live! He has to know that I would do whatever he wanted to keep them safe!''

He slowly looked down at her. His left hand still rested on the mantel, but it was stretched out flat, fingers wide, pressing hard against the rough wood. The other was clenched in a fist to stop him from reaching for her. ''Listen to me. This all happened last week, before the hit on the safe house. Giamo knows now that you're not staying with your parents. He knows that they have no idea where you are. He's not going to bother them, I promise."

"He could use them," she whispered, "to get to me."

"No. Threatening them would accomplish nothing, because there's no way to let you *know* he's threatening them. Do you understand?"

She stared up at him for a long moment, then asked in dismay, "So no one's going to watch them? No one's going to protect them?"

"Yes, someone's watching them. They're not in custody, but a couple of men are watching their house. But they're not in any danger. *You're* the one Giamo wants." As he gazed into her soft, teary brown eyes, he moved closer, and his voice grew husky. "But you're not in danger, either, Tess. I'll take care of you. I'll keep you safe."

She believed him. He saw it in her eyes as trust slowly replaced fear. She believed that her parents were safe, believed that *she* was safe.

Swallowing hard, he raised one hand to her face, wiping away the single tear that had formed at the corner of her eye, then left it there, his palm warm against her jaw, his fingers gentle on her cheek. He shouldn't be touching her, he acknowledged, not even this little bit. But not even the certain knowledge that it was wrong could stop him, could make him withdraw.

Tess sighed softly, and through his small contact with her, he felt the tension drain away. She needed comfort, needed to be touched, to be stroked and held, and he needed to do it. Just once, he promised himself as he brought his other hand to rest on her back, wordlessly urging her closer. Just once he would take what he wanted—a touch, a kiss, a taste—and worry about the price later. Just once he would forget right and wrong, would indulge in being a fool, would trade good sense and propriety for bone-deep, heart-racing, knee-weakening pleasure.

A shiver of anticipation tickled down her spine when she realized dazedly that he was going to kiss her. Because she was upset? Because he knew she wanted it, needed it? Or because he wanted it himself? Maybe next week or tomorrow or ten minutes from now the reason would matter, but not now. Nothing mattered right now but the feel of his mouth, gentle, tentative, brushing against hers.

His tongue touched her lips, moistened them, parted them, only to reach the barrier of her teeth; then his mouth covered hers. He allowed her just a taste, as quick as a sigh, and left her craving more. Then, before she could find the breath to protest his leaving, he kissed her again, hard, firm, and his tongue coaxed its way inside her mouth, sensuously twining with hers, stroking, exploring, arousing. He tasted warm, dark, wild, like a violent summer night's storm, and he made her hunger, made her respond with a mindlessly hot fervor, made her whimper deep in her throat.

She was as sweet as he'd thought she would be, as passionate as he'd known she could be. When she drew his tongue deeper into her mouth, he obliged her, tangling both hands in the silken web of her hair, using the faint pressure of his fingers to hold her steady while he deepened the kiss. When she pressed her body against his and he felt the soft, rhythmic rocking of her hips against his hardness, he groaned, frustrated with the clothing that kept them from duplicating the actions of their long, slow, thrusting kiss.

With aching slowness he slid one hand from her hair down her throat, letting it rest on her breast, soft and protected by her sweater. Even through the bulky knit he felt her nipple harden beneath his palm, felt it grow as rigid with excitement as his own flesh. He rubbed it, dragging the heavy sweater back and forth, using its nubby texture to intensify his caress.

Suddenly touching wasn't enough to satisfy his feverish need. He needed to kiss her breast, to suckle it, to savor its sweetness, in the same agonizing way he needed to be inside her. But even as he pushed her sweater up and out of the way, baring one small, delicately veined breast, a tiny voice in his head reminded him once more how wrong his actions were. Wrong. Improper. Dangerous. She was a witness, for God's sake, and it was his job—*his job*—to protect her!

Tess felt his emotional withdrawal seconds before the physical one. Breathing raggedly, he pulled his mouth from hers and gently drew her sweater back into place. For one long moment he held her against his arousal, then slowly he took a step away from her. She felt as if the rug had been pulled out from beneath her, leaving her unsteady, weak, disoriented. Searching his eyes, dark and shadowy and filled with emotions, for the reason, she thought she recognized desire, dismay and regret before he backed away from her. ''Deke?'' she whispered.

Her unspoken questions echoed in his head. Why did you stop? What's wrong? Don't you want me? And what answers could he give? *Of course I want you. I want to make love to you. I want to undress you and look at you and touch you and hold you. I want to kiss your breasts and stroke your body and explode inside you. I want to stay there, deep inside you, until your body and your life and your heart feel empty without me. I want to love you...but it would be wrong.*

All the desire, all the longing, all the savage aching in the middle of the night, in the bright morning and in the lazy warm evenings, couldn't change the fact that it was wrong. That she was a witness and he was a marshal. That it was all right for him to want her but all wrong for him to take her. That if he did take what she offered, if he made love to her, if he opened himself to her, it would cost him his soul.

Tess waited for him to speak, but he said nothing. He simply stood a few feet away and warily watched her, offering no excuse, no explanation, no apology—not that she wanted an apology. No. All she wanted was to finish what they had started. To feel his mouth and his hands on her body. To see him naked and boldly aroused, his body hard and rigid and thick for her.

Flushed with the heat of longing, she smoothed her sweater and took an awkward step away. "I—I'll fix lunch now."

He waited until she had reached the kitchen door before he spoke. "Tess..."

She stopped and turned back.

"That won't happen again."

Her smile was faint and tinged with regret. "I was afraid you would say that."

"It's *wrong*."

"That's a matter of opinion."

"Well, that's my opinion, and my boss's and the whole damn Marshals Service!" he said heatedly.

She smiled again, still faintly, still regretfully. "But it's not between you and the boss and the whole damn Marshals Service. It's between you and me. For your information, I wasn't kissing a marshal. I was kissing a man."

He dragged his fingers through his hair in frustration. He should have known she would argue the point with him; she'd argued about everything else. "You can't separate the marshal from the man—*I* damn sure can't. The only reason I'm here is to protect you. That means I'm working twenty-four hours a day. There are certain standards of conduct that I have to adhere to in the performance of my duties—"

"Standards of conduct?" she interrupted. "Performance of your duties? What is this? You get into an argument you can't win, and you start talking like a government manual."

Jaw clenched, he closed his eyes and counted silently to ten, then to twenty. When he opened them again, he scowled fiercely at her and said through gritted teeth, "It won't happen again."

Tess studied him for a moment, clearly considering his vow. Then she shook her head. "Maybe it won't. But if it doesn't...that will be a loss for both of us, Marshal."

Turning, she disappeared into the kitchen, leaving him staring after her.

He really had a way about him, she thought grimly as she put a pot of water on the stove to boil. Take her breath away in a first-class seduction, end it abruptly enough to leave her dizzy, then tell her it couldn't happen again. That kissing her didn't conform to the standards of conduct he had to adhere to in the performance of his duties.

She put a baking sheet with four sourdough rolls in the oven, banged the door shut and turned the oven on. The worst part, she grudgingly admitted, was that she could see his point. She had met Scott Rowan very briefly, but she suspected that the gray-haired marshal would have been appalled by the scene in the living room. Making out with the witness certainly wasn't in keeping with the efficient, purely professional image the Marshals Service wanted to project.

But it wasn't as if Deke did this on a regular basis, with every female witness he was assigned to protect. She had to believe that. This attraction between them was something special, something neither of them could control. She had to believe that, too. So what if it was unprofessional? *She* would never tell anyone. And although she was the first to admit that her experience with men was limited, she had enough to know that this chemistry between them was rare. She had kissed enough men in her life, and none of them—including her ex-husband—had elicited that kind of wickedly powerful response in her. Only Deke had . . . and he didn't want it to happen again.

She wouldn't make any promises. If it didn't happen, she would regret it. But if it did . . . she would make the most of it.

While the water heated, she emptied a can of peas in a colander to drain, then began dicing onions and celery. She added pasta to the boiling water, cut a thick slice from the ham in the refrigerator and chopped it into cubes. Last, she mixed a dressing, drained the pasta and stirred everything together into a salad.

She set the table, poured a glass of milk for Deke and iced tea for herself, then got the rolls from the oven. "Lunch is ready," she called.

Deke was staring at the ceiling. He wasn't sure he could eat. There was still a tight feeling in his stomach, the sick kind of dread he got when he knew he'd made a serious mistake. He could count the number of times he'd experienced this particular feeling: when he'd found out the truth about Anthony Giamo, the day his unit had arrived in Vietnam, a few months after his marriage and the first time he'd made love to Angela. But was his mistake this time in kissing Tess—or in telling her that it couldn't happen again?

For the first time since he'd met her, he wanted to go to bed *alone*. He wanted to burrow under the covers and pull his pillow over his head and forget how she'd felt, so soft and warm and giving, and how she'd tasted, so sweet and addictive, and how she'd sounded, so helplessly aroused. He wanted to sleep for the next three weeks, wanted to avoid even the slightest contact with her. If he could do that, maybe he would survive this.

But he couldn't do that. He couldn't leave her alone for any length of time, except at night. He couldn't avoid her because of his job. His damn job. If not for the credentials he carried, he would have no problem. Without them, if he wanted her so badly that it was burned into his soul, he could take her. If he wanted to spend the rest of his life making love to her, why not?

But if not for the credentials he carried, he grimly reminded himself, he wouldn't be here with her. If not for them, he never would have met her.

With a sigh, he started for the kitchen. He would sit across from her, and he would eat the lunch she had prepared. If he could stomach his own rare attempts at cooking, he could stomach this.

* * *

After lunch Tess sat at the dining table, her feet propped on the chair across from her, and watched Deke do the dishes. It was one of the few agreements they'd reached without arguing. If she cooked the meals, he would clean up afterward. It seemed a fair deal to her, since washing dishes was one of her least favorite chores. Still, she wouldn't have minded helping him if he'd been willing to accept it.

"Do you wear that gun all the time?" she asked idly, twisting the salt shaker in slow circles on the tabletop.

He barely glanced at her. "Just about."

"Even when you're back in Atlanta and not working? Even if you just run up to the grocery store for a six pack of beer some night?"

"Even then."

"Why don't you wear a shoulder holster? All the cops on TV do."

He glanced at her again, for a second longer this time. Was she bored? Making idle conversation? Or, as he suspected, trying to put the awkward incident in the living room behind them and regain some sense of balance? Well, if she was trying to smooth things over, the least he could do was cooperate. "Shoulder holsters look good for TV but they're uncomfortable as hell, and they make it easier for someone to get your gun away from you. And unless you can afford custom-tailored suits, your coat snags on them and they're pretty obvious."

"How many cops can afford custom-tailored suits?"

"Not many. The ones who come from money. Or marry it." His dark eyes turned shadowy. "And the ones who sell out for it."

Tess bent one knee up and leaned her elbow on it. "What if the man who gave our location to Giamo is one of your friends?"

"If he is—if he was—he destroyed whatever friendship we might have had the day he made the deal with Giamo," he said harshly.

"Don't you care what his reasons were for doing it? Don't they make a difference?"

"No."

"Is it that simple for you? Black and white, no shades of gray?"

He rinsed the last dish, then dried his hands and faced her. "He's a *cop*, one of the good guys, and he's dirty. He betrayed everyone he works with, everything we believe in. He almost got you killed. His reasons don't matter. *Nothing* can justify what he's done." He gave a disgusted shake of his head. "Damn right, there are no shades of gray."

"Country, duty, honor, justice—that's what you believe in, isn't it?" She stood up and pushed her chair into place beneath the table, then gripped the back. "What about extenuating circumstances? They're a part of justice. Don't you believe in them?"

Their gazes met, his dark and flashing with indignation, hers cool and steady. "No," he said bluntly. "Not for a cop."

It was probably that single-minded determination that made him a good marshal, Tess considered thoughtfully. Professionally, regarding her safety, that was great; he would keep her alive or—God forbid—die trying. On a personal level, though, she found such single-mindedness daunting. How could she ever convince him to let the attraction between them develop when he was focused so narrowly on professionalism and conduct and propriety?

Because that was what she wanted—a chance for those feelings to fully develop. Involvement. A relationship. An affair.

She silently repeated that last word, testing its flavor. Affair. She wanted to have an affair with Deacon Ramsey. She shook her head in bemusement. For a long time after her divorce, she'd thought she would never want another man, would never care for another man. Deke had already proven her wrong on the first count, and, without even being aware of it, he was well on the way to proving her wrong on the

second, too. She admired him. She felt a very deep respect
for him. She trusted him more than she had ever trusted any
man.

And let's not forget desire, she added with a wry private
smile. Heaven help her, she could never forget the desire,
whether he was ignoring her or scowling at her or not even
in the same room with her.

But *he* could forget. She looked at him, still standing in
front of the sink, the expression in his eyes now distant and
grim, completely unaware of her presence. He could forget
that he'd held her, that he'd kissed her and touched her
breast with such sweet caresses. He could forget the heat
he'd set pumping through her veins, the fever that had made
her burn. He could forget his body's own impressive response to their kiss.

Maybe she should simply concentrate on getting through
the next two and a half weeks. Maybe *she* should forget that
he'd held her, kissed her, made her burn.

But she couldn't do that, because her last words to him in
the living room had been God's truth. If they forgot, if
nothing else happened between them...it would be a loss for
both of them. A loss that Tess wasn't sure she could endure.

Chapter 6

After four sleepless hours in bed Tuesday night, Deke finally gave up, left the bed and, swearing silently, put on his jeans. He could thank Tess for his restlessness, he thought sourly as his fingers awkwardly fumbled over the cool metal buttons that fastened his jeans. She seemed to be sleeping peacefully—he'd heard no sound from her room since she'd gone to bed hours earlier—but she was responsible for the frustration that made sleep impossible for him tonight.

Since the brief exchange following Monday's kiss, she'd behaved the same as usual—quiet most of the time, giving in occasionally to a need for conversation, paying little attention to him. She hadn't mentioned the kiss again, hadn't done anything to seek another one, even though she'd made it clear she wouldn't object. She hadn't shown much interest in him at all.

He, on the other hand, had spent the past thirty-six hours in a state of arousal so intense that it was truly painful. Before then, he'd simply had fantasies, strictly imagined, existing only in his head. Now he had sensations—taste, scent,

touch—to go with them. Now he knew just how silky her
hair was, how soft her skin felt, how sweet her mouth tasted,
how firm her breasts were, how hard her nipples got. Now
he knew that she wanted him, that she would welcome him
into her bed and her body.

And it was slowly killing him to stay away.

Leaving the gun on the nightstand, he opened the door
carefully and made his way through the darkness to the
kitchen, fumbling for the light switch on the wall.

"Don't turn the light on, please."

For just an instant he froze and cursed his decision to
leave his pistol in the bedroom. In the next instant he recognized the voice as Tess's and made out the shadowy shape
of her sitting at the dining table. His heart beating rapidly—because she'd given him a start, or simply because she
was there, he didn't know—he went to the cabinet to the
right of the sink and took out a glass. When he opened the
refrigerator, the bright light made him squint as he filled the
glass with milk. As soon as he shut the door, his eyes ad-
justed once again to the night's darkness.

When he sat down across from her, he saw a glass of
orange juice and a bottle of aspirin on the table in front of
her. "Do you have a headache?"

"It's going away." Her voice was soft and hushed. "I
know I didn't wake you this time. I've been sitting here very
quietly for the last half hour or so."

He didn't offer a reason for being up, and she didn't seem
to expect one, only turned once again to look out the window. The moon was nearly full, and its light shone with an
eerie daylike brightness, but softer, hazier, on the meadow
behind the cabin. It came through the window, too, throwing exaggerated shadows across the table, bathing Tess in its
cool, gentle light and leaving him in darkness.

"I've never been an outdoors type of person," she said,
still speaking in a hushed tone, as if afraid to disturb the
night quiet. "My hobbies run toward reading and watching
TV, not hiking or camping or anything like that. Still..."

She sighed. "This place is beautiful. When this is over, if—" she paused, gave a little shake of her head, then continued "—if I get through it okay, I want to come back here. I want to hike into the forest and find the mountain lake that this place is named after. I want to see every bit of natural beauty there is to see."

She found beauty outside the window, he acknowledged, but he didn't look out. He didn't need to. He'd found his own definition of beauty across from him, in the delicate moonlit lines of her face, in her warm, clear brown eyes, in the sensuous curve of her mouth. Sitting there with her hair finger combed and wearing no makeup and a candy-striped robe, she was the most beautiful woman he'd ever seen.

And she could be his.

The thought came from nowhere, a treacherous sly whisper, and brought a sudden empty feeling to his chest, as if his heart had stopped beating and his lungs had stopped accepting air. Then, over the rushing in his ears, he heard himself swallow, heard his heartbeat begin again, pounding, throbbing, pumping heat and desire and lust and hope through his body with his blood.

Hope. They were two intelligent, mature people who were attracted to each other. Two people old enough and experienced enough to understand exactly what that meant. Two people strong enough to make that decision and deal with the consequences.

And those consequences might not be as dire as he'd forced himself to believe. When the case ended, he would be out of her life. He'd told himself that repeatedly, but it wasn't necessarily true. If Tess wanted him now—and she'd made it clear on Monday that she did—why wouldn't she want him when the case ended a month or two months from now? What would stop them from continuing to see each other, from building something long-term between them? God knows, they already had a hell of a foundation laid.

He smiled bitterly. He was trying to justify taking her to bed, making love to her, because he knew his self-control was getting ragged. He was weakening, searching for ways to have what he wanted without losing his self-respect, both personally and professionally.

What if she did still want him afterward? It didn't change the fact that he was a marshal and she was a witness in his custody. It didn't change the fact that he was on duty twenty-four hours a day and that his behavior had to be above reproach the entire time. It didn't change the fact that all he owed her—all he was morally and ethically allowed to give her—were the basics: shelter, food, safety.

And none of *those* facts, he thought bleakly, changed the fact that he was going to make love to Tess Marlowe. Maybe not tonight, maybe not this week, but soon. It would happen soon.

Tess sat in silence and watched him, even though she could make out nothing of his expression. When she'd heard his bedroom door open a few minutes ago, she had felt like a giddy teenager with her first serious crush. The longing to see him, the shivery excitement of being with him, the agonized uncertainty—does he like me? does he want me?—all were there.

But she wasn't a giddy teenager. She was a woman, all grown up, married and divorced, in hiding to save her life . . . and aching to get her heart broken.

She was falling in love with Deke Ramsey. If she kept to herself for the next sixteen days and didn't speak to him, didn't look at him or touch him or think of him, maybe she could stop the damage before it was done. But if they talked, if they shared their meals, if he continued to look at her with hunger in his eyes, if he gave her a chance to seduce him away from his principles and standards, she would lose her last chance at walking away from this chapter of her life unscathed.

But whatever pleasure she could get in the process would be worth the pain that followed. She knew that instinctively, in ways that she couldn't explain to anyone, not even herself, but trusted all the same.

"Have you been sleeping okay?" Deke's voice sounded rusty, a harsh intrusion in the darkness.

"Yeah. I still have the dreams, but they're not as vivid, not as frightening. I guess in time they'll go away completely." She took a sip of juice, then linked both hands together on the tabletop. "Life is funny, you know? In all the years I've worked in that office, I never worked late until the night Walt Davis was killed. The only reason I was there then was that I'd had a dental appointment the day before, and I'd taken the afternoon off. I had to stay the next night to catch up on my work. If not for that toothache, I wouldn't have missed work, I wouldn't have stayed late the next night, and I wouldn't have seen Walt Davis murdered. I wouldn't have been involved in Anthony Giamo's arrest, and he wouldn't have tried to kill me, and we wouldn't have been forced to come here." She shook her head slowly. "All because of a toothache."

"Another couple of weeks and everything will be normal again."

She shook her head once more. "No, I don't think so. I think you were right that day in the safe house when you said that nothing will ever be the same again. I'll never forget seeing Walt Davis die, watching the water in the fountain turn red with his blood. I'll never forget how cold Giamo was about it, as if he'd just squashed a bug instead of putting a bullet in a man's chest and another in his brain. I'll never forget the woman—how she screamed, or the terror in her voice when she yelled at Giamo. I'll never forget that those men tried to kill us."

"Maybe things will never be the same, but they will be normal again. The dreams will go away, the fear will fade. Even the memories will grow dim and hazy, as if they happened to someone else. You'll go back home, back to work, pick up your life where you left off." And maybe he would be there to help her. Maybe he could give her other dreams, other memories, to replace the bad ones.

"But I'll be different. Because of everything that's happened since that night, I'll be a different person."

"In what ways?"

"I'm not sure. I think I have a finer understanding of how precious life is and how easily it can be taken away. I think I appreciate it more. I want to enjoy it a little more." She shifted positions, drawing her feet onto the seat and tucking them beneath her robe for added warmth. "You know I was married before and that my husband divorced me."

It was a statement, not a question, and Deke treated it as such, making no response. He hadn't forgotten how annoyed she'd been when he had told her about the background investigation the U.S. Attorney's office had ordered on her.

"We were together eight years. We met in college and got married as soon as he graduated. We probably never should have done it, never should have had more than a brief affair. But we were young and foolish, and marriage seemed so romantic. It was okay the first few years. The next few years we drifted apart from each other. Will had his interests and priorities, and I had mine. His included a brilliant career, making as much money as he could, advancing in his firm as quickly as he could. Mine included having a family. The more we argued, the less we could compromise. He spent the last few years of our marriage looking for comfort and companionship and sex with as many other women as he could find."

She fell silent for a moment, then looked up at his shadowy outline and smiled apologetically. "I'm not sure why I'm telling you all this. Blame it on the moonlight. It makes me feel . . . free."

His throat dry, he reached out and touched his fingers to her hands, still tightly clasped. "Go on."

"I've never told anyone that—about his affairs. I think my parents and friends suspected it, but I never told them. I was ashamed, I guess. All his other women made me feel like a terrible failure as a wife, as a woman." Again she paused, and her fingers unconsciously twined around Deke's. She was telling this badly, in awkward starts and stops, but there was a point, she suddenly realized, that she wanted to make, something she wanted—needed—him to understand.

"I knew, of course, that things couldn't go on the way they had been, but I'd never thought about asking for a divorce. That's simply not the way it's done in my family. Then one day—it was in spring, one of those beautiful days when the sun is shining and a breeze is blowing and you would give anything to be able to spend the afternoon in the park with a book and a blanket and a kite—on one of those days I came home from work, and Will was packing. He'd gotten this promotion he'd wanted, and with it came a transfer to Philadelphia. He had stopped by the lawyer's office on the way home and started divorce proceedings. He was taking his current lover with him."

Still unaware that she was squeezing his hand, she broke off to stare out the window. Deke watched her, aching to use the hand that clutched his so tight to pull her around the table and onto his lap, to hold her close, to offer her soft words and softer kisses, to chase away the painful memories with gentle caresses and heated loving.

But he did none of those things. He let her hold his hand, and he patiently waited.

"I never told anyone the truth, not all of it. I said that we were divorcing because of his transfer, because we'd grown apart, because we wanted very different things from life, because I wanted a family. I never told them that he'd spent more time in other women's beds than he had in ours. I never told them how deeply that hurt me, how it made me doubt everything about myself. I kept all that secret."

Without giving up her hand, Deke moved to the chair at the end of the small table, putting himself at a right angle to Tess. "His affairs don't make you any less a woman," he said quietly, his voice sharp with intensity. "They just make him more a fool. You can't blame yourself for that. You can't accept responsibility for his failures.''

She smiled wanly at him. ''No, you're right, I can't. For four years I let Will and the divorce rule my life. I rarely went out with other men, and I never let any of them get close. I was afraid to get involved again, afraid that if the next relationship ended badly, I would be forced to admit that the divorce was my fault, that Will was innocent and I really was to blame. I was afraid to risk another failure. Even though it meant always being alone, I thought that was better than taking a chance and losing again. But I was wrong.''

That was the point of her story. She knew now how precious life was, knew that she could die tonight, tomorrow or next week, knew that something so fragile and dear should be treasured, enjoyed, lived to the fullest. She knew never being hurt again wasn't worth being alone forever. Keeping her heart and her ego and her pride safe wasn't worth giving up all chance for happiness.

And Deke understood. She was willing to risk making love with him, willing to risk an affair with him, even though it might end in heartache. Even though it might be wrong, even though it might bring far more pain than pleasure, she was willing to take that risk.

But was he?

His body found the answer long before his mind did. Without thought or intention, he pulled his hand back, still trapped in the strong grip of her delicately shaped fingers. As her fingers began to loosen, he twisted his hand until he was the one who held her, and he pulled her from her chair. At the same time, he stood up and guided her smoothly, naturally, into his arms, where in spite of—even because of—the difference between them, she fitted perfectly.

Monday's kiss had been hesitant, then urgent. There was no hesitancy tonight. He slid his fingers into her hair and gently pulled her head back and covered her mouth with his—closed at first, simply nuzzling the soft sensual lines of her lips, then open, his teeth nipping at her lower lip, his tongue wetting it from end to end. He let one hand glide from her hair down her back, lower still to the slight curve of her hips. Molding his fingers to her bottom, he pressed her against him, hip to hip, belly to belly, thigh to thigh, hardness to softness. He wanted her to know how much he wanted her, how desperately he needed her. He wanted her to know that simply looking at her made him hard. There was no need for caresses or kisses. His desire for her was so great that with one look, he grew hard, swollen and stiff and throbbing to find completion within her. He had spent the last eight days trying to ignore it, trying to control it, trying—when all else failed—to hide it. Now he would spend the next only-God-knew-how-many days trying to satisfy it. As long as she wanted him. As long as she would have him. Forever.

His tongue glided across her teeth, and his hand shifted from her hair to her jaw, his fingertips gently rubbing, gently coaxing her mouth open. He pressed his tongue into her mouth, past her teeth and into the moist welcoming heat. Soon he would probe that other moist, welcoming, heated place inside her. Soon he would fill her, would sheath his hardness intimately in the most feminine part of her, and there he would find death and life, completion and renewal, ending and beginning.

He explored her mouth and savored its textures—her tongue rough and bold, the roof firm and ridged, the insides of her cheeks soft and yielding. He tasted the orange juice she'd drunk, tasted hunger and urgency and pleasure. He thrust deeper, and she welcomed him, hungrily lured him in.

For a moment her hands clutched at the waistband of his faded jeans, low on his hips, for support; then she twined one arm around his neck, the tips of her fingers disappearing into the unruly waves of his dark hair. She moved her other hand over his chest, brushing in a tantalizingly brief caress over his nipple before reaching his forearm, strong and smooth and hard with muscle.

He felt even better than he looked, she marveled. His skin was warm from the fire burning inside and stretched taut over granite-hard muscles. There was no softness anywhere on him, just bone and muscle and satiny skin and coarse swirling hair that curled around her fingers as they stroked. She longed to step back and look at him, longed to slowly, leisurely explore every inch of his body, first with her hands, then her mouth, then with her own body. She wanted to touch his nipple again and watch it harden, wanted to rub her own nipples, already swollen and achy, across his. She wanted everything.

His breathing was ragged when he tore his mouth from hers. For an instant she feared there would be a repeat of Monday's scene, an unbearable rejection, but he made no effort to push her away. Instead he drew in a deep, desperately needed breath, his lungs filling, his chest expanding, and he laid his hand gently over her breast, feeling the pounding of her heart through the soft, crinkly, candy-striped cotton. "Are you sure you want to risk this?" he whispered hoarsely.

She moved, rubbing her breast against his big palm. The action was all the confirmation he needed. Capturing her hands, he raised each one to his mouth, placing an open, wet kiss in the center. Then he drew her with him, not to the bedroom, as she'd hoped, but closer, to the chair he'd vacated only moments earlier. He sat down and pulled her onto his lap, his hands helping to settle her across him, raising her gown to free her legs so she could face him, straddle him.

When he kissed her again, Tess moaned and rubbed her body against his. In the process of getting positioned, her gown had been lifted to her hips, and now her robe fell open, leaving the triangle of silken curls between her thighs and the vulnerable femininity underneath exposed. The thick, rigid length of his arousal pressed against her, separated from her only by the worn fabric of his jeans. Each time she moved, his denim-encased flesh rubbed the small erect nub of her own flesh, and she felt his heat, potent and dangerous, seeping into her.

She was tormenting him with the slow, involuntary rocking of her hips. He didn't know, though, just how intimate her actions were until he slid his hand between their bodies, intending to reposition himself inside his jeans for more comfort, and his fingers, instead of fumbling between soft layers of denim and candy stripes, found softer layers of warm, moist, swollen, feminine flesh.

His first impulse was to jerk back as if burned. Indeed, so hot was the dampness generated by passion that he might have been. His second was to touch her again, to stroke her gently, to make her writhe and groan, to take from her mouth the harsh cries of completion. But he'd waited for her too long, needed her too much. If he touched her there again, he would empty himself into the faded denim that held him without feeling the exquisite pleasure of her body gloving him.

He ended the kiss slowly, dipping his tongue into her mouth once more, then again for another taste, then biting gently at her lower lip. With his heavy breathing echoing in his ears, he guided her back until she was arched over the support of his other arm. Disregarding the belt to her robe, he simply pushed the fabric to each side. Her nightgown underneath was pale pink cotton and fastened with a row of tiny white buttons. His fingers worked awkwardly and freed two buttons before he ducked his head impatiently and, through the fabric, bathed the clearly visible peak of one breast with his tongue.

Tess gasped, increasing the arch in her back in a silent plea for more, and after unfastening several more buttons, Deke gave it, suckling first one nipple, then the other, drawing each crest deep into his mouth, holding it gently between his teeth while his tongue worked its magic.

"Please, Deke," she whispered, her voice quavering and weak. "Please..."

He'd waited long enough, he knew with a fierce surge of pain. If he didn't bury himself inside her within the next few minutes, he was going to explode where he was. Swiftly, he got to his feet, lifting her with him, then letting her slide to the floor, her body touching his for every agonizingly slow inch.

He led her to her bedroom door, where he left her with a murmured, "Wait a minute." Then he disappeared into his own room. Only a moment later he returned, his pistol nearly concealed in his right hand. He didn't wait to put it down before reaching for her again, but pulled her against him, wrapping his arms around her, kissing her greedily, backing her blindly toward the bed.

Tess heard the soft clunk as he laid the pistol on the nightstand; then he turned all his attention to her. While his mouth on her ear sent uncontrollable shivers down her spine, his hands found the knot that fastened the belt of her robe and nimbly untied it. Slowly he pushed it off her shoulders and down her arms to her fingertips, where it fell without a sound to the floor.

She reached for the hem of her gown, intending to pull it over her head, but he stopped her. "No. I'll do it." In his own way, in his own time. He stepped away from her long enough to open the curtains on both windows, letting in the cool glow of the moon. He wanted to see as much of her as possible, but without the harsh intrusion of the electrical lights.

For a long, still moment he stared down into her face, lost in her sheer beauty, his body's urgent demand forgotten. She was so beautiful, so delicate, so perfect. Then she touched him, no more than the brand of her palm on his ribs, and the moment ended, swept away by renewed desire. Still holding her gaze, he slid his hand inside the open bodice of her gown, covering her breast, capturing her nipple gently between two fingers. He watched her lips part, heard her breath quicken, saw her eyes flutter shut.

With his other hand, he slowly unfastened another button, then another, until the last was free. All he had to do to see her, every seductively lovely inch, was push the fabric from her shoulders to the floor. But he forced himself to leave it where it was. When it was time, he would bare her, but not yet.

Tess shivered when his arms slipped inside her open gown to wrap around her waist. When he began lowering her to the bed, she gasped at the sensation of falling and caught his shoulders for support. As she sank onto the mattress, he parted her legs with one muscular thigh, then settled, half on her, half off.

He was big, both in stature and sexually. She savored every sensation, from the fiercely strained way he was kissing her to the satiny fire of his chest rubbing against her breasts, from the erotic press of his manhood on her thigh and hip to the sheltering weight of his body bearing her deep into the soft mattress.

His hands roamed restlessly over her body, blazing a trail from cheek to throat to shoulder to waist to hip, then back again. Murmuring wordlessly beneath his kiss, she caught his hand and guided it to her breast. She wriggled underneath him, burning, aching, throbbing, seeking relief that only he could bring her, bringing him torment that only she could relieve.

At last, lungs bursting, heart racing, she forced herself free of his kiss. "Now, damn you," she whispered fiercely, raising her hands to cup his cheeks. "I need you now."

He rolled to his side and freed his hands to undress while Tess slid her gown off and tossed it aside. His jeans were old and well-worn. A solid tug on the first button pulled the remaining ones free, too, and he kicked them off before returning to her. "You are so beautiful," he murmured, skimming his hand over her belly to the silken dark curls. Gently he probed beneath them. Even more gently he stroked the sensitive flesh there before dipping inside. She was hot and moist, her muscles flexing convulsively. She was ready for him.

Powerfully he rose over her, bracing his weight on his arms, positioning himself between her open thighs. The long, thick length of his arousal probed where seconds ago his finger had been, sliding carefully inside her, bit by bit, savoring, shuddering, until at last he was sheathed completely within her. With great effort, he held himself still, then lowered his head until his forehead bumped hers. "Oh, Tess," he sighed. "Oh, lady..."

He kissed her very gently, a brush of lips on lips. Tentatively he shifted inside her, felt her body straining to conform to his intrusion. Forty-two years of living had never prepared him for this, he thought dazedly. Marriage, Angela, every affair he'd had since he was eighteen—all were meaningless compared to this. To Tess.

She found his nipples and made him shudder. Slowly she dragged the abrasive surface of her tongue across one, delighting in the way it puckered and hardened, just as hers had done for him. His groan, deep and hoarse, gave her a heady sense of power. Testing it, she caught his nipple between her teeth, gently, the way he had, and suckled it.

Muttering an oath, he forced her head to the mattress and clamped his mouth over hers, his tongue stabbing savagely into her mouth, an action that his hardness mimicked lower. She met every thrust of his hips, arching her back, finding and matching his rhythm, and she urged him on, locking her legs around his hips, allowing him deeper penetration, caressing his chest and his back and his face, suckling and biting his tongue.

The sensations built quickly in her belly, spiraling, burning hotter and brighter, making her gasp for each sweet breath, and they spread through her with every rapid beat of her heart, with every deep furious thrust of his hips, until she couldn't endure any more. Color exploded behind her tightly closed eyes, and strained, whimpered cries escaped her and were instantly swallowed by his kiss. Trembling, out of control, helpless, she clung to him.

In some small part of his mind, he knew he should stop, should give her a moment to catch her breath, to let the release that was sending violent shudders through her subside, but he, too, was beyond control. In and out, sinking, filling, withdrawing, returning—it was as necessary to him at that moment as breathing, as living. He experienced the same feelings she had, in the same way, building, intensifying, overwhelming. Letting her take his weight, he slid his hands beneath her to cup her bottom and lifted her to meet him, opening her more to him, cradling her for one last impossibly deep thrust. His fingers gripping soft flesh, his body strained and tightened. For a second there was nothing, then fulfillment, sharp, violent, intense, as he emptied himself inside her.

For a long time he lay heavily on her, still cradling her, still buried deep within her. He knew he was too big, knew he should roll off and let her breathe, but he knew, too, that these few moments wouldn't hurt her, and he needed them—needed to lie there until the shudders stopped, needed to feel every inch of her body against his, needed to feel the weakening but still detectable clenching of her muscles around his now-softening flesh.

Tess stroked his back in slow, easy circles, then slid her hands over his sweat-slicked skin to his hair. She loved his hair, she thought drowsily, thick and dark and untamed. And she loved his shoulders, broad and strong, and his chest, satin-soft and hard-muscled. She loved touching him and kissing him and arousing him, and, God help her, how she had adored making love with him! "If I died right now," she said, stroking both hands through his hair, "I would die a happy and very satisfied woman."

His chuckle was low and unintentionally seductive. "That's a hell of a thing to be thinking about at a time like this."

"Four years. That's how long I've waited."

He moved carefully onto his side, shifting her with him, keeping their bodies joined. Tenderly he brushed a strand of hair from her forehead, then pressed a kiss where it had been. "Was it worth it?" he asked softly, the smugly amused tone of his voice making it clear that he already knew the answer.

"Absolutely."

He kissed her again, this time on the cheek. "Do we have to wait four years to do it again?"

Just as she felt him stirring inside her once more, he rolled onto his back, lifting her with him. "How old are you?" she asked, drawing her knees in close to his hips and carefully rising over him.

"Forty-two."

She felt him growing, lengthening, to fill her once more. Bending low, she gave him a kiss. "I'm impressed," she said in a sultry voice, then shifted her hips experimentally. "I'm *very* impressed."

It was nearly ten o'clock when Deke awakened Wednesday morning. For a long moment he kept his eyes closed, making use instead of his other senses. He was lying on his back, a fluffy pillow beneath his head, the covers pulled to his chest—with Tess snuggled close within the crook of his arm. She had pillowed her head on his shoulder, and one arm, so light he barely noticed it, lay across his stomach. Her body was soft and warm against his, and her breathing was slow, deep and easy, signaling that she still slept. She needed the rest, he thought with a thoroughly satisfied smile.

But his smile faded when he thought about last night's loving. Did he regret it? Had he given in to desire and thrown good sense and morals and professional conduct right out the window? Had he made a vital mistake?

He searched within himself and found no regret, no dismay. While there was no doubt that morally and professionally this was wrong, there was no doubt, either, that it was the best thing he could have done. Naturally he couldn't condone an affair between a marshal and his witness, but this was different—there were extenuating circumstances. This wasn't a casual affair, begun to ease the boredom of confinement. He and Tess had shared something last night that most people searched all their lives for and never found. There was no way he would let it end when this case ended, no way he would let it end until his life ended, too.

Finally he opened his eyes and looked at her. She seemed so delicate, so incredibly fragile. Looking at her like this, innocent and vulnerable and naked, he was struck with a sense of wonder that last night's loving had been so easily accomplished. She was so small, and he was big and hard, and yet they had fitted together so perfectly not once, but twice.

And his body was starting to ache to do it again.

Turning his head the other way, he checked the clock on the nightstand next to his gun. It was a few minutes after ten. His agreement with Scott had been that he would call in between ten and noon on the appointed days, and this morning was one of those days. If he didn't call within that time frame, his boss would assume something had gone wrong and would call for assistance. So, as enticing as a morning of long, slow loving sounded, it would have to wait.

He eased his arm from beneath her and slid out of bed, tucking the covers around her. Carrying his jeans in one hand and his pistol in the other, he walked naked to his own bedroom, gathered some clothes, then took a quick shower, shaved and dressed.

When he returned to Tess's room, she was stirring, half-awake, still half sleeping. She smiled when the mattress sank underneath his weight and blindly reached for him. When her hand encountered jeans instead of bare skin, she sighed regretfully and opened her eyes. "Good morning."

For a moment he simply looked at her. Her hair was tousled, the look in her eyes drowsy and warm and uncertain.

The only man she'd been with in the last twelve years had been her ex-husband, he reminded himself. She'd had no experience with the awkward morning-after rituals.

He leaned forward and kissed her, brushing his lips along her jaw, finally reaching her mouth for a lingering taste, then murmured an intimately soft, "Good morning."

"When I woke up alone, I thought maybe I'd dreamed last night."

"No." He brushed his fingers through her hair, tucking it behind her ear. "We have to go into town as soon as you're ready. I've got to call in."

"Why don't we just skip it and stay here?"

"Because if Scott doesn't hear from me within—" he glanced at the clock "—an hour and twenty-five minutes, he's going to be on the phone to the local sheriff's office. You don't want to explain to some deputy why we missed checking in, do you?"

"No, I guess not." She started to push the covers back, then remembered at the last moment that her safe, plain, unsexy pink nightgown was on the floor instead of on her body. Tugging the covers back in place, she extended one hand. "Would you hand me my robe?"

His dark eyes moved over her with intense warmth. "I saw you last night, Tess—all of you." But he leaned down anyway and retrieved the pink-and-white robe for her.

"Do I have time to take a shower?" She dropped the blankets and shrugged into the robe, giving him a brief glimpse of her small breasts, their rosy nipples flat and soft and waiting to be aroused.

His mouth had gone dry, hungering for a kiss, and it made his voice raspy when he replied, "You can have about forty minutes."

She was ready in less than thirty, wearing faded jeans and an oversize black T-shirt. Deke stood at the front door, his jacket on to cover his holster, and watched as she leaned against the back of the sofa for support while she put her shoes on. The scooped neck of her shirt slipped off one shoulder, revealing that it was bare, meaning that her breasts were bare, too. All he had to do was slide his hands underneath the loose shirt and he could touch them, could stroke her nipples into hardness, could make her legs go weak, could make the heated moisture that meant she was ready to take him pool between her thighs. . . .

He shifted his gaze elsewhere as the uncomfortable swelling started in his groan. He had thought making love to her last night would take the edge off his need, but he'd been wrong. Now that he knew what it was like to glove himself deep within her, to have her legs wrapped tightly around him, to hear her soft, helpless cries and to feel her body quivering and clenching around his hardness in release—to fill her with his own sweetly liquid release—now he wanted her more than ever. A hundred times, a thousand, wouldn't be enough.

"I'm ready," Tess said, slipping her arms into her own jacket.

Making love hadn't changed one thing, she thought a few minutes later. Deke was no more talkative on this drive into town than he'd been before. She wondered what he was thinking about, then wondered exactly what it was he'd offered her last night besides sex. Was last night's incredible lovemaking all he intended to give her? Or was he planning an affair that would run the duration of this assignment? When he took her back to Atlanta, safe and unharmed, would he walk out of her life? Or would he give their relationship a chance to survive and grow under the circumstances of their normal lives?

None of the answers really mattered. She had made her position quite clear to him last night: she was willing to have an affair. There would be no demands for promises or pretty words. She would accept responsibility for the decision to have the affair, and she would accept responsibility for the consequences, good or bad.

Four years ago that idea would have frightened her. Before she got emotionally and physically involved with a man, she would have insisted on promises, assurances that she wouldn't be hurt. Four years ago the loving alone wouldn't have been enough for her. It wouldn't have been worth the risk—not even the *simple* risk—of pain. But now, knowing that Deke might very well never touch her again, knowing that in a few weeks he could walk away from her as coldly and as permanently as Will had done, knowing that she could very likely end up with a broken heart...now the prospect of pain didn't matter. If she loved Deke and he left her, yes, it would hurt, but she would have a heart full of precious memories. She would have this brief time of loving, and it would be worth whatever heartache waited ahead.

They went to a different pay phone this time, one located in front of a drugstore in the heart of downtown Altus. Deke parked in the side lot, shut off the engine and turned to Tess. "You'll have to get out with me this time." The phone wasn't visible from the parking lot, and he wanted her in his sight at all times. Besides, after he'd made the call, he had an errand to run inside.

She nodded and climbed out, locking the door behind her. He met her at the back of the truck and slipped his arm around her shoulders, holding her close. Was he as hungry to touch as she was, she wondered, or simply playing his role in their husband-and-wife-on-vacation charade?

While he was on the phone, she leaned against the brick building, one knee bent, foot placed flat on the wall, and watched the traffic as she listened with half an ear to his conversation. The people who passed on the sidewalk all seemed to know each other and spoke warmly. Most of them offered a polite hello or a nod in greeting to her, and in spite of Deke's warning last week not to be friendly, she returned them.

After a few moments, when it became clear that Deke was winding up the phone call, she touched his arm, waited until he looked down at her, then whispered, "Ask him about my parents."

He nodded and did so. A moment later he confirmed that he would call Friday, then hung up. "Your mother and father are fine. I told you, they're not in any danger from Giamo. He's not a stupid man. He knows we have you in custody, and he knows that your parents have even less idea where you are than he does."

She sighed softly. He was right—she knew in her heart he was—but she couldn't stop worrying. She changed the subject as he took her arm and led her into the drugstore, wandering down the aisles toward the back. "What do we need here?"

When he didn't answer, she looked up at him and saw a faint red tinge beneath the bronze of his cheeks. Then she saw the Family Planning sign that hung above the aisle they were in and her own cheeks turned red.

"I didn't exactly come on this trip prepared," he said uncomfortably. "I should have thought about it last night, but..." He'd been beyond thinking of anything last night except how beautiful she was, how badly he wanted her and how exquisite it had felt to be inside her.

Tess's blush deepened. She hadn't given any thought to birth control, either. What a failure she was as a responsible, modern woman. Then the other implications of his purchase occurred to her: if he wanted to buy something now, then he must plan to continue making love to her for the next two weeks, at least. And if he hadn't used anything last night, there was a possibility—slim, but there all the same—that she could be pregnant.

Smiling slightly, she waited while he made his selection from the wide display, then walked with him to the cash register. Throughout her twenties, all she'd thought of was sweet-smelling babies who grew into chubby-cheeked toddlers and obstinate children and rebellious teenagers. After Will had made it clear that he had no intention of ever becoming a father, she had become obsessed with what she was missing.

But in her thirties she'd given up the dream. First she'd found out about Will's affairs, and she'd known that bringing a helpless, innocent child into their marriage would be a mistake. Then had come the divorce. She had finally accepted that she would probably never have children, would never know the pleasure of being pregnant or the thrill of giving birth, the joy of holding a tiny human being and knowing that he had been created, partly of her and partly of her husband, by love.

She knew it wasn't likely that she'd gotten pregnant last night. Her cycle was irregular and difficult to predict, but for heaven's sake, she was thirty-five years old, and studies had shown that women in their mid-to-late thirties and older had more difficulty conceiving than younger women. Still . . . it was a lovely thought. A lovely possibility.

Deke laid the small box on the counter, and a clerk maybe half his age rang it up, calling out the total. Deke didn't use a wallet but carried his money loose in his jeans pocket. In the right pocket were several hundred dollars of the money Scott had given him—government money. Taxpayers' money. In his left pocket was the twenty-dollar bill that was all the cash he'd had when they left Atlanta. He pulled it out and handed it to the clerk, then stuffed his change into the same pocket.

Taking Tess's arm, he guided her out of the store. "Do you need anything before we leave town?"

Still thinking about babies and making love, she shook her head.

"You have everything you need for dinner tomorrow?"

Thanksgiving—she'd almost forgotten about it. Wistfully, she glanced over her shoulder at the pay phone before he pulled her around the corner into the parking lot. "Could I call my parents?" she asked, then quickly continued before he could turn her down. "I wouldn't tell them where we are or anything, I promise. I just want to let them know that I'm okay and not to worry about me and to have a nice day tomorrow."

"No."

"Deke . . ."

He shook his head. When she laid her hand on his arm and looked up at him beseechingly, he muttered an oath. "It's bad enough that I slept with you, Tess. Don't ask me to do this, too."

She drew back, stunned, then whirled and started toward the Bronco. She hadn't gone three steps before he caught up with her, but he didn't try to touch her, didn't try to explain.

The silence between them was cold and stony and lasted until they reached the cabin. There, when Tess would have stormed into her room and slammed the door, Deke caught the collar of her jacket and pulled her back to face him. "Don't think because you let me make love to you that I'll break all the other rules for you, too. I can't do that, Tess. I can't jeopardize your safety and my job any more than I already have."

"No one forced you to sleep with me!" she said hotly. "*You* were the one who kissed *me*. *You* were the one who seduced *me*."

His smile was bleak. "Lady, you seduced me the first time I saw you, and you didn't even know you were doing it. I didn't have any choice last night. Even though I knew it could cost my job, not making love to you was costing my sanity. I needed you so desperately. . . ."

Tess lowered her gaze, ashamed to look at him. She had known all along about his standards of conduct, about his principles and dedication and loyalty to his job. She had known that making love to her would compromise them. And when she had asked if she could call her parents, she had known it was against the rules, had known he had to tell her no, but she had hoped that the fact they were now lovers would sway him. She had tried to use what had happened between them last night to her own benefit.

"I'm sorry." She tried to smile, but it wasn't much better than his. "I was wrong to ask you to let me call them."

"Yes, you were. The calls I make to Scott are different. I know the phone lines into our office are secure. No one can tap into those calls and listen in or trace them and find out where we're calling from. I can't say the same about your parents' phone." Then he sighed and slid her coat down her arms. "And I was wrong for what I said. It sounded harsh, and it diminished what happened last night, and that's not what I meant to do."

This time her smile was more successful. "Now that we've both apologized, what would you like to do? Have a late breakfast? An early lunch?"

His gaze, dark and warm, locked with hers. "What I'd really like to do is get my hands underneath that shirt and find out for sure if your breasts are really bare." He cleared his throat, but it did nothing for the hoarseness that had crept into his voice. "Then I'd like to kiss them, to kiss you, everywhere—your face, your ears, your throat, your nipples, your belly, between your legs. . . ." He shrugged. "But if you'd rather have lunch . . ."

The rest of his compromise was lost in a sudden kiss as Tess told him wordlessly, with her hands and her body and her tongue in his mouth, exactly what she would rather do.

Chapter 7

Over the years Thanksgiving had meant various things to Deke. As a boy there had been the Thanksgiving when his father had taught him and his brothers thankfulness for their country, for their freedom and for their lives. Poor in money, they were rich in the things that counted: love, family, happiness. As a teenager he'd been thankful that his mother had been able to keep the family together for one more year. As a twenty-year-old it had been gratitude that he'd made it through the hell that was the war in Vietnam for nine months and twenty-one days without getting wounded.

Today, he thought, lying on the braided rug in front of the fireplace with Tess in his arms, their clothes in a tangle, their skin slick with sweat from recently satisfied passion, today he had something more precious than his father's teachings, than his family or his life, to be thankful for: today he had Tess.

She was lying beside him the way she slept at night, snuggled close, her head cushioned on his shoulder, one leg nestled intimately between his thighs. Her breathing was still uneven, but it was slowing, returning breath by breath to normal.

The cabin was warm from the fire before them and from the oven in the kitchen behind them, and enticing aromas filled the air—pumpkin pie cooling on the counter, turkey breast turning golden in the oven, Rose Conrad's special dressing recipe redolent with sage and other spices he didn't recognize. There would be candied sweet potatoes, too, and sourdough rolls with honey butter and pecan pie—a typical holiday celebration, scaled down for two.

Idly he thought of his family back in Atlanta. Dinner would be served at promptly one o'clock, so his mother and sisters-in-law would be busy in the kitchen, while the kids played outside and his brothers watched football on TV. That was the way Thanksgiving always was at home, and he had always enjoyed it, had never wanted it any other way. But there was something to be said for preparing a small dinner together, then making slow, leisurely love in front of the fireplace while it cooked.

"I wish I could have let you call your parents."

"I know." Tess stretched out one leg, propping her foot on the hearth next to his. Like the rest of him his feet were big, longer and broader than hers.

"You have small feet."

"I prefer dainty," she said airily. When his hand covered her breast—not touched, she thought ruefully, but literally, completely covered it—she sighed. "But I don't guess I can claim to have dainty breasts, can I? It sounds funny."

"I prefer small," he said, playing with her nipple. "I suppose you've heard the saying that more than a handful is wasted?"

"That's a sexist statement," she said. To prove it, she slid her hand down his chest, over his belly and through the thick dark curling hair until she cradled him in her palm. Even in a semiaroused state, he was definitely more than a handful—and definitely not wasted. "Deke?"

"Hmm." She started to withdraw her hand, but he captured it and guided it back. Her lazy, gentle caresses felt too good to give up.

"Why were you so mean to me in the beginning?"

"Mean? Me?"

"You didn't want to be in the safe house with me, and you made sure I knew it. You wouldn't talk to me, and you were nasty and ill-tempered all the time."

Slowly he released her and turned onto his side to face her, propping his arm beneath his head. "I told you yesterday. You seduced me the first time I saw you. If I was mean or ill-tempered, it was only because I was trying to keep some distance between us. I was trying to keep from grabbing you and unzipping my jeans and . . ." He shrugged.

"Was it so important to you that you stay away from me?" She smiled faintly. "I know you don't make a habit of seducing the witnesses you guard."

"You're wrong. I do."

For a moment she thought he was joking, and her smile grew. Then she realized that he was as serious as she'd ever seen him. She sat up and reached for the nearest piece of clothing—his shirt. The short sleeves fell past her elbows, and the hem reached practically to her knees.

"Maybe 'habit' isn't quite the way to describe it," he said with a grim smile as he picked up his jeans. Ignoring the navy blue briefs on the floor, he stepped into the jeans and buttoned them, then sat down facing her again. "But it's happened before. Her name was Angela. She was a witness in a drug-smuggling investigation. Her husband, who she had recently divorced, was one of the major suppliers at the time, and she had agreed to testify against him."

"And you had an affair with her." Why did it hurt so much to say that? she wondered. It had happened in the past, long before she'd known Deke Ramsey even existed. She'd realized all along that there had been other women before her, just as there would be other women after her.

But the circumstances of his affair with *this* woman were too similar, too close to home.

"We had her at a safe house in Jacksonville, and I...I fell in love with her." He was staring at the fire, thinking back six years, remembering without pain, without bitterness, without that horrible sense of loss that had plagued him for so long. As he had told Tess would happen with her own memories, his had grown dim and hazy, as if they had happened to someone else. As if some other man had fallen in love with Angela Wright and had an affair with her. As if some other man had been devastated by losing her. As if some other man had taken years to get over her. But it had been him. "And yes, we had an affair."

"That must have been kind of tough, with the other marshals around." She heard the quaver in her voice and prayed that he didn't.

"They knew what was going on. We were all friends, buddies. They looked the other way."

"And after the trial? What happened?" Did he continue seeing her? Did he try to build a normal relationship with her? Or had he ended the affair with the trial?

Deke leaned back against the hearth and stretched his legs out in front of him. "She entered the relocation program. She had to, to keep someone in her husband's organization from killing her. I never saw her again."

"If you loved her," Tess said softly, hesitantly, hating the words with a passion, "why didn't you relocate with her?"

Finally he looked at her. "Because I didn't love her that much. I couldn't make that kind of sacrifice."

She shivered and folded her arms over her chest for warmth. "Well...I can see why your boss might want to start letting you guard only men from now on."

"Don't joke when you don't mean it, Tess." He watched her for a moment, his dark eyes studying her face, then tried to call Angela's image to mind. It wouldn't come. He could describe her—hair color and style, bone structure, eye color, height, weight, body type—but he couldn't conjure up a picture to go with that description. All he could see was Tess. "You asked if it was so important to me that I stay away from you. My affair with Angela was a serious error in judgment, but one that could be dealt with because I'd had a spotless record up until then. But if it happened a second time..." He shrugged.

"And now it has." She said it flatly, without a hint of the darker emotions that swirled inside her. "So what will happen now? Do you expect me to keep this a secret?"

"I expect—"

A knock at the door interrupted him. He rolled to his feet, picked up the holster he'd left on the floor and slid the gun free. "Go to your room and close the door," he ordered in a whisper, and Tess jumped to her feet, grabbing the rest of their clothes in her arms, and obeyed.

Deke went to the front window and lifted the curtain slightly. There was a pickup parked behind the Bronco, and a young man dressed in a flannel shirt, jeans and work boots stood on the porch, his hands in his back pockets. He looked totally harmless, but Deke didn't put much stock in appearances. Sliding the safety off his gun, he went to the door and unlocked it, then opened it little more than a foot. The gun was out of sight in his right hand. "Can I help you?"

"Sorry if we disturbed you. We're restocking the firewood," the young man said. "Do you need anything else? Sheets, towels?"

Looking past him, Deke saw the manager who had checked them in come from the woodpile on the west side of the house. The older man lifted his hand in a wave, then climbed into the truck. "No," he said, relaxing his grip on the pistol. "We're fine, thanks."

He watched the young man return to the truck, waited until they drove away, then closed and locked the door. He replaced the safety on the pistol, set it down and called to Tess to come out again.

She had taken advantage of the interruption to get dressed, Deke noticed regretfully as she came into the living room, carrying his shirt in one hand. "Why the clothes?"

"In case that was the bad guys and they killed us, I didn't want to be found dead wearing your shirt and nothing else," she said flippantly.

He began walking toward her. "You know, I can remove those clothes as easily as you put them on."

"But you won't."

"You're right." He laced his fingers behind her back and pulled her slowly toward him. "If I kiss you a little and caress your breasts a little and rub you a little here—" he moved his hips against hers "—you'll take them off of your own free will."

She shrugged, acknowledging the correctness of his assumption. Then she grew serious and reached up to rest her palm along his smooth-shaven jaw. "Deke...I won't tell anyone."

"About what?"

"This. About us."

He gave her an odd little half smile. "You think they won't know anyway the first time they see us together?"

"I don't want you to get into trouble. I'm as responsible for this as you are. You love your job. What would you do if you lost it?"

The smile grew. "I don't know. Maybe come up here and apply to the sheriff's department. Then we could hike into the forest and find that mountain lake together." He lifted his hands and combed them through her hair. "Don't worry about me, Tess. I'm not going to lose my job. I'm not going to get into trouble. My boss likes me. I'm very good at what I do."

Besides, how could they fire him for making love to the woman he was probably going to spend the rest of his life with?

He kissed her gently, then released her, pulled his shirt on and followed her into the kitchen. There she checked the turkey in the oven, then made a rich sweet syrup for the sweet potatoes, and while she worked, sniffing, tasting, stirring, bending for one item, stretching for another, Deke sat at the table and watched. She could feel his gaze, as warm and tender as a caress, and she avoided meeting it, because she knew what she would see. Desire. Lust. Affection. Hunger.

But not love.

Angela. Even the name made her nose wrinkle in distaste. What had she looked like? She had probably been beautiful, she thought with a scowl, with breasts and curves and long, long legs—the kind of woman who made men's heads turn. It would take an extraordinary woman to make Deke forget his principles and his duty and fall in love with her.

And there was absolutely nothing, she thought sadly, about *her* that was extraordinary.

But he hadn't entered the relocation program with Angela. He had loved her, but not enough for that. She took some solace from that knowledge. That meant the other woman hadn't been the great love of his life. It meant he might fall in love again.

She had never known how greedy she could be. Here, at the worst time of her life, she'd been given a lover better than any she might have created in her fantasies: he was gentle, sweet, tender, considerate, talented and gorgeous, too. And she wasn't satisfied with that. She didn't want just a lover, just an affair. She wanted a future. She wanted love. She wanted . . . God help her, she wanted marriage and babies and forever.

And she had no right to expect any of that. After the trial, scheduled to begin two weeks from today, she had no right to expect anything.

"Tess?" Deke had watched the expressions cross her face while she worked—a sweet smile that faded into bleakness, then, for just an instant, pain so harsh and deep that he felt it all the way across the room. "What's wrong?"

She lifted her gaze upward, controlling the excess moisture in her eyes, then glanced over her shoulder at him. "I was just thinking. The trial begins two weeks from today."

He didn't believe her answer. That might be cause for fear, but not pain, and damn sure not the kind of pain he'd seen. But he couldn't call her a liar, couldn't try to coax the truth from her, not when the look in her eyes was so vulnerable. "Does that concern you?"

She sighed deeply, grateful that he'd accepted her response without question. "Do you know that the preliminary hearing was the first time I'd ever been in a courtroom? Even when I was divorced, my attorney handled it for me. I didn't have to appear."

"You'll do fine at the trial. You were very impressive at the hearing."

Again she glanced at him. "Were you there?"

He nodded.

"Will you be at the trial?"

"I don't know. But security will be very tight at the courthouse, especially in that courtroom. There will be at least two, probably four, marshals in the courtroom, and they'll be using metal detectors." But that wasn't what she wanted to know, he realized. She wasn't asking witness to marshal, but woman to man. Lover to lover. "I'll be there. I'll clear it through Scott."

She left the stove and pulled a chair over so she could sit facing him. "Will he go to prison?" she asked. "You know the details of the case. You understand the evidence in ways that I don't. Tell me what you really believe. Will Giamo go to prison?"

He laced his fingers through hers. "It's a strong case, Tess, and you're an excellent witness. If everything goes well, yes, I think he'll be convicted and sent to prison."

"And what could go wrong?"

He didn't want to give her anything else to worry about, but he wouldn't keep her in the dark, either. "Anthony Giamo got rid of Walt Davis because he knew too much about Giamo's business. He murdered Donald Hopkins and tried to kill you to keep you from testifying against him. The man is not above bribing a juror or a judge."

"Or trying to kill me again."

He tightened his grip on her hand. "I won't let that happen."

She raised her free hand to touch his face, her fingertips trailing along his jaw. "You're one man, Deke," she said softly. "Once we leave this cabin... how can you prevent it?"

"Once we leave this cabin, it won't be just me. There will be plenty of other marshals to help. Trust me, Tess. Nothing is going to happen to you."

She sighed softly, kissed the hand that held hers, then returned to check the turkey once more. Using thick pot holders, she removed it from the oven and left it on the stovetop, put the yams and the extra dressing in to bake and started on the pecan pie. "Let's talk about something more cheerful. Why did you join the Marshals Service?"

If she had asked him that question ten days ago, he would have refused to answer it. A week ago, he probably would have given some flip response that made it clear it was none of her business. Today he told her the truth. "My father was very patriotic—flying the flag, my country right or wrong, that type. He thought there was no place in the world as good as the United States, no country that gave as much to its people, no country so deserving of respect and loyalty, and no honor greater than serving it. He tried to teach that to the five of us, and I guess it sank in with me. When I graduated from high school, I joined the marines and went to Vietnam. After college I knew I wanted to go into some type of federal law enforcement, and the Marshals Service seemed the most interesting."

"When did you father die?" Her voice was soft, encouraging him to continue talking. He rarely opened up about himself, and she wanted to learn as much as she could about him. She wanted to know everything.

"When I was fourteen. He was killed in an accident at work. It almost destroyed my mother. If she hadn't had five kids to take care of, I think she would just have given up and died alongside him. But she knew if she did, we would have to be split up. No one would have taken in five boys, and once the family had been separated, we never would have gotten together again."

"So she held on for the kids' sakes, and you helped her."

"Why do you say that?"

She smiled gently. "Because that's the kind of person you are. You feel responsible for others."

"Yeah, I helped her." His expression grew distant and grim as he remembered the way he'd helped. By confronting Anthony Giamo when his father's boss, a man who worked for Giamo, had refused to pay the last week's salary and the benefits still owed to James Ramsey. By impressing the older man with his cocky, brash behavior, with his willingness to fight for what was rightfully his, with his street-smart, not-afraid-of-anybody attitude. By accepting a job with him, something totally innocent at first that, over the next two years, grew into something serious enough that now it could damage his career and place his integrity in question.

He squeezed his eyes shut and rubbed them hard with the heels of his hands. It was ironic that something he'd done as a kid could come back to haunt him twenty-six years later. At the time it had simply been a means of survival, a way to help keep the family together. He'd been too young and too needy to worry about right and wrong.

The fact that the joint FBI-Marshals Service investigation hadn't yet turned up anything to connect him to Giamo was good news. The fact that they were still looking—and he knew they must be, because Scott would have told him if he'd been cleared—wasn't. Even though he would never do anything to harm Tess or any other witness in his custody, even though he would rather die than misuse his authority for profit, even though his only real crime twenty-six years ago had been that of youth, of ignorance—in spite of all those things, if he could be linked to Giamo, he would become the prime suspect in Tess's attempted murder. Scott would be forced to pull him off this assignment, and to avoid suspicion when they replaced him, they would have to move her again, would have to find a new place for her with new people who didn't know her as well as he did. People who might not have as much invested in keeping her safe as he did.

"Would you mind setting the table?"

Tess's soft voice penetrated his bleak thoughts with a warmth he badly needed. He scooted his chair back with a scrape and went to stand behind her, sliding his hands to her hips and pulling her back snug against him. When he placed a shivery kiss on her neck, she laughed, and her hands stilled.

"What are you doing?" she asked even as she tilted her head to give him better access.

"Forget the table," he murmured in her ear, slowly bringing his hands up beneath her shirt, over her belly, stopping just below her breasts. "I'm cold, Tess. Come make me warm."

She twisted in the circle of his arms to look at him. His words had been true, she thought. His dark eyes looked cold, haunted, hopeless. "Do you want to talk?"

"I want to make love to you."

"Is that going to make whatever's bothering you go away?"

"It would make me feel better."

"It would make *me* feel better if we talked first and loved later."

He dropped his arms and took a step back. "That's because you don't know what we'd be talking about."

"Try me."

With a shake of his head, he turned to the cabinet that held the dishes and began removing what they needed. He'd been stupid to go to her, to call her attention to his mood. How could he look in her eyes and tell her that the investigation into the leak of the safe house location and her own near-murder was likely to reveal *him* as a suspect? Not only would he lose any chance of making love to her again, he would also lose her trust and her respect. Instead of desire and fondness in her big brown eyes, he would see fear—fear of *him*.

He couldn't bear that. He couldn't tell her.

But he owed it to her. If he was a suspect, she deserved to find out from him, not from total strangers when they came to take her away from him.

But he needed a little more time with her, he silently argued. He needed to try again and again to satisfy this need she'd set burning deep inside him. He needed *her*.

Tess watched him carry the dishes to the table, then slowly turned back to her dinner preparations. What had brought that haunted look to his eyes? They had been talking about his father's death and how his mother had handled it, how he had helped keep the family together afterward; then, the next thing she knew, he was coming to her with that look. Was it connected to his father's death—grief after twenty-eight years? Sorrow over the means his mother had used to support her five sons? Sadness that he hadn't been able to help more?

Whatever it was, he would tell her if he wanted her to know. She certainly wasn't in any position to insist on an answer, to demand a look into his soul.

She got out a serving platter and the sharpest knife in the drawer. "If you'll carve the turkey, I'll put the rolls in the oven and make some tea."

Deke took the knife, picked up a fork and lifted the turkey breast onto the platter. "What is Thanksgiving like at the Conrad house?" he asked as he began slicing.

"Probably the same as at the Ramsey house, only quieter. We always spend Christmas with my dad's brothers and sisters and their children and grandchildren, but Thanksgiving is always just Mom and Dad and Mom's parents and me."

"And for eight years, ol' William."

She smiled broadly. "My dad used to call him William. It made him mad."

"Which was probably why your dad did it."

She filled two pans with water and set them on the burners to heat. "Probably. Dad never was very fond of him. In the mornings we always watched the parades on TV, and in the afternoons Dad and Granddad and Will watched football, while Mom and Grandma and I sat at the dining table and talked. It was always very..." She sighed softly and used the same word she'd used a moment earlier, but this time with a negative flavor. "Quiet."

Deke supplied the reason behind the difference. "No kids. I remember the Thanksgivings before my nieces and nephews were born. Holidays just seem more special when you have kids around."

When the water began to boil, Tess added tea bags to the first pan, turned off the heat and set it aside. In the second pan, she stirred in a cupful of sugar, lowered the heat and continued to stir until it was completely dissolved, leaving a clear, thick syrup. She set that aside, too, and put four rolls onto a baking sheet and slid it on the bottom rack in the oven. "You like kids, don't you?"

"Sure."

"Then why aren't you married and raising a few?" Her tone was casual, but that was the only thing about her question that was. If he said he'd never married because of Angela, because he'd never gotten over her, because he'd never stopped loving her, it would absolutely break her heart. But she wanted to know.

"Isn't there a saying, 'lucky in cards, unlucky in love,' or something like that?"

"Something like that."

He grinned at her. "Did I ever tell you I'm a hell of a poker player?"

Which meant he considered himself unlucky in love. So Angela *was* the reason, Tess thought darkly. Damn her!

"I was married once, when I was in college. It lasted two years, and the happiest day of the whole thing was the day we got divorced."

"Bad choice, huh?"

"Very bad." He finished slicing the meat and cut a small piece, offering it to her from his fingers. "The honeymoon was okay, but it went downhill from there. We fought like cats and dogs for eighteen months."

"Then?"

"Then?" he echoed.

"You said you were married two years. What about the other six months?"

The easy banter faded, and he grew more serious. "Then she found someone else, and I quit caring enough to mind. Finally she divorced me and took off with him. And, like you and Will, I haven't seen her since."

No wonder he'd understood so clearly about her own failed marriage, Tess thought. He'd been through it himself. He must have felt some of the same feelings she had—the frustration, the anger, the bitterness, the determination not to let it happen again.

Then he'd met Angela, and that relationship had ended badly, too. It was almost enough to make her feel sorry for him. But she couldn't summon up any sympathy whatsoever regarding Angela. She was too envious of the other woman, still too hurt by hearing his declaration of love for her.

The buzzer on the stove went off, snapping Tess out of her thoughts. She reached for the pot holders, but Deke already had them. "You take care of the tea, and I'll get this."

She removed the tea bags and poured the strong flavored brew into a pitcher, added the syrup, then filled it to the top with cold water. By the time she'd filled two glasses with ice and set them and the pitcher on the table, Deke had all the hot foods there, too.

"So . . . what's the rule?" she asked, picking up the conversation again as she sat down. "Two strikes and you don't try again?"

He gave her a questioning look as he poured the tea.

"A divorce and an unhappy love affair," she explained. "Two strikes. Does that mean you've given up on falling in love and getting married and having children and living to see your grandchildren?"

He handed a glass of tea to her, then sipped his. It was typically Southern—strong and very sweet. "That's an odd question coming from someone who gave up after one strike."

"Yes," she agreed after a moment's silence. "It is. I'm sorry."

"Not everyone falls in love, Tess, and hardly anyone lives happily ever after. Those are fantasies." Fantasies that he was beginning to buy into. He couldn't deny that in the last few days, the prospect of commitment, of permanence, had grown more appealing. There would be pleasure in waking up every morning with the same woman. In having children with her, sharing a home and a future, goals and dreams, with her. No longer being alone but part of another person, half of a couple. Being a husband, father, lover, friend, protector.

As she dished out turkey, dressing, candied sweet potatoes and hot rolls, she wondered if his cynically shaded words were a warning to her. *Don't fall in love with me. Don't dream of a future with me. All we agreed to was an affair—no promises, no assurances, no guarantees.*

"If kids mean so much to you, why didn't you go against ol' William's wishes and have them anyway?" he asked. "I assume that, like most women, you were responsible for the birth control while you were married. Why didn't you 'forget' it and get pregnant anyway?"

Tess's cheeks flushed pink. "I thought about it. It certainly would have speeded up the divorce."

"That's right. Instead of wasting eight years of your life on the bastard, it would only have been six, or maybe even four. So why didn't you?"

"I read somewhere that the most precious gift you can give your child is to love his mother—or, in my case, his father." She paused, a thick piece of turkey suspended in midair from her fork. "By the time children became such an issue with us, I honestly can't say that I still loved Will, and it was quite apparent that he no longer loved me."

But she could love again, Deke thought. She was too warm, too passionate, too giving, to spend the rest of her life alone. She could love a man and give his children that most precious of gifts. If she never did, it would be a great loss. And if she did it with any other man but him, it would be *his* great loss.

Was he falling in love with Tess Marlowe? Instinctively, he shied away from the question. He cared for her. He desired her. He needed her. He found great comfort and greater pleasure in the idea of making love to her six weeks, six months, six years from now—or even longer. He thought of her in terms of permanence, always, forever. But did he love her? When he'd sworn, after Angela, that he wouldn't risk the pain and heartache of loving again, had he been foolish enough not only to fall in love again, but to fall in love with another witness?

Caring, desire, need, permanence, always, forever—they certainly seemed to add up to love, but he couldn't, for his own sake, put that name on what he was feeling. What if he was wrong? What if she never learned to love him? What if, like his ex-wife and Angela, he invested his time and his emotions and, God help him, his *self* in Tess, and it ended as badly, as painfully, as before?

"Why are we talking about such serious topics?" Tess asked, smiling faintly at him. "How about something not so grim?"

Deke slowly, very slowly, smiled back. "All right. Why don't we discuss in explicit, erotic detail exactly what I'm going to do with you after dinner?"

She felt the tingling that he could start with just a look, felt the flames he stirred to life with no more than a word She took a sip of tea to ease the dryness of her throat, but when she spoke, her voice was still husky. "By all means," she invited. "Tell me more."

After dinner they put away the leftover food, rinsed the dishes, then went into the living room. Outside, the skies had darkened, the sun giving way to rain-heavy clouds. Inside, Deke added another log to the fire, and Tess gathered the plump pillows from the sofa and dropped them to the floor, making a comfortable place to lie and watch the fire. By the time she finished turning off the lamps, he was doing just that, and she joined him.

For a long time he simply held her. There was such pleasure in that, she thought, resting her cheek against the nubby weave of his turquoise shirt. Will had never been a particularly physical lover. He'd had little time to waste on soft caresses or comforting embraces, and if they weren't a prelude to sex, she could just forget them.

Sex. The word made her sigh. It sounded mechanical and cold and so unemotional. No woman should ever have to describe the physical relationship she'd shared with her husband as "sex," but that was precisely what it had been with Will in the last years of their marriage: a cold, mechanical and unemotional act. In the beginning it had been different—never as nerve-tingling and toe-curling and exciting as it was with Deke, but at least deserving of the word "intimacy." But those last few years, they'd had sex. Nothing more.

She sighed again. She could lie here the rest of the day and compare Will to Deke, and her ex-husband would come up short in every area: tenderness, generosity, understanding, strength, character, dedication, loyalty, decency, goodness.

But it wasn't really fair to compare them. She felt nothing for Will—truly nothing save a little pity that he would probably never know the kind of peace and happiness and satisfaction she'd found these last few days. What she felt for Deke couldn't be adequately described in words. There were names for each feeling—respect, desire, admiration, passion and a host of others—but no single word, not even love, that truly encompassed them all.

Deke slid his fingers into her hair, wrapping and twisting until the delicate silken strands trapped his hand. "You sound..." Not sad, exactly, but a little blue. "Melancholy. What are you thinking about?"

That I love you more after less than two weeks than I ever loved Will. She smiled secretly at the impulsive answer. That was probably the last thing in the world he wanted to hear from her—even less than he would want to hear, *I've changed my mind and decided not to testify.* She shifted against him, sliding her hand underneath his shirt to rest on the warmth of his stomach, and replied, "Shortcomings."

"Yours, mine or the world's at large?"

"None of the above."

"Uh-huh." She felt his response in gentle vibrations in his chest. "Then it must be ol' William's."

She didn't reply.

"Considering that you've been divorced four years, that you haven't seen him since then and that the last few years of your marriage were unhappy, you seem to think about him a lot." He wove his fingers deeper into her hair. "Do you still love him?"

"No."

"Not even a little?"

"No."

"If he returned, you wouldn't take him back?"

"No."

He smiled faintly. He'd known those answers already— had known that Tess couldn't make love to him the way she did if she still cared for her ex-husband—but he'd wanted to be sure she knew that, too. "Then why is he on your mind?"

"I don't know. I guess because we've been talking about our pasts—about your ex-wife and Angela. Because for a very long time he was a very important part of my life. Because he influenced a great many things about me. He helped make me who and what I am today. And, I guess, because until Tuesday night, he was the only man in my life."

"Only?" Deke echoed. "As in lover?"

"Yes."

"You've never been with any man but him . . . and me?"

"Yes."

"How many thirty-five-year-old women can truthfully claim to have had only two lovers?" he asked wonderingly.

Tess lifted her head, and he quickly released his hold on her hair so it wouldn't tug at her scalp. Her smile was sweet and sheepish and embarrassed. "How many thirty-five-year-old women would *want* to truthfully admit to only two lovers?"

"A lot. Sexual freedom isn't all it's cracked up to be, sweetheart. After too many casual affairs, you begin to lose respect for your partners and for yourself."

"And do you speak from experience?"

He was silent for a moment before he answered. "Not recent."

Was this a casual affair? she wanted to ask. Would he soon lose respect for her, and for himself for sleeping with her? That was the phrase he'd used yesterday: slept with—*It's bad enough that I slept with you, Tess*—while she called it making love. And didn't that simple fact answer her questions?

Everyone deserved at least one wild, passionate fling, she comforted herself, and if this was hers, so be it. And if she never found another man after Deke walked out of her life, at least she would have her memories. At least she would know how wonderful and exciting passion and loving could be.

She raised up, supporting herself on one elbow, and looked at him. His eyes were closed, his breathing smooth and even. That was another part of the Thanksgiving Day ritual, she thought with a smile—falling asleep while your stomach was full and the room was warm and quiet.

But Deke wasn't asleep, as his lazy smile indicated.

With her hand beneath his shirt, she tweaked the hair on his chest. "You owe me something."

"What?"

"All those explicitly erotic things you promised at the dinner table."

He thought of the things he'd told her, of the heat he'd ignited in both of them, and his smile deepened. "Why don't you get me started?"

For a moment she simply looked at him; then a slow smile curved her lips. She'd been welcome to touch him since they'd first made love, and she'd done it, but not as freely or as often or as intimately as she would have liked. Sitting up on her knees, she shook her hair back to its natural smoothness, then slid both hands underneath his shirt and over his chest, taking the fabric with them. She needed help from him, just the awkward lifting of his head and shoulders, to pull the garment off; then she dropped it on the floor, a brilliant splash of color on the worn boards.

His skin was warm and smooth, sprinkled with coarse dark curls and marred only by a jagged scar two inches long on his ribs. "Did you get this as a marshal?"

He shook his head.

"In Vietnam?"

Again he shook his head.

She smiled slowly. "Wrestling with your brothers?" She ran her fingers over it, tracing it from one end to the other, then lowered her head and repeated the action with her mouth.

"That's the right answer. You win the—" He swallowed the words and breathed in sharply when her tongue touched the old wound, tenderly bathing it. "Prize," he groaned.

She raised her hands to his shoulders, kneading the hollows formed by his collarbones, then glided them lower, over solid muscle and the distinctive ridges of his ribs, careful not to touch the flat disks of his nipples. "You're a handsome man, Deacon Ramsey," she said hoarsely, drawing one fingernail across his stomach and watching his muscles tighten and quiver in response.

He closed his eyes and tried to regain control, but it was a lost cause. She'd hardly touched him, and already he was having trouble breathing; already his heart was racing. She hadn't touched him at all, not even a light caress, below his stomach, and already his manhood was swollen and hard. When would he stop wanting her like this, with this wild, reckless hunger that threatened to destroy him? he wondered hazily, then rephrased the question more accurately: would he *ever* stop wanting her like this? Only when he was dead, he suspected.

Leaning forward, she placed a kiss, soft and gentle, on his nipple, and it began changing. Her next kiss was still soft and gentle but openmouthed, moistening the nub of flesh, and it grew hard and the dark circle around it pebbled and tightened. Turning to his other nipple, she suckled it, too, making it hard and taut.

Deke reached for her, catching her upper arms, intending to pull her down and kiss her madly while undressing her, while burying himself inside her. But with remarkable strength for someone so delicate, she captured his hands and held them away. "I'm in charge here," she murmured, lifting his right hand to her mouth. She kissed the palm, then nibbled one blunt-tipped finger and took a bite of the meaty flesh at the base of his thumb. After returning both hands to his sides, she again began to brush sensuous kisses across his chest, leaving a burning trail from one nipple to the other and down to the waistband of his jeans.

She sat back on her heels, silhouetted by the bright fire behind her. She was smiling with sweet anticipation, looking beautiful and sexy and innocent, delicate and strong and aroused. This was why his marriage had failed, Deke thought as he stared at her. This was why he'd let Angela disappear from his life without a trace. For Tess. So that he would be free to love her when he found her.

With finely boned fingers she outlined his hardness through his jeans, her movements causing the fabric to tighten and tug and caress the naked flesh underneath with its roughness. Biting back a moan, he reached for her again, but she moved swiftly, evading his hands. "I bet I can find those handcuffs you threatened me with last week," she warned from her new position between his legs. "I'm not above using them, either."

She moved back, taking a seat on the stone hearth, and began unbuttoning her blouse. Her gaze never wavered from his as she slid each small button from its fastening. When the blouse hung open, alternately revealing and shielding her breasts with each movement, she paused to roll down the cuffs, smoothing each sleeve down her arm. She pulled it off slowly, folded it and laid it on the stone beside her. Next she stood up, unbuttoned her jeans, slid the zipper down and began sliding them off, taking her skinny silver panties with them over her hips, down her thighs, pooling at her ankles, where she stepped out of them, scooped them up and neatly laid them aside, too.

For a moment she stood there, naked but for her socks, the firelight dancing over her body, its golden glow lighting her here, shadowing her there. Deke could do nothing but stare. He couldn't have reached for her if his life depended on it, could only stare and hunger and ache.

She knelt at his side once more and touched him with a heat that burned even through his jeans. She rubbed his thighs, feeling the strong, knotted muscles there; then for a painfully long moment, she simply laid her hand over his arousal, letting her fingers mold to the shape of him, feeling his size and his heat and the faint, tiny tremors that pulsed through him.

This was torture, he thought, his head back, eyes closed, lips parted to help him breathe. Pure, sweet, incredible, intense, worth-dying-for torture. If she continued this much longer, she could make him beg and plead in a way that was totally foreign to him. She could ask for his soul, and he would gladly give it.

She unbuttoned his jeans, one slow button at a time, pushing the fabric aside to reveal his skin. He was naked underneath, she realized when she reached the dark, swirling nest of hair that cradled his hardness, and she remembered that when he'd put his jeans on after their lovemaking this morning he'd ignored the briefs. The discovery made her shiver. Any man in tight, button-fly jeans made an erotic picture, but Deke in tight, button-fly jeans and absolutely nothing else was enough to make her tremble uncontrollably.

Gently she reached inside his open jeans and stroked him, from the blunt tip that was moist with desire to the warm heaviness lower, cradling his weight in her palm, tenderly caressing. "The male body and the changes it goes through with arousal are fascinating," she said, almost too hoarse to speak. "The way you get hard and taut and swollen..." She touched the tip of her tongue to her lips, easing their dryness.

With a heavy groan, he arched against her caress and tried to speak her name, but it faded away with a soft hiss. When she guided his rigid length to the opening of his jeans and bent to taste it, he arched again, this time against her mouth, and swore viciously. His hands were knotted in fists, and beads of sweat were forming on his forehead from the effort required to stop himself from grabbing her and thrusting deep inside her.

After a long, deep, intimate kiss flavored with the very essence of him, Tess sat back and found one of the small plastic packets he'd left on the floor earlier. Her hands trembled so badly that she had trouble opening it, but at last she was able to slide its contents out. When she positioned it at the tip of his manhood, he began hastily, awkwardly, struggling out of his jeans. They finished at the same time, and he reached for her, lifting her into place, sliding her along his length, groaning at the exquisite sensations of her.

It was over almost before it started. With a great shuddering heave, he stiffened beneath her, his body pumping with his sweet, hot release and fueling her own response, making her gasp and tremble and finally collapse helplessly on his chest.

Deke brushed her hair back from her sweat-dampened face, then stroked his big hands down her back and murmured low, soothing words in her ear until the convulsions eased and faded. He kissed her—a deep, gentle mating of their tongues—then held her, still intimately joined with him, while he rolled onto his side. He lifted her leg higher on his hip, supporting it there with his arm, and slid his hand carefully between their bodies to boldly caress between her thighs.

"The male body and its changes may fascinate you, sweetheart," he murmured, their faces so close that she could feel his lips brush her with every word, "but that ain't nothing compared to what happens with yours. As soon as your heart rate returns to normal, as soon as you can breathe deeply instead of those erotic little gasps, as soon as your body quits trembling and the muscles down here—" he gestured with his hand between them "—quit clenching around me, as soon as lethargy takes over and you get all warm and sleepy and comfortable and relaxed...I'm going to do to you what you just did to me. I'm going to show you all the changes in your body when I love you. I'm going to make your breasts tingle and your nipples grow hard and ache to be kissed. I'm going to make the muscles in your belly quiver helplessly every time I caress you. I'm going to make you hot and moist and eager to take me. I'm going to make you want to beg to have me, the way I wanted to beg you. I'm going to torment you until you think you can't stand it another second, and then I'm going to satisfy you. I'm going to make you whimper and shudder and explode...."

As his fingers continued to stroke her sensitive core, he closed the last tiny distance that separated their lips and took the cries of her second completion from her mouth. An instant later with a hoarse cry of his own, he joined her, his release spilling over once again.

Moments later, her body still sheathing his, their mouths close, their breath mingling, they were both asleep.

Chapter 8

Tess was moving cautiously when she got out of bed Friday morning. The soreness between her thighs was minor and eclipsed by the memory of the long, intense lovemaking that had caused it. The stiffness in her joints was more uncomfortable and a reminder that, at thirty-five, she was too old to be making love all through the afternoon and most of the night on a braided rug on a hardwood floor, she thought with a wry smile.

Still lying in bed, Deke detected the change in the way she moved. "Did I hurt you?" he asked swiftly, a frown darkening his eyes.

"No." She smiled ruefully. "But the next time we decide to do that when we have two beds within twenty feet, by all means, let's use the beds."

He watched her pull her gown on, then bend to pick up her robe from the floor. "Come over here and I'll rub you."

She caught the sly gleam in his eyes and backed away. "You have to call your boss this morning, remember? We don't have time."

"For a simple back rub?" he asked innocently.

"The way you make me feel every time you touch me, it wouldn't stop at a simple back rub, and you know it," she admonished him. "Now you'd better get dressed or *you'll* have to explain to some local deputy why we missed checking in."

"I should have told Scott I'd check in every third day between two and four in the afternoon," he said grumpily as he threw the covers back and got up.

Within an hour they were dressed and on their way to town. Tess twisted as far as the seat belt would comfortably allow so she could watch Deke. It was one of her newfound pleasures—simply looking at him. He was so handsome, so dear.

"It's funny, you know," she said softly.

He glanced at her. The scowl that she'd thought was permanently etched into his face in their first days together had been replaced these days by a gentle smile and the deep, intense warmth in his dark eyes. "What is?"

"This should be the worst time of my life. I saw a man murdered, and I'm in hiding to save my own life. I should be terrified . . . but all I can think about is making love to you."

He squeezed her hand, then continued to hold it. "You were celibate for four years. You've got a lot of time to make up for." He said the words lightly but still felt their sting. Was that all he was to her, a means of satisfying four years of pent-up desire? A warm, eager body that fit so well with hers, that gave her the things she'd needed and done without for so long?

No. She cared—she *had* to. She couldn't look at him the way she did, couldn't touch him, couldn't make love to him, the way she did, if she didn't care.

But there was a big difference between caring enough to have an affair and caring enough to spend the rest of her life with him. In almost getting killed, she had found the courage to release the fears and constraints that had kept her from men since her divorce. She'd found the courage to initiate this affair with him. When the trial was over, when the danger was gone from her life, would she want to continue exercising that courage? Would she want to find out what she'd been missing all this time with other men? Would she have any interest in immediately tying herself down again with one man? Would she *care* enough?

A lot of time to make up for. Tess gave him a long, chiding look. "You make it sound like I'm using you. Is that what you believe?"

He took his eyes from the road for a moment to return the look. "No, I don't."

"Good."

He grinned slightly. "Do you want to ask if *I'm* using *you*?"

"No, I don't."

"Why not?"

"Because you haven't taken anything that I haven't given willingly. If you were simply using me to get what any other woman could give you, you would have gone to any other woman. To one unconnected with your job, to one who wouldn't make you feel as if you'd compromised your principles."

He raised her hand and kissed it, then laid it flat on his thigh and returned his own hand to the steering wheel. "You're an intelligent woman, Tess."

"Yes," she agreed with a smug smile, "I am."

The regular trips to town and back had depleted more than half the tank of gasoline, so Deke pulled in at the first station they reached. In case they needed to make a sudden and unexpected departure, he wanted the Bronco gassed up at all times. When that was taken care of, he moved the truck to the pay phones near the driveway and left Tess sitting inside, the engine running and the radio on, while he went to the phone.

"Have a nice holiday?" he asked Scott after the preliminary greetings were taken care of.

"As nice as it could be with the in-laws visiting. How about yours?"

"It was okay." He smiled at the understatement. "Any word on the investigation yet?"

"We're still trudging along. Listen, you know a cop named Drake?"

He searched his memory for the name, then for a face to go with it. "An Atlanta vice cop? Big guy, used to play football?"

"That's the one. He passed along a bit of information to McNally that he thought we might be interested in."

For the next five minutes Deke listened and said nothing. His hand slowly clenched around the receiver, and he shivered as a chill seeped through him, leaving him cold and numb all the way through. When his boss stopped talking and waited for a response, he had to try twice to get the appropriate words out. "I'll talk to her," he said in a flat, emotionless tone. "I'll see—" He broke off, looking at Tess, sitting safely in the truck and singing along to some song he couldn't hear as if she didn't have a care in the world. That would change soon. Everything would change. *Everything*.

The thought brought a pain so sharp he had to look away. He tried to breathe deeply to ease it, but it seemed there were bands around his chest, refusing to let him fill his lungs.

"Deke?" Scott questioned. "Are you there?"

"Yeah, I'm here." To his own ears, his voice sounded strained and harsh, but his boss didn't seem to notice.

"So…talk to her and let us know what she decides, okay? Lay it all out for her. I don't want her claiming later that she didn't understand."

"She'll understand. I'll give you her answer Sunday."

"Couldn't you make it tomorrow?"

"For God's sake, Scott, you don't expect her to make a decision like this overnight, do you?" he exploded. "I'll give her a couple of days to think about it and let you know Sunday." Before his boss could comment on the loss of his temper, Deke said goodbye and hung up.

Tess was still singing, slightly off-key, when he got into the truck, fastened his seat belt and began backing out without even glancing at her. Slowly she reached across to turn the radio down, then hesitantly turned to him. "Bad news?"

He breathed in, then noisily exhaled. "Yeah, bad news."

"Did they catch the guy who sold out? Was it a friend of yours?"

"No. It's got nothing to do with that."

"Is it your family? Has something happened?"

"No."

"Is it *my* family? Did Giamo—"

"Tess," he interrupted sharply, then winced. "I'm sorry. Let's go home."

Home, she silently echoed, settling back in the seat. Not "back to the cabin," as he would have said a week ago, but *home*. With a sigh, she leaned over and turned the volume on the radio up again, but she'd lost her pleasure in the music.

Maybe he would tell her what was wrong when they reached the cabin, but she wouldn't hold her breath waiting. She wished he wouldn't do this—wouldn't get upset about something and refuse to discuss it with her. He'd done it Thanksgiving Day, when they were talking about his family, and now again today. Didn't he trust her enough to confide in her? Or, for him, did their closeness stop the moment they got out of bed or put their clothes on?

No, that wasn't true. He was as gentle with her out of bed as he was in. Everyone had the right to keep a few secrets— even *she* had one left. She hadn't told him yet—and maybe never would—that she loved him.

After three more songs and countless commercials, they reached the cabin. Inside, Tess hung up their jackets while Deke made a quick walk-through, checking the window and door locks. When he returned to the living room, she was sitting on the hearth, her hands pressed together between her thighs, her expression tense and anxious.

She was waiting for him to tell her the bad news, Deke thought, but God help him, he didn't want to. He didn't want to say anything, to do anything but hold her close. But he had to. It was part of the job.

He sat down beside her and started to reach for her hands, then clasped his own together instead. Trying to think of an easy way to say what he had to was futile, so he took a deep breath, cleared his throat and simply said it. "A vice detective with the Atlanta Police Department got word from one of his informants that . . . Giamo has put out a contract on you. Apparently, the first time he used his own boys, and when they didn't get the job done, he turned to professionals."

A bit of the color drained from her face, but she wasn't overly concerned. "By a 'contract,' you mean to have me killed."

He nodded.

"But . . . that's not news. We've known all along that he would try again. That's why you brought me here. So . . ." She shrugged in bewilderment. "What's the bad news?"

"According to the informant, this murder-for-hire *will* be carried out. If—if they don't get to you before the trial, then . . . they'll do it afterward."

"But that doesn't make sense." She smiled, but it wasn't steady, and neither was her voice. "The purpose of killing me is to stop me from testifying, so what good will it do *after* the trial? Giamo will already be in prison. I mean, it's unnecessary."

"It's called vengeance, sweetheart. If they can keep you from testifying, great. But if they can't . . . you'll be punished for it." He reached for her hands then, sandwiching them between his own. They were as cold and clammy as his. "You have two options. The first is to forget about testifying. Giamo would probably still go to trial, and there's a chance he might even go to prison. But to be safe, you would probably have to leave Atlanta, because even if you don't testify, you're still a threat. You saw what he did."

"But Atlanta's my *home*," she said in dismay. "I've lived there all my life. My family is there, my friends, my job." And *he* was there. How could she leave all that behind? How could she pack up and run away like a frightened little rabbit and leave Deke and her parents and her grand-parents?

She freed her hands and stood up to pace the length of the room. At the front, she stopped beside the window and lifted the curtain a few inches so she could see out. It was quiet and peaceful outside, the Bronco the only thing out of place in the wilderness setting. She had been planning to come back here when she was free, to play tourist and see all the sights. Now he was telling her that she should run away and hide for the rest of her life. She should let Anthony Giamo frighten her out of her home, not just for these few weeks, but for the next however many years until he died and it was safe to return.

Slowly she turned, lacing her fingers together in front of her. "And what's the other option?" she asked quietly, calmly.

He couldn't look at her, couldn't meet her gaze and let her see how abhorrent he found this idea. He couldn't let his personal feelings sway her from the right choice. "You could enter the relocation program after the trial."

As his precious Angela had done, she thought. "What exactly does that mean?"

"It means we give you a new identity—a new name, a new home, a new background. We would provide you with all the necessary papers and would handle any problems that might come up. You would be settled someplace far from Atlanta, and you would never be able to go back there. You would have to cut off all contact with your family and your friends and your past. You would never be able to see or talk to your parents again. For all practical purposes, Tess Marlowe would be dead."

She stared at him for a moment, then began laughing softly. "You're joking, right?" Then the amusement faded and was replaced by anger. "You know how I feel about my family! How could you ask me to walk away from them? I'm their only daughter, their only granddaughter! If I left, they would have no one!"

"Tess, I'm not asking—"

"You people are supposed to protect me! You're not supposed to let anything like this happen! You promised me! Damn you, Deke, you *promised* me that nothing would happen!" She ran her fingers through her hair, tugging at the ends. "How is it that no matter what I do, *I'm* the one who gets punished for Anthony Giamo's crime? Why am *I* the one who has to lose everything when I didn't do anything wrong?"

The tears burst free then, streaming down her cheeks, scalding and full of pain. She stood there near the window, her entire body shuddering with the sobs, making no effort to dry the tears, to stem their flow, and Deke sat on the hearthstone, aching to go to her and struggling not to, because he already knew what her choice had to be: she would have to relocate.

It was that clear. Simply refusing to testify and leaving Atlanta wouldn't be enough to guarantee her safety. Maybe Giamo would be satisfied with that choice, but Deke wouldn't allow her to bet her life on it. It was just as likely that the old man would have her tracked down and killed anyway, just for added insurance.

Like Angela, she had no other choice. She had to enter the program. And like Angela, they would move her, would give her a new name and a new history, and some lucky marshal somewhere would know who she was and would be in regular contact with her, but it wouldn't be him. He would never be allowed to know what part of the country she was living in, much less what her new name was. He would never know if she was all right, if she was happy or sad. He would never know if she needed him. He would never know if she found someone to love, if she had children, if she died.

He had lost her, just as he had lost Angela. Even though Tess was standing not ten feet away, he knew that was going to be the eventual result. A few more weeks was all he had. That had been enough with Angela, but God help him, not with Tess.

He lost the battle to protect himself and went to comfort her instead, knowing as he folded her into his arms that every moment he held her now was going to cost him dearly when she was gone. Still, he drew her close and stroked her hair and whispered soft, meaningless words into her ear while her body trembled against his and her tears soaked his shirt.

When her tears were all cried out, dry sobs still shook through her. Deke raised her chin and dried her cheeks with his fingers, gentle around her puffy eyes, then led her to the couch, where he leaned back against the sofa arm and cradled her once more to his chest.

They sat like that for hours, neither speaking. What was there to say? Tess thought miserably.

Just this morning she had talked blithely about the "worst time of her life." She hadn't known then that there were varying degrees of "worst." She hadn't known then that Anthony Giamo could take everything she held dear and leave her with nothing. She hadn't known then that a future with Deke—even if he'd wanted to share one—was out of the question. If she left Atlanta without testifying, she would be leaving him behind, along with her family. If she testified and entered that program, she would still be leaving him behind. If he had refused to relocate with Angela, whom he'd loved, then it was damn certain that he wouldn't even consider going with *her*. After all, he didn't love *her*.

She sighed softly, and Deke ceased stroking along her spine. "Do you want some lunch?"

She shook her head.

"Do you want to talk?"

For a moment her fingers, curled through a belt loop on his jeans, tightened, pulling the fabric tighter and pressing the pistol he hadn't removed earlier into his side. Then they nervelessly relaxed, easing the pressure. "What is there to talk about?"

"Do you have any questions about witness relocation?"

She kept her eyes locked on his rich burgundy-colored T-shirt. If she met his gaze, if she looked into his warm, intense, caring dark eyes, she would dissolve into hysterical tears again at the thought of everything she was going to lose. "I can't do that, Deke."

"You can't talk about it?" He raised his hand to her hair, smooth and straight and silky.

"No. I can't do it."

"You have no other choice, Tess."

She shook her head. "If I refuse to testify, why do I have to leave Atlanta?"

"Because if you stay, you'll be an easy target for Giamo. The government has other evidence linking him to Davis's murder, but without your testimony, the case loses a lot of its strength. As paranoid as the old man is, even if he were tried and acquitted, he might still consider you a threat. He would see killing you as a means of eliminating that threat, and that would go a long way toward protecting him against similar problems in the future."

"What do you mean?"

"Say Giamo's acquitted, and five years from now, someone with knowledge of his activities agrees to offer testimony against him. You think that witness isn't going to be intimidated right out of the courtroom when he hears that the last time people tried to testify against Giamo, all of them ended up dead?"

"So how would my leaving Atlanta change any of that?"

He sighed wearily. "Distance provides security. If you're living in the same city, you're more dangerous to him—and easier to get to. Once you decide not to testify, you lose your protection. It would be as easy as killing Donald Hopkins was. But if you moved away and cut off all ties to the city, he would have to track you down before he could have you killed. He may not be that paranoid or that vengeful.''

She pulled out of his arms and moved to the opposite end of the sofa, leaning, like him, against the arm. He missed her warmth instantly but let her go. That was something he was going to have to do permanently soon.

''But what if he's convicted without my testimony? What if the evidence is enough to convince the jury? Why couldn't I stay then?''

''The U.S. Attorney can't guarantee that there will even be a trial without your testimony. It's unlikely but possible that the charges would be dropped—and that would put you in even more danger.''

''Why?'' It seemed simple enough to her. ''There would be no trial. Giamo would be free, and so would I.''

''You could always change your mind and decide to testify later, and if you did, the U.S. Attorney could refile the charges. Giamo would be right back where he started—facing life in prison.'' He paused grimly. ''Relocating is your only choice, Tess.''

She sat in silence for a long time, staring into the distance, seeing nothing. Yesterday was the first Thanksgiving she'd ever spent away from her parents, and it had been bearable only because she'd spent it with Deke. If she took his advice and relocated, she would face a lifetime of Thanksgivings—and Christmases and Easters and Fourths of July and birthdays and anniversaries—without her parents, without Deke, without anyone she loved.

''My father's parents died when I was little. I don't remember them,'' she said softly. ''But my mother's parents have always been there. They've always been a big part of my life. My grandmother is seventy-seven years old. My grandfather is seventy-eight. If I do what you say, I'll never see them again. I wouldn't even be able to go to their funerals when they died. I wouldn't even *know* when they died.''

He said nothing.

"If I met someone and got married," she continued, still speaking in that soft, empty voice, "my parents could never know their grandchildren. They've waited so many years for grandchildren, and they wouldn't be allowed to know them, to even know they existed. And my children could never know their grandparents. They could never know what wonderful people they are. They could never know my aunts and uncles and cousins. God, they could never even know anything important about me, about their own mother!"

She jumped to her feet and started for her bedroom. At the door, she stopped and looked back at him. "I'm sorry, Deke, but I won't do it. I won't even think about it." With her shoulders rounded by despair, she went into the bedroom and closed the door behind her, shutting him out.

He stared at the door for a long time, then covered his face with both hands, hiding his own despair. Damn Scott Rowan for forcing him to take this case! And damn himself for not being able to keep Tess at arm's length. He'd known from the beginning that she was dangerous, that she was a more serious threat to his heart than he'd ever faced before, but he'd let need blind him to the reality of their situation.

And the reality was, he'd lost her. Oh, she might rebel against the relocation program now, but in the end, common sense, decency and an innate need for security would win out. She would realize that relocation was the only way she could stay alive. She would realize, too, that she couldn't turn her back on the case and walk away. She was too honest, too upright, too decent, to let Anthony Giamo get away with murder, no matter what the cost to her. She would realize that living without her would be difficult for her parents and her elderly grandparents, but nowhere near as difficult as weekly visits to her grave. She would realize that, no matter what the circumstances, being alive was always better than being dead.

Silently he cursed the Fates that had taken her to that vantage point at that particular moment on that deadly night. All because of a toothache, he thought bitterly. A simple thing like a toothache had changed her life irrevocably—and had destroyed his. Getting over Angela was going to look like a piece of cake when he faced the impossible task of getting over Tess.

And that, he realized bleakly, answered yesterday's question. He wasn't falling in love with Tess Marlowe. He'd already fallen.

Hopelessly. Bitterly. Impossibly.

Tess came out of the bedroom as the sun began setting and went straight into the kitchen without glancing at Deke. Her eyes were still puffy from more tears, her head ached, and her stomach was rumbling from hunger.

She took the leftovers from yesterday's dinner out of the refrigerator and put the potatoes and dressing in the oven to heat. After wrapping several thick slices of turkey in foil, she put them in, too, then set the pecan and pumpkin pies and a container of whipped cream on the table. She filled two glasses with tea, drank half of hers to wash down two aspirins, then refilled it. Finally she sat down at the table to wait.

She was moving stiffly, Deke thought as he watched from the doorway. Not this morning's stiffness from too much loving, but the kind that came from rigid control of muscles and nerves and emotions. He knew how she was feeling: that if she relaxed her control, she would shatter into a million jagged pieces.

She looked unapproachable. He wanted nothing more than to gather her into his arms, to assure her that she could let go and he would keep her together, that he would protect her. But one of her anguished cries from this morning kept him in the doorway, several feet distant: *Damn you, Deke, you promised me that nothing would happen!* He had made her promises: I'll keep you alive; I'll keep you safe; I won't let anyone hurt you. And at the time he had believed them. Now they both knew that they were lies, empty lies.

He couldn't keep her safe. He couldn't protect her. He couldn't end this nightmare for her.

And so he kept his distance.

Tess knew he was standing there watching her, knew, too, that he wasn't going to come any closer. So this new turn of events was going to affect not only her future, but also her present. The affair that she'd thought she could count on at least until the trial began was going to end now, crushed under the weight of this new threat against her.

She couldn't blame him. He'd already been involved once with a woman he'd lost to the witness relocation program. She could understand his wanting to end this relationship before it, too, followed the same course. Even though he didn't love her the way he'd loved Angela, he did care for her. She knew that in her soul.

Except that she wasn't going to enter the relocation program. She didn't know what she *would* do, but this afternoon, alone in her bedroom, she reaffirmed that decision. She couldn't do it. She didn't care enough about justice, about right or wrong, about seeing Anthony Giamo pay for his crimes, to give up her family...to give up Deke. She would not do it.

God, there had to be an easier answer! There had to be some way out of this, some way to keep her family and her future and her life intact!

But she didn't know what it was, and judging from his expression, neither did Deke.

I'm sorry, she wanted to cry. Sorry we made love, sorry you cared, sorry you feel so responsible! But she said nothing.

When the oven timer went off, she slowly stood up and walked over to it, shutting it off with a twist. Bending, she checked the food, then carefully withdrew each dish with the pot holders, set it on the table and turned off the oven. Finally she looked at him, gesturing to the empty seat across from her.

After a moment, although he'd never felt less like eating in his life, he sat down. He let her fill his plate and picked up his fork, but each bite was tasteless, and simply chewing was an effort. After a sampling of each dish, he set his fork down and watched her. She seemed to have a healthy appetite tonight in spite of everything else, he thought as she cut her second slice of turkey into bite-sized pieces.

She noticed him watching her and smiled edgily. "They say crises bring out the best in people. They bring out my appetite. You may have noticed that I had no problem eating at the safe house even when I was afraid. When I found out about Will's first affair, I gained ten pounds. When he left me, I gained twenty. Be grateful that you won't be around to see what I look like in two months."

He leaned back and folded his arms over his chest, controlling a surge of anger at the flippancy of her last remark. "Relocating won't be so bad. You've lived in Atlanta all your life. It will give you a chance to see some other places."

"I've seen other places. There's this nifty little concept called a vacation, where you pack your bags and go off to someplace new for a week or two or three, and you have a good time, and you see other places and other things, and then you go home again. They're fun. You ought to try one sometime, Marshal."

It was the first time she'd used his title since they'd made love, and it grated, making his jaw ache from clenching it so tightly. His hands formed into tight fists of fury. "You'll meet new people, have a new job, make new friends," he continued, his voice showing the strain he was trying to hide. "You'll have a chance that thousands of people would jump at—to start a completely new life. You'll have no past, no mistakes, no bad marriage, no failures. You'll be a brand-new person with a clean slate, starting over again. You'll find someone to marry, and you'll have children, and it's true that they won't get to know their grandparents, but you'll still have them, and they'll love you, and you'll love them."

Her tautly controlled composure shattered then, and she hit the tabletop hard enough to rattle the dishes. "I don't want to love anyone!" she cried. "It's not worth losing them!"

"Tess—"

"Tell your boss to forget it! I won't let them move me and make me a brand-new person! I won't give up the people I've loved all my life! I won't let Anthony Giamo do that to me!"

Leaning forward, he caught her hands when she tried to jump up from the table, and he held her forcibly in her seat. "Tess, you don't have a choice! Damn it, it's the only way to make sure you're safe!" Then his voice softened. "It's the only way to keep you alive."

"Why didn't they explain all this to me in the beginning?" she demanded, her voice breaking. "Why didn't they tell me, 'Oh, by the way, Miss Marlowe, we think you should understand that you're risking your life by talking to us. If Anthony Giamo doesn't destroy you, we will'?"

"Because the danger didn't seem to exist in the beginning. People testify at murder trials all the time without serious repercussions. You just had the bad luck to get tied up with someone as cold and brutal and heartless as Giamo."

"Maybe." The look she gave him was damning. "Or maybe they thought if they told me the truth, if they explained all the risks and dangers, I wouldn't testify. Maybe they thought my dying was worth convicting Giamo." She dropped her gaze to their hands. His fingers were gripping her wrists tightly, tighter than was necessary to restrain her. What was he feeling? she wondered. Surely this had to bring back painful memories of Angela. "Do you ever regret not going with her?"

He stared at her bowed head. The question was unexpected, and it took him a moment to realize who she meant. "No," he answered honestly. If he had disappeared with Angela, he never would have met Tess. Maybe, if he'd gone, he would have been happy for a while, at least, but he knew now that his life would never have been complete without Tess.

"How could she leave her family like that?"

"All she had was a sister and a grandfather."

"How many doesn't matter." She looked up at him then. "It couldn't be any harder to leave a family of ten than it is leaving a family of only two. How did she do it?"

"I don't know."

"When you met her, did you know what was going to happen?"

"Yes."

"How could you fall in love with someone you knew you would lose?"

"Tell me how to stop from falling in love," he said grimly. "I could put the information to good use." Twice he'd fallen in love, and both times he'd lost. But it wouldn't happen again. After Tess, he would never love anyone again.

They sat in silence for a long time; then Tess sighed. "You can let go of me now."

Hesitantly he did so.

She picked up her fork and finished eating, then cut a large slice of pumpkin pie and buried it on her saucer beneath whipped cream. When she'd eaten half of it, she licked a bit of cream from the fork, then shifted her gaze to Deke. "I said something this morning that I shouldn't have."

Damn you, Deke, you promised me . . . He avoided her eyes, not wanting her to see that the remark had hurt—not because she'd blamed him, but because he had let her down.

"I know none of this was your fault. I know there's absolutely nothing you could have done to make it turn out differently. All you can do is wait for Giamo to act, then try to protect me from him, and that's what you're trying to do, even now."

"I made promises I couldn't keep," he said, his fierce scowl back for the first time in days.

"No, you didn't. You said you would protect me, and you have. You said you wouldn't let anything happen to me, and you haven't. This is beyond your control, Deke. You could no more stop Giamo than I could."

"I'm sorry."

She smiled sadly. "So am I." More than he would ever know.

That night Tess went to bed alone. She had wanted to ask Deke to lie with her, to simply hold her, but he'd shown no desire to do either of those things all evening. He'd sat in the armchair, lost in a world of his own, one as bleak and grim as hers had become, if his expression was anything to judge by. When she told him she was going to bed, he'd barely nodded, and he hadn't offered to go along.

Now it was 2:00 a.m. She had dozed a bit, dreamed and awakened in tears, then repeated the cycle. Now she lay awake in the darkness, staring at nothing, searching for a way out of the nightmare her life had become. But she couldn't find one. She had two choices, Deke had told her, and both were bad. Both were unacceptable.

There had to be a third choice. Dear God, there had to be! But if the Marshals Service couldn't think of one, how could she?

She needed Deke—not only in her future, but now. She needed to feel his arms around her, needed the familiar strength of his body next to hers, needed his heat to chase away the chill inside her. She needed . . .

The bedroom door creaked when it opened, and he stood there, as if in answer to her silent plea. He came to the bed, laid his pistol on the nightstand and tugged off the sweatpants that were all he wore. Tess scooted back and lifted the covers so he could slide underneath with her. He took a moment to remove her nightgown, then settled into bed, holding her close.

His caresses were soothing, not sexual, in nature. So were his kisses. But the arousal that branded her thigh was definitely sexual. "Deke?" she whispered.

He quieted her with the brush of his lips over hers.

He continued caressing her, but didn't touch her breasts, didn't stroke between her thighs, where she needed him to touch her most. Maybe he didn't want her anymore, she thought sadly, but then she reached low and closed her hand around his manhood, gently judging his size and heat, and she knew that wasn't true.

He pulled her hand away, then nuzzled her hair from her ear. "You don't need that," he murmured. "Not tonight."

"I do," she weakly protested. "I need you. I need you to hold me."

"I'll do that all night."

"I want you inside me."

"Oh, Tess..." He felt her hand take him again, and he groaned. He'd come to comfort her, to comfort himself, not to make love to her, not to torment himself with the achingly sweet experience that soon he would never have again.

She pressed a kiss to his chest, moistening his skin with her tongue, gliding across to his nipple.

"I made you sore last night," he said, his resolve fading under her determined assault.

Groping under the covers for his hand, she guided it between her thighs. "Do I feel sore?"

The velvety soft feel of her, hot and moist and swollen around his fingers, shattered his control. He had already lost her, but for two more weeks she was here, and she was his. For two more weeks he would love her in every way, every day, saving up memories for when she would no longer be there.

He fastened his mouth over hers, his tongue thrusting to meet hers, while one hand tormented her breasts and the other made long, frantic strokes from deep inside her out to the sensitive bud above. The flames fanned to life quickly, licking over their bodies, burning from inside out, searing with need. He shifted into position over her and, with one long, complete movement, entered her fully and without protection.

Tess realized it and wondered if he had, praying he hadn't. Just once let him be careless and too aroused to remember, she prayed silently. Whatever happened in the future would be easier to bear if she had a child—Deke's child—to love. Even if she had to raise him alone, she could give him the most precious gift: she loved his father. Dear God, how she loved him!

He knew what he'd done and was counting on his self-control to do no harm. Making love to her was always intensely satisfying, but there was an added potency to feeling her glove him without that thin barrier. The simple idea of being unprotected inside her, of the faint possibility that he could empty his seed into her, made him shudder almost beyond control.

When the tremors of impending fulfillment began rocking through him, he gritted his teeth on his body's protest and withdrew from her heat, reaching in the dark for the nightstand. Tess touched him as he tore open the packet, pleading in an aching whisper, "Not this time," but he completed the task.

"I have to," he murmured regretfully as he turned to her. He would like nothing better than to see her grow big and round with his baby, but he couldn't. By the time she found out she was pregnant, she would be living her new life, and he wouldn't be there to watch her belly grow larger, to see his child born, to help him grow up. The only thing worse than losing Tess would be losing her and their baby.

Release came, shuddering through him and arcing into her. She moaned, clinging to him, panting, shivering, and she cried. Tears of love, of sorrow, of completion and of loss.

The loss of her identity. The loss of her life. The loss of her love. And the loss of her last chance to have a child.

* * *

The next morning Deke found her in the kitchen fixing breakfast when he woke up. She was wearing black sweatpants and a long, ribbed sweater in bright, vibrant fuchsia. Her socks were fuchsia, too, and the leather tennis shoes by the dining table were black. The color was a vivid contrast to the paleness of her face.

"Don't you think that outfit's a little subdued?" he asked dryly.

She was standing in front of the stove, turning strips of bacon in the skillet with a fork. When she finished, she pushed up a sleeve of her sweater, then looked down at the garment. It was one of those colors so bright that looking at it almost made her wince. Other than an apple-red Georgia Bulldogs T-shirt, it was the only piece of clothing she owned that wasn't a soft hazy pastel or a safe classic navy blue, gray or brown. "What would you know about subdued? I've seen all those shirts you brought. Lemon yellow, bloodred, royal blue—" she gestured with the fork at the shirt he was wearing "—emerald green. You're certainly not going to fade into the woodwork in any of those."

He moved to stand behind her, his hands on her shoulders. "How are you feeling?"

She let him rub her neck while she considered possible answers. Relieved that he had come to her last night. Satisfied that he still wanted her. Disappointed that he'd refused to increase her slight chances of getting pregnant. And terrified as hell about their future—*her* future, she amended. "I'm okay."

She didn't look it, he thought, but he saw no sense in pointing that out. If the truth were told, he probably looked pretty bad this morning, too. And he felt every bit of it.

"How about a massage?" He turned her in his arms and moved his hands with smooth, firm pressure over the delicate bones of her face, easing the tension in her forehead, her jaw, her shoulders. When he slid his hands beneath her hair to her neck, her head fell forward, her forehead resting on his chest. His cheek found its own resting place in the sweet silkiness of her hair.

His fingers worked their magic, chasing stiffness from taut muscles, replacing it with sweet, lazy, welcome peace. She stood limply, her hips braced against the counter, her head against his chest, her hands spread flat across his stomach, seeking added support. He urged her closer as his hands began to make slow circles down her spine. Her body was soft and warm, small and delicate, so perfectly designed, in spite of the difference in their sizes, to accept his.

"I think the bacon's burning," he murmured in her ear.

Eyes closed, she shook her head. "I think that's me."

With a soft laugh, he kissed the top of her head, then turned her to one side so he could remove the bacon strips from the skillet. She gave a relaxed sigh, then moved out of his arms and turned her attention to cooking again.

Instead of the small kitchen table, they took their breakfast into the living room, where Deke had built a fire. "It seems awfully cold for November," Tess remarked with a shiver, choosing a seat on the braided rug near the fire's heat.

"You're in the mountains. Winter is a little fiercer up here than in Atlanta."

"I wish it would snow—really snow."

"It will, but not this early."

"I wish we would have a blizzard and get snowed in until next spring."

He smiled faintly. "And come out to find that life has gone on, that the trial has taken place without us, that Giamo's in prison and you're safe and sound forever and ever."

She simply nodded.

"You'll be all right, Tess," he said quietly. "You'll survive."

This time she knew he wasn't talking about the ordeal of protective custody or the trial. He was talking about relocating, about starting over, about living her life surrounded by strangers, a stranger even to herself. She didn't tell him that it wasn't going to happen, because he would argue with her, and she didn't want to spoil the day with arguments. She simply nodded again and agreed that yes, she would survive.

The day passed slowly. Tess sat on the sofa, her sweater and socks brilliant splashes of color against the subdued cushions, and pretended to read. Deke alternately sprawled in the armchair or paced the room or stood at the front window, one shoulder against the wall, and stared outside. He didn't pretend to do anything but brood.

He had thought she would want to talk more about her options, would want his advice, but she hadn't said a word on the subject since breakfast. He had to admit that he was hurt that she didn't trust his judgment on this. Maybe relocation wasn't the solution she wanted, but didn't she know that if there was a viable alternative, he would have found it for her? Didn't she know that the last thing he wanted in this world—except for seeing her hurt—was to let her go?

When bedtime came, he greeted it with relief. There would be no wasted hours tonight in the loneliness of his own room, longing to go to her but holding back. There would be no futile argument over whether she needed him simply for comfort or for loving. He followed her into her room, undressed, removed her clothes and made love to her through half the night with a fierce, almost desperate urgency.

And when they were sated, their passion spent, he held her, still fierce, still desperate, through the rest of the night.

Chapter 9

When they reached the pay phone at 10:15 Sunday morning, Tess stopped Deke before he could leave the truck. "I want to talk to your boss," she said, moistening her lips nervously.

"Why?"

"Please? Just for a minute?"

What could she possibly have to tell Scott? he wondered. The details of their affair? That would serve no purpose. Besides, she'd promised not to. Was there some question about relocating that she'd found difficult, under the circumstances, to ask *him*? "You shouldn't be out like that, even for a minute."

"It can't be any more dangerous than going to the grocery store or the drugstore with you. Please, Deke."

He relented, because he knew she was right. "All right. But stay here until I get him on the phone." Pocketing the keys, he got out and circled the truck to the phone, dropping in some coins, dialing the number from memory. Scott

answered on the third ring. "It's me," Deke said unneces-
sarily.

"Is everything okay?"

"Okay? I had to tell someone who thinks the sun rises and
sets on her family that she's never going to see them again,"
Deke said bitterly. "Yeah, sure, everything's fine."

"She agreed to relocate."

"She hasn't agreed to anything. She wants to talk to
you."

"About what?"

"I don't know. Want me to put her on?"

At his boss's affirmative answer, he gestured to Tess to
join him. She did, pulling her jacket tighter against the cold,
and hesitantly took the receiver from him. "Mr. Rowan?"

"How are you, Miss Marlowe?"

He was coolly polite, with just the right degree of distance in his voice, like Thad McNally. "I'm fine," she replied. "But the chances of staying that way seem to be
getting worse every day."

"We'll do our best to take care of you. Did Deke explain
the situation to you?"

"Yes, he did."

"And you understand?"

"Yes."

"Then you've decided to enter the relocation program."

She smiled faintly at his assumption, as if that were the
only choice an intelligent person could make. "No, Mr.
Rowan, I haven't." Clutching the receiver, she turned to face
Deke as she spoke, her gaze steadily meeting his. "We only
discussed two choices. Not testifying and leaving Atlanta,
or testifying and entering your program and leaving Atlanta.
I don't like either one."

"Well, I'm sorry, Miss Marlowe, but sometimes—"

"So I've chosen the third option," she interrupted.

"Third option?" Deke mouthed at the same time his boss
repeated it on the phone.

"Yes. I've decided to go through with my plans to testify against Anthony Giamo. . . but I'm not leaving town afterward. I'm not changing identities or giving up my home or running away to hide."

"Do you understand what you're saying?"

She smiled faintly at the doubt in his voice. It was much milder than the fury darkening Deke's eyes. "Yes, I do. It took me a long time to reach this decision, but I think—"

Deke snatched the phone away from her in midsentence. "We've got to go, Scott. Someone's waiting here to use the phone," he lied. "I'll call you back when they're gone." After slamming the receiver down, he dragged her to the Bronco and lifted her roughly inside, then closed the door so hard that the truck rocked back and forth. A moment later he was seated on the other side, twisted in the seat to face her. "What the hell do you think you're doing?"

"I'm making the only decision I can live with," she said calmly.

"*Live* with?" His echo was harsh. "Lady, you're choosing the one sure way to be dead before your next birthday! You can't do that!"

"The decision is mine, Deke, and I'm the one who has to live with the consequences. I'm the one who loses."

"Yeah, you're going to lose your damn life!" Shaking his head, he swore savagely. "Is that what you want? Do you have some death wish I don't know about?"

She touched his hand, but he jerked it away. Undaunted, she laid her hand on his thigh. "You know how sometimes you have to make a decision, and you don't know what to do, and you get this awful feeling inside, like being sick to your stomach? And if you make the right decision, it goes away, and if you don't, it gets worse until you do whatever is necessary to change it?"

He scowled fiercely at her. Although he would never admit it, he knew precisely what she was talking about. He'd felt it himself only a few days ago when trying to deny what was between them.

"Well, that's the way I've felt ever since you told me about this murder-for-hire thing Friday. No matter which of your options I considered, the feeling never got better... until I realized last night, while you were asleep, that there was one other choice. I could stand up to Anthony Giamo. I could do the right thing, and not run away or change my name or anything like that. I could do what I have to do, in the only way that I can accept. I understand that it means taking a big risk. I understand that it means living with the danger, but... it made the sick feeling in my stomach go away."

"You're a fool, Tess," he ground out. *"They will kill you."*

"I know they'll try. And maybe this time they'll succeed." She turned her head away for a moment, hoping to hide and control the tears that were filling her eyes. "But do you remember what you told me about relocating?" She waited, but he made no effort to respond. "'For all practical purposes, Tess Marlowe would be dead.'"

"But I didn't mean—"

"I know what you meant. Tess Marlowe would cease to exist, and Jane Doe would spring into life at the age of thirty-five with no background, no parents, no history. But I know the other meaning is true, too. Living without my parents and grandparents, without the rest of my family and my friends—" and without you, she added silently "—that would be worse than being dead. That would be like living without a heart, without a soul. It would mean living without hope."

"You'll make new friends," he began, biting off the words savagely, but she stopped him with a shake of her head.

"But I can't make a new family. Deke, I couldn't live that way. It isn't simply a matter of not wanting to disappear. I *couldn't* do it. You could give me a dozen new identities and a dozen new homes and a thousand new friends, but I would still worry about my family. I would still contact them. I would still see them. I cannot cut them out of my life completely. All your work would be wasted.''

"Damn it, Tess—"

Leaning forward, she placed her fingers over his lips. "I would still worry about you, too. I couldn't cut you out of my life, either, unless . . ." She looked down, then up again. This time he saw that her eyes were bright with tears. "Unless that was what you wanted."

Yes, it was what he wanted, if it would keep her safe, if it would keep her alive. He would give up everything—his love, his happiness, his future, even his life—if it meant Tess would be safe.

He grasped her hand and pressed a kiss to her palm, then twined his fingers through hers. He stared at them for a long time, then raised intense dark eyes to hers. "I'll go with you."

It was Tess's turn to stare. His words echoed in her head, quietly spoken, with no hint of anger, no argument, no deceit. Just a plain, simple offer that filled her with warmth and wonder and love. "You would . . ." She cleared her throat. "You would relocate with me?"

He nodded.

"You would give up your family and your friends and your career and your home to move with me?"

He nodded once more.

She settled against the door behind her and considered it. He'd loved Angela, he had told her, but not enough to relocate with her. Yet he had just offered to go with *her*. Did that mean he loved her, more even than Angela?

Or did it simply mean he was that concerned about this threat against her? Did it mean he was willing to sacrifice himself to see that she was safe? Did it mean he was *that* dedicated, *that* principled, *that* duty-bound?

It didn't matter. She loved him more than ever for offering, but it didn't change her mind. She wasn't going to hide for the rest of her life. She wasn't going to let Giamo defeat her.

She leaned forward once more and wrapped her arms tightly around him. "Thank you," she murmured, brushing a kiss over his cheek. "But no thanks."

Deke stared at her. "What the hell do you mean, no thanks?" Didn't she know what that decision had cost him? He was as close to his family as she was to hers. He liked Atlanta as much as she did, valued the good friends he'd made there, loved his job. He was willing to give all that up for her, to go with her and take care of her and keep her safe and love her, and she said thanks, but no thanks?

"It would be so much easier with you there," she explained patiently, "but harder, too. Because I would still miss my family. I would still tell them my new name and where I was living. I would still be a part of their lives, and if you were with me, that would endanger *your* life. I couldn't do that."

"And you can't send Giamo to prison, then sit back and wait for them to kill you, either," he said harshly. "Tess, don't be a fool. Standing up for a principle is fine. Dying for one isn't."

But he wasn't reaching her. He could see it in the stubborn set of her jaw. She'd made up her mind, and nothing was going to change it. Or so she thought, he corrected with a scowl. He still had nearly two weeks until the trial began to make her see reason. Nearly two weeks to make her accept the fact that she was going to relocate, whether she liked it or not.

In a surge of restless energy, he left the truck and called Scott again.

"Let me talk to Tess again," his boss said without greeting.

Deke signaled to her, and she got out and came to the phone. "Yes?"

"Miss Marlowe, surely you understand the—the—"

"Stupidity?" she offered helpfully.

"The folly of what you're suggesting. According to this informant—who happens to be very reliable—this contract

Giamo has taken out on you is good at any time, before, during or after the trial. If you refuse to join our program, we cannot offer you protection once the trial is over. You'll be a sitting duck.''

"Better than a scared rabbit," she said dryly. Switching the phone to her other hand, she reached out to hook her fingers in the front belt loop of Deke's jeans. "I understand all that, Mr. Rowan. Deke has explained the choices and the risks and dangers, but it's my decision. You can't force me to assume a new identity. You can't force me to leave Atlanta. Look, this whole situation has turned my life upside down. When it's over, I want to live as normal a life as I can. That doesn't mean pretending to be someone else."

His sigh was weary and strained. "Very well. I'll tell the prosecutor what you've decided. He'll probably think . . ."

When he let the thought trail off, Tess finished it. "He'll think I'm as crazy and foolish as you and Deke do. But at least I'll be crazy and foolish in familiar surroundings, with familiar people."

"Would you please put Deke on the phone again?"

She offered the receiver to him, then slid her arms around his waist. He held her there. "Yeah?"

"What do you think?"

"She's stubborn, hardheaded and a damn fool."

Scott made a sound of agreement. "Will she change her mind about the program?"

"Yes."

"What makes you so sure?"

Because he was going to force her to. Because he wasn't going to stand by and let her make a decision that would undoubtedly cost her life. Because he'd waited his entire life to find her, and he damn sure wasn't going to lose her now. "Just trust me."

"All right." Scott's chuckle was short and bitter. "Frank Harris is really going to love this. It makes the government look bad when one of their witnesses is executed after the trial."

"That's not going to happen this time. I'll talk to you Tuesday." He hung up and held Tess a moment longer before hustling her to the truck.

"Stubborn, hardheaded and a damn fool," she said with a faint smile. "You have such a way with words, Marshal."

He glared at her. "I'm not in the mood for teasing, Tess."

Her smile grew warmer, sexier. "What *are* you in the mood for?"

"We're going to have a serious talk when we get home."

"We've been having serious talks for days now."

"Damn it!" Shaking his head, he clenched his jaw and started the engine, then backed out.

"It's hard for you to understand, isn't it?" she asked softly, sympathetically.

"Why you would deliberately risk your life when protection is available?" he asked coldly. "Damn right I can't understand why anyone would be that stupid."

"Why did you refuse to go with Angela?"

"That's got nothing to do with this."

"It has a lot to do with this," she argued. "Why did you refuse? You *loved* her, yet you let her disappear from your life. Why?"

"I wasn't prepared to make that kind of sacrifice."

"What kind?"

"My family, my identity, my job." Then he glanced at her. "But my life wasn't in danger, Tess. Angela's ex-husband wasn't interested in me. He didn't even know I existed."

She sighed softly, rubbing her fingertips over her temples. "Then let's simply agree to disagree, all right? I don't want to fight with you, Deke. I don't want to try to make you see this from my point of view, and I don't want you trying to frighten me into accepting your point of view."

"Frighten?" he repeated sarcastically. "Sweetheart, you don't know the meaning of the word 'frighten' yet. That'll come after the trial, when you're on your own and you leave your house or your office some night and some bastard blows you away."

"Maybe that won't happen," she said stubbornly.

"It *will*. Giamo wants to make an example of you. He wants you dead."

"Maybe he'll change his mind. Maybe he'll decide it isn't worth the risk of facing another murder charge."

"I've known Anthony Giamo a long time, and I've never known him to change his mind," he drawled sardonically. Then the anger returned to his voice. "Damn it, Tess, you say you love your family too much to cut them out of your life. Just consider this. When they kill you, it's your family who's going to have to identify your body. Maybe they'll use a .22 like they did with Donald Hopkins. That's fatal, but nice and neat. Or maybe they'll pump a dozen rounds from an AK-47 into you. Also fatal, leaves a lot of holes, but still not too messy. Or maybe they'll use a shotgun. As small as you are, that'll cut you right in half. But no matter how they do it, it's not going to be a pretty sight for your father or your mother to see."

She folded her arms over her chest and stared stonily ahead. "Then maybe I'll tell my parents that if anything happens to me, they should get in touch with you and let *you* identify my body. After all, you know it better than they do. Then you can have the satisfaction of saying, 'I told you so,' even if I am too dead to hear."

Deke felt the force of her words as sharply and painfully as a blow. His hands tightened around the steering wheel until his knuckles were white, and the color drained from his face. He took the turn off the highway to the resort much too fast, sending the Bronco skidding across the narrow road, then swerved back to the right side and onto the grassy shoulder, where he brought the truck to a sudden stop.

For a long time he didn't look at her. He was breathing deeply, ragged shuddering breaths, and his hands were trembling. Hell, his whole body was trembling. He was furious with her, so furious he couldn't speak, but underlying that was a pain, a deep, relentless pain that she could think, even in anger, that he was capable of finding satisfaction in her death because it proved him right.

Finally he spoke in a whisper so cold, so empty, that it made her shiver. "Damn you, Tess. Damn you to hell."

She reached for him, but he flinched, as if even the thought of her touch sickened him. Unhappily, she let her hand fall back to her lap.

After a moment, he checked over his shoulder, then pulled onto the road again. A few minutes more and they were at the cabin. Inside, she tried once more to approach him, and once again he rejected her. "Leave me alone, Tess," he said wearily. "Just leave me alone."

He let his anger simmer for the rest of the day, rebuffing her strained apologies, ignoring her later attempts at conversation, refusing to eat the lunch she'd fixed, eating dinner only because his hunger demanded it, but without looking at her or speaking to her or acknowledging her presence at the small table in any way.

When he did accidentally glance into her face as she was rising from the table, what he saw there stunned him. Her mouth was a narrow downturned line, her expression one of sorrow, and her eyes... God, her beautiful, soft brown eyes were haunted and bleak, as if the joy and laughter and smiles were gone forever.

His throat closed over the lump there, and his chest constricted. He hadn't meant to punish her for her angry remark, only to nurse his own pain, but that had been the result just the same. Silently calling himself every vile name he could think of, he stood up, too. "Tess."

She stopped halfway between the table and the door, and waited, staring sightlessly.

Hesitantly he approached her, reaching out to stroke her hair from her cheek but stopping short of actually touching her. "I'm sorry."

"No..."

"Yes. Our time together is too important to waste on petty insults and hurt feelings. I knew you didn't mean what you said in the truck. It just—God, it hurt that you could say it, even if you didn't mean it. If anything happened to you..." This time he did touch her, his fingers brushing feather lightly over her cheek; then he finished in a husky, choked voice, "I don't think I could stand it."

She laid her hand over his, pressing it to her face. "I know you could never take satisfaction in anyone's death. I was just..." She shrugged helplessly, unable to finish.

"You were reacting to a very emotional, very traumatic event. It's all right, sweetheart." He brushed his lips over her hair, then gave her a slight push toward the living room. "Go sit down. I'll be in as soon as I do the dishes."

"Let them wait and come sit with me." She heard the all-too-apparent plea in her voice but wasn't embarrassed by it. "I'll help you with them in the morning."

He slid his arm around her shoulder and walked to the living room with her. They wound up lying on the sofa, Deke in back, his arms wrapped around Tess's slight body to hold her close, watching the fire. All the lights were out except in the kitchen, giving a warm, peaceful, golden glow to the room.

"Deke?"

"What?" His breath made her hair flutter and tickle his jaw.

"I need to do laundry."

He was still for a moment; then he laughed.

"You find that funny?"

"I was expecting some serious pronouncement, and you're worrying about laundry."

"Considering that I have less than two days' worth of clean clothes left, I think that's serious enough. You don't want to see me running around here naked."

He swept his hand over her body, from her breast to her stomach to her hip. "On the contrary, I like seeing you naked. You're beautiful."

"Do you really think so?" she asked shyly, turning her head just enough to catch a glimpse of him.

"Haven't people told you that before?"

"My parents, but they're obligated to think so."

"What about ol' William? I know the guy was a bastard, but surely he told you how beautiful you were at least once."

She sighed and snuggled closer to him. "Will was taken with a lot of things about me—the fact that I was smart enough to help him study in college, that I was foolish enough to totally adore him when we were first married, that I was old-fashioned enough to want to be his wife first and a person second, that I was tolerant enough to look the other way when I found out about his affairs . . . but he was never impressed with the way I looked."

He turned her onto her back, still supporting her with one arm, and drew just one fingertip over her face. "Your ex-husband was not only a bastard, but a stupid one at that. You deserve better."

"Yes," she softly agreed; then her eyes fluttered shut as he traced his finger across her brows.

For a long time he continued the gentle caresses—along her jaw, over and down her nose, back and forth across her lips. Her eyes remained closed, and her breathing grew slow and deep. He thought she was falling asleep when, in a soft, hesitant voice, she spoke. "Can I ask you one question?"

"You can ask me a thousand questions."

Slowly she opened her eyes to look at him. "On the way home today . . ." She paused, hesitant to refer to the things they'd said to each other on that short drive. "You said that you'd known Anthony Giamo a long time."

He thought back to the conversation and knew that she was right. He'd been so angry at the time that he hadn't even realized he'd said it. "Yeah."

"Did you arrest him or something?"

"No."

"Then how do you know him?"

When he didn't answer for a long time, she looked up at him. He was staring at the fire, his expression grim and more than a little regretful.

"Never mind," she said quickly, turning onto her side to face him. "It doesn't matter."

"It does." He gently lifted her away and sat up, then moved to the other end of the sofa, stretching his legs out. Tess sat up, too, and faced him, her legs tangled with his. "I thought about telling you this Thursday when we were talking about my family—hell, you should have known even before then. Before you left Atlanta with me. But...I didn't know how you would react to it. I knew you had a right to know, but I couldn't take the chance that you would turn away from me, that you would stop trusting me."

She thought back to Thanksgiving Day and immediately remembered the haunted, hopeless look in his eyes and the sound of his voice when he'd come to hold her. *I'm cold, Tess. Come make me warm.* "Nothing you could do would ever make me stop trusting you."

"Wait until I finish, then tell me that." He tilted his head back and studied the beams that crisscrossed the ceiling. "I was fourteen when my father died. He worked in construction, and there was an accident on the site. He was killed, and several other men were injured. The company owed my mother some money—his final paycheck, payment for some vacation time he'd saved, some other benefits—and they refused to pay her. Any fool could see how distraught she was. Just getting out of bed in the morning took all her energy. They figured she wouldn't find the strength to fight them for the money, and they were right. But they didn't count on me."

Silently she studied him, watching the emotions cross his face—sadness, anger, bitterness, regret—and she wished she hadn't brought up the subject. Knowing how he'd met Anthony Giamo wasn't worth making him relive an unpleasant past.

"Without my mother's knowledge, I went to see Dad's boss. Remember, I was only fourteen." He shook his head ruefully. "I was a cocky son of a bitch. I told him I wanted every penny he owed my father and I wanted it *now*. The guy laughed and threw me out of his office. So I went to see *his* boss. I lied my way in to see him. I told him about my father's death, how Mom was taking it so hard, how it would be nearly impossible for her to raise five boys by herself and how she needed every bit of help she could get. I wasn't asking for anything that wasn't rightfully ours, I told him, and if we didn't get it, we would have to 'take steps.' I was bluffing, of course. I had no idea what steps we *could* take if he threw me out. All I knew was that what they were doing was wrong. They were stealing money my dad had earned and taking advantage of a widow's grief."

"That man—you father's boss's boss—that was Giamo." She didn't need to see his slight nod of confirmation.

"He was amused by the idea of being threatened by a kid. Fortunately for me, he was also impressed. I found out later—much later—that men who threatened him usually disappeared or wound up dead. Anyway, he said he would look into it, and he did. The next day one of his people delivered a check to my mother. It was everything the company owed Dad and then some. Not long after that, about the time the money ran out, he sent one of his men to pick me up, and he offered me a job. It was perfectly legitimate—doing yard work, running errands, that sort of thing. I worked for him part-time for almost two years.

"When I turned sixteen and got my driver's license, he changed my job, gave me a raise and more responsibility. Instead of cutting the grass or cleaning the pool, I made deliveries." He glanced at her to see if she understood what he meant by that innocuous term. From the lack of change in her expression, he saw that she didn't. She was as naive now as he'd been twenty-six years ago. "I collected packages from Giamo's various businesses and delivered them to various others, and I picked up envelopes from shop owners, businessmen and politicians, and delivered them to Giamo.''

Slowly, understanding dawned in her soft eyes. ''You were sort of a . . . what's the word?''

''Bagman,'' he said dryly. ''Numbers runner. Either one fits. Remember, Giamo has always controlled the gambling around Atlanta. As for the envelopes, I found out one day they usually contained large amounts of cash—payoffs, protection, kickbacks.''

''You were only sixteen!'' she protested. ''What kind of man uses a sixteen-year-old boy for such a job?''

''A smart one. A kid's more easily intimidated than a man, less likely to try to rip him off, and if he got caught, back then the courts were a lot more lenient.'' He rested his arm on the back of the sofa. So far, Tess's only reaction had been dismay. That was because she hadn't yet realized the implications of what he was telling her. She wasn't devious enough, didn't have the criminal bent that would lead her to such a realization without help—help that he would have to provide her.

''You didn't know what you were doing, did you?''

He shook his head. ''Looking back, I can't believe how naive I was. I'd heard rumors even then about Giamo and the kind of man he was, but I didn't believe them. He was always genuinely nice to me, and he helped us when we needed it badly. At fourteen I couldn't have gotten a regular job, not a steady one, and without the money he paid me, we couldn't have gotten by.''

Tess laid her hand over his on the sofa back. ''So what happened?''

''I only did the new job for a couple of weeks. When I finally figured out what was going on, I confronted the old man, and he confirmed my suspicions. That amused him, too, that I could be so stupid and that it mattered so much. I quit my job that day, and I never saw him again. And I never told anyone about it, besides Scott and now you.''

"You didn't really do anything wrong, Deke. You were hardly more than a child," she said comfortingly. "You can't blame yourself for that."

"You're missing the point, Tess."

She looked blankly at him.

"Right now about half the manpower of both the FBI and the marshals' offices in Atlanta is tied up searching for someone who knew you were at that particular safe house at that specific time who also has ties to Anthony Giamo." He paused, then painfully continued, "If they find out that I used to work for him...I'm going to be their prime suspect."

"But you obviously aren't the leak," she said, her tone reasonable and matter-of-fact. "Beyond the fact that you aren't capable of selling your principles and honor for money, you were there when they tried to kill me. You came closer to getting killed than I did. If you'd set up something like that, you would at least have had the sense to be someplace else when it happened."

"Sweetheart, if they find out that I used to work for Giamo, they're also going to find out that I didn't want to guard you. I was damned if I would spend twenty-four hours a day with you without a fight, and Scott and I had it in his office. And I can guarantee they're going to find it curious as hell that less than thirty-six hours after I objected so strenuously to being sent to that safe house, someone made a hit on it."

She was silent for a moment, considering everything he'd told her; then she shook her head. "But they would need proof. That's not enough to pin anything on you."

"No, but it's enough to get me pulled off this case. It's enough to make them recall me to Atlanta and keep me as far away from you as they can."

Her fingers tightened around his hand. "But I wouldn't let you go. I don't care if they suspect you. I don't care if they don't trust you. I *know* you didn't do anything wrong."

Earlier she had been insecure when he'd told her she was beautiful. Now it was his turn. "Do you really believe that?"

She smiled wanly. "There are very few things I'm certain of at this point in my life, but one of them is you. You're a good man. You're honorable and trustworthy and loyal and upstanding. You could never do what this unknown person has done. You could never profit from your position. You could never deliberately hurt an innocent person or allow it to happen."

He smiled, too, feeling as if a great weight had been lifted from his shoulders—and his heart. He should have known all along that he could trust her with the details of his long-ago association with Anthony Giamo. He should have known that she would continue to trust him, that her belief in him would never be swayed. He should have had faith in the woman he loved.

Tugging on her hand, he pulled her to him, fitting her snugly between his legs, sliding his arms around her to hold her close. "You're a remarkable woman, Tess Marlowe," he said in a low, amused, aroused voice. "Remarkable."

She kissed his chin. "Now that the mutual admiration society is back in session, why don't you take your clothes off and show me something I can really admire?"

With a laugh, he struggled to his feet, taking her with him, and started toward the bedroom. "I'll do more than show you, sweetheart," he promised huskily.

The bedroom was cool and dark, but he remedied both those problems by leaving the door open so warm air and gentle light could filter in from the living room. He stood her on the woven rug beside the bed and kissed her, but he made no move to undress her. He found something erotic about fondling her through the barrier of her clothes, something that made him appreciate her bare skin even more when she was naked.

Tess welcomed his tongue into her mouth, stroking it with her own, suckling it hungrily, while her hands, palms flat, rubbed sensuously over his chest. She loved the feel of him, so strong and solid and finely muscled. His body was powerful, but he was capable of such tenderness. Even in the midst of a jarring, control-shattering release, he was gentle.

Working blindly, she located his holster and found the strap that held his gun in place. Flipping it up, she withdrew the pistol and laid it on the nightstand behind them, then tugged his shirt free of his jeans, sliding her hands underneath to repeat her caresses on his satiny warm skin.

He drew his mouth from hers reluctantly and dragged in a sweet breath. The scent of her was in his lungs, the taste of her in his mouth, the need for her in his soul. She was as addictive as any drug could possibly be. Every time he touched her, he longed to stroke her again. Every time he kissed her, he hungered for more. Every time he lay cradled so deeply within her, he ached to experience that pleasure again and again until he died.

And every time he thought of losing her, he lost a bit of himself.

He nuzzled her hair away from her ear and traced the outer edge with his tongue, making her shiver. Her hands were on his nipples now, teasing them, torturing them, so he laid his own hands over her breasts, rubbing the nubby weave of her sweater over their sensitive peaks. "Do you like that?" he murmured in her ear, his voice a mere whisper in the night.

"I'd like it better if you were touching my skin," came her strained, breathless reply.

"Soon. Don't you know that anticipation is half the fun?" He slid one hand lower until it was insinuated snugly between her thighs. The warmth that surrounded his fingers was erotic and surprising in its degree. Hot, he thought with a lazy smile. She was hot and growing moist, and only he could cool her. Only he could satisfy the need burning inside her, could quench the flames and bring her peace.

And then, with a touch, with a kiss or even a look, he could set her afire again.

Tess wriggled, moving against his hand, but fully clothed, all she succeeded in doing was intensifying the ache. "I've anticipated enough," she whispered, her breath coming rapidly. "I need you now."

"Soon." He freed his hand and popped loose the snap at the top of her jeans. The zipper made a rusty, raspy sound as he pulled it down; then he slid his hand inside the soft, faded denim and underneath the elastic band of her silky panties to the silkier curls below. For a long moment he simply cupped his hand over her, pressed intimately close by the layers of clothing. His eyes were closed, his cheek resting against her hair, and his breathing was tautly controlled as he shuddered with the demands of his arousal, powerfully swollen and still growing.

Tess leaned against him, unable to depend on the muscles in her legs, which had gone weak the instant he'd positioned his hand. With trembling hands, she raised his shirt so she could feel his bare skin, so she could touch her tongue to the already erect peak of one small brown nipple. When she drew it into her mouth, he tensed with a groan that vibrated through him. When she scraped her teeth over it, he swore softly and stroked through the curls that protected and sheltered her femininity. He made contact, and she gasped, clutching a handful of his jeans with one hand.

"Oh, please," she whispered, stiffening as he continued to caress the small nub that had become the very center of her being.

"Do you like that?" he asked with a low chuckle.

She couldn't answer. The sensations his agile fingers sent shimmering through her were too strong, too incredibly intense.

"If you don't, I could stop." He laughed again, smugly pleased with the power he held over her, deeply aware that in a moment she would tense and cry out and shudders would wrack her body, and then she would demonstrate an equal power over him.

When he acted as if he might withdraw his hand, she held him there, and as he'd predicted, a moment later every muscle in her slim body drew taut and her hips arched helplessly, seeking more, silently pleading for that last stroke, that last caress, that would bring her to a blinding release.

And, as he'd predicted, when the trembling eased, she turned to him with a passion that was almost violent in its intensity. She kissed him, rubbed and stroked and tasted him, arousing, tormenting, biting him. She undressed him with agonizing slowness, kissing and caressing each bit of his skin as it was exposed—except his manhood, where he needed her attention the most. She removed his jeans and briefs carefully, without touching him, and when in frustration he caught her hand and tried to guide it to his groin, she simply laughed and twisted free and continued to leave a trail of damp kisses in the coarse hair that was scattered over his chest.

"Do you like that?" she asked in a sultry voice, settling on her knees and dropping a gentle kiss to his hip.

"Damn it, Tess..."

She sat back and looked up at him while her fingers trailed down his thigh and muscular calf. "Do you want something?" she asked, all sexy, sensuous innocence.

He grasped her shoulders to pull her up, but she refused to move. "Anticipation," she reminded him with a sweet, alluring smile.

He looked down at her in the gentle light. She could cut him to shreds with that smile, he thought. She could cut out his heart and keep it for her very own, and he would never feel a thing but the sheer mindless pleasure of loving her.

His hands relaxed on her shoulders, sending a silent message that she received with another sweet smile. His need was still strong, she knew, the hunger twisting in his belly as it had done with her, but he was willing to endure, willing to let her do whatever she wanted to please him.

She leaned forward and took him in her mouth in a deeply intimate kiss that left him trembling. She made no other contact with him, no caresses, no steadying hands for support. Just a kiss, long and deep and hungry.

He slid his hands into her hair, groaned her name and tried, with what little strength he possessed, to pull away, but she didn't need his warning. She knew what she was doing, knew what was happening within his body as surely as he'd known with her, and she welcomed his release.

She gave him no chance to recover. Rising smoothly to her feet while the tremors still ricocheted through him, she drew him onto the bed beneath her. Before he could think, before he could react, before he could protest, she moved into position over him, taking him deep inside her, and brought them both to another blinding completion.

That night, her body close to Deke's, her arms and legs tangled with his, his seed deep inside her, she slept. Restfully. Peacefully. Hopefully.

Chapter 10

Tess opened the dryer and pulled out an armload of clothes, dumping them on the folding table before placing a load of wet clothes inside and restarting the dryer. She and Deke automatically divided the clothes, with him folding his and her folding her own. It should have been a pleasant enough task, but she found little pleasure in it.

Since awaking this morning, she'd been edgy, restless. She'd half expected a stern admonishment from Deke about their failure to take proper precautions with their lovemaking last night, and knowing that in this mood she would have turned it into a fight, she was relieved it hadn't come. Still, a fight would give her an outlet for this excess energy that was making her skin crawl.

Shaking out a pair of jeans, she lined up the seams and neatly folded them, laid them on the table, then put her hands on her hips. "You're a gorgeous man," she began, watching as he folded his own jeans. "And a pleasant companion and a fabulous lover..."

He grinned, his dark eyes alive with warmth and amusement. "But?"

"But I would give almost anything to see and talk to someone—*anyone*—besides you for just five minutes," she finished with a sigh.

He didn't take offense. As much as he loved her, as much as he enjoyed being with her and making love to her, he, too, was beginning to long for another face, another voice, another place besides the cabin. "Nine more days and we'll be out of here."

"Oh, wonderful," she said sarcastically. "*Only* nine more days."

"Then the trial, then . . ." He hesitated, centering his attention for a moment on the clothes he was folding. "Then your new home. Your new life."

She stiffened. She had been foolish to think he'd accepted her decision not to enter the relocation program simply because he'd dropped the argument yesterday. But *he* was foolish if he thought she would change her mind. She wouldn't. She couldn't. "I'm not going anywhere," she said flatly.

"You don't have any choice. You're not the only one involved here, Tess. You've got to think of the others affected by this decision."

"I *am* thinking of them—of my parents and my grandparents. And of you."

He kept his voice neutrally pitched. "What about the baby you might be carrying?"

For a long time she stared at him; then her hand dropped protectively to her stomach.

"You know it's possible that you're pregnant. What if you are? What will you do then?"

"I—I won't make any demands on you."

He ground his teeth and gestured impatiently. "That's not what I mean, damn it, and you know it! Giamo has hired someone to kill you. And, lady, if you're pregnant and they kill you—the baby dies, too."

She hugged her arms to her chest. "I-I'm probably n-not," she stuttered. "Without using one of those home tests, I wouldn't even know for at least two months, and I'm not sure how accurate they are. My cycle isn't regular—"

"If you don't relocate immediately following the trial, you won't live two months," he said harshly. "Damn it, Tess, I don't want to find out that we were going to have a baby at your autopsy. I don't want to have to bury you *and* our unborn child."

She shuddered with the chill his tortured words sent through her. She hadn't considered the ramifications of her actions last night, hadn't thought of anything beyond the fact that she desperately wanted Deke's baby. But he was right. If she was pregnant, the baby would take priority over everything else—her own desires, her family, even her life. She would have to do whatever was necessary to protect and nourish the life inside her. She would have to take whatever steps were required to make her child safe, to ensure that she stayed alive to love him, to take care of him.

She would have to enter their damn program, assume a new identity, begin a new life.

If she was pregnant, she reminded herself. There were no guarantees. Her luck had been so bad lately that she wouldn't let herself hope, wouldn't let herself dream, that even now Deke's child was growing inside her.

But if it was...if there was even the possibility, how could she risk its life?

She lifted her distressed gaze to his. "Is that why you let me make love to you last night without...? Because you knew if I got pregnant, I would have to protect the baby and therefore protect myself the way you want?"

"I couldn't have stopped last night if my life had depended on it," he said huskily.

"So the idea of using that occurred to you later."

"Not 'using' it, Tess. You can't deny that it's a valid consideration that affects your decision."

"No." She spoke softly, distantly. "I can't. But you know I'm probably *not* pregnant."

"Probably not," he agreed, regret heavy in his voice. "But you can't risk your life in the six to eight weeks it will take to confirm that. You can't risk the baby's life."

"No," she repeated. "I can't."

"Of course..." He stopped, cleared his throat, looked out the window. "If you are, you could remain in Atlanta...and have an abortion."

The distress that lined her face deepened. "You know I could never do that, Deke."

He hadn't thought it would be an option, but he was grateful all the same to hear her say so.

"I'll make you a deal. Until I know for certain one way or the other, I'll do whatever you say. I'll leave Atlanta, change my name, change my life. But if I'm not pregnant . . . I'll give up the new life and go back home, go back to being Tess Marlowe again. All right?"

No, it wasn't all right, but it was the best compromise he was going to get at this time. It was better than yesterday's unyielding stance. "All right," he agreed.

He was leaning forward to kiss her when the laundry room door swung open and the manager, tall and lanky, stepped inside. "Mr. Marshall. Ma'am." He offered Tess a polite nod. "I thought that was your truck parked outside."

"What can we do for you?" Deke asked, subtly moving until he was between Tess and the other man.

"I was just on my way down to your cabin. I have a message for you. You got a call from a man named Scott—said you have his number. He wants you to call him as quick as you can."

Deke felt alarm race up his spine. Scott would never have called here unless it was urgent. Had there been another threat against Tess? Had they uncovered his ties to Giamo in their investigation and decided to pull him from this assignment? Had something gone wrong with the case?

"You can use the phone in my office if you'd like. I'm going out to check the cabins, so you'll have some privacy. The door's unlocked—just go right in."

"Thanks. We'll do that."

As soon as the manager left, Tess asked, "What's wrong?"

"Your guess is as good as mine." He gathered their neatly folded clothes into the laundry basket he'd found in his closet and shoved them under the table, then grasped Tess's arm and left.

They walked the hundred yards to the office at a rapid clip. As the manager had said, the door was unlocked and no one was inside. Deke reached for the phone on the counter and dialed quickly, calling collect this time. "What the hell's going on, Scott?" he demanded as soon as his boss accepted the charges for the call.

"It's Frank Harris. He was injured in a hit-and-run accident this morning. He's in critical condition."

The news was bad, but it could have been worse, Deke acknowledged grimly as they returned to the laundry room. Although less than an hour ago he'd been wishing to see another place besides the cabin, he didn't like the idea of taking Tess away from it now. She was safe here, and God help him, he needed to know that.

But Julia Billings had given them no choice. She wanted to see Frank's witness—no, he corrected, *her* witness—and she wanted to see her today.

Tess walked beside him, glancing at his face, trying to read his expression. He'd said very little on the phone, each response growing more clipped, more abrupt. When he'd hung up, he hadn't said much, either. "Well?" she asked at last. "Are you going to tell me?"

"Do you remember Frank Harris?"

"The assistant prosecutor?" She nodded.

"He was involved in an accident this morning. He was hurt pretty badly."

"I'm sorry."

They reached the laundry room, and he followed her inside. The dryer holding the last of their clothes had stopped, and he took them out, dumping them on the table. "It was a hit-and-run, and of course it can't be proven, but Giamo seems the most likely suspect."

"Why would they do that? Are they trying to delay the trial?"

He shrugged. "Maybe." Or maybe they were trying to draw Tess out of hiding. Giamo's lawyer had to be smart enough to know that Harris's replacement would have to talk to her. Maybe they were looking for a chance to get her out in the open, so they could try once more to kill her. "The trial is scheduled to start next week. There's no way Frank's going to be well enough to handle it by then. He probably won't even be out of the hospital for a month or longer. That leaves the government with two options: to request a continuance until he's better, which might be six or eight weeks or even more, or to assign another prosecutor who will have to hustle to familiarize himself with the case and the evidence and the witnesses."

"And I assume they've chosen to assign someone else." She folded the last of her lingerie and added it to the basket.

He nodded. "The U.S. Attorney is going to take it herself. She's probably already more familiar with it than anyone else in the office, but she still needs to interview the witnesses for herself—starting with the most important one. You."

"So we're going back to Atlanta."

"No." Basket in hand, he gestured with a nod for her to precede him out of the laundry room. "It's still too risky to take you into Atlanta. We're meeting her at a farm we use occasionally as a safe house. It's about twenty miles west of the city."

When they reached the cabin, Deke left the laundry in Tess's room, then followed her into the kitchen. She stopped in front of the refrigerator, her hand on the handle, but didn't open it. "Will *this* safe house be safe?"

"No one knows we're going there but Scott and Julia."

"How well do you know Julia?"

"I met her when I transferred to Atlanta four years ago."

"But how well do you know her?"

He looked down at her for a moment, then walked away to lean against the counter on the opposite side of the room. She turned to watch him. "When I first came to Atlanta, I had an affair with her that lasted nearly a year. When it ended, we remained friends as well as colleagues."

Rubbing the side of her nose with one finger, Tess solemnly considered her reaction to this news. She was surprised—somewhat foolishly, she decided. Deke was a handsome, sexy, intelligent man. Of course there had been women, probably quite a few of them, in his life. And who could be better suited to him than one who understood the requirements and demands of his job?

And she was grateful that he'd told her the truth without prompting. It was a sign of his trust in her that there had been no evasion, no trying to hide the truth.

And she was jealous as hell. She could deal with Angela, whom he'd loved, because she was gone, disappeared, out of his life forever. But Julia.... He still saw her. He called her friend. He liked and respected her. She was still in his life, and Tess felt a savage need to be the only important woman in his life.

"Did you love her, too?" she asked, aware that there was a definite catty flavor to her question but not caring.

"No. But did I care for her? Yes. Do I still care for her? Yes, in the same way I care about Scott and Thad and my other friends. *Friends*, Tess. Not lovers. Not loved ones."

And which was she? she wondered. Lover...or loved one?

"I trust her. She's one of the best prosecutors I've ever met, and she's one of the best friends I've ever had. You'll be safe with her."

"Are you sure?" she questioned. "Has she been cleared in their investigation?"

"I don't know. I didn't ask. But I can promise you, as sure as I know that Scott or Thad didn't leak the location of the safe house, I know that Julia didn't do it, either."

She smiled a little bitterly. "Don't make promises you can't keep," she reminded him.

He crossed his arms over his chest and studied her. "Are you jealous because I slept with her?"

"Why do you ask that?" she challenged.

"Why else would you be so determined to dislike her without even meeting her?" he countered.

She closed the distance between them in two steps and grasped his open jacket with both hands. "Yes, damn you, I'm jealous," she blurted out, tugging at the leather. "At least I don't have to face your ex-wife or Angela and know that they were your lovers, too."

He laughed softly and lifted her off the floor for a kiss. "I didn't even know you then, sweetheart. And remember—the emphasis is on *were*. Past tense. You have no cause to be jealous now." He set her down again and slid his hands up from her hips to tangle in the fabric that bloused where her gold T-shirt was tucked into her black denim jeans. "I told Scott we'd meet Julia at four. It's about a two-hour drive from here, but we'll allow an extra half hour for circling Atlanta. That gives us an hour for lunch. Are you hungry?"

They left the cabin a few minutes before 1:30. Tess stood at the top of the steps, staring out over the clearing, while Deke locked the door. He came to stand behind her, sensing her reluctance to leave. He wrapped his arm around her, the crook of his elbow around one shoulder, his hand resting on the other. "It'll be all right, Tess."

With a sigh, she clasped his forearm with both hands and leaned back against him. "I wish I shared your optimism."

"We're just going to talk to Julia, then came straight back. We'll still stay here until the trial starts."

"I know. But I don't want to leave. I feel safe here. I feel as if nothing can touch me here. Nothing can touch *us*." And she was afraid that when they left something *could* come between them. Here it was easy for Deke to be attracted to her because she was the only other person around. But what would happen when they weren't alone? When he could have his choice of any woman in central Georgia, would he still want *her*?

"It'll be all right, sweetheart." He kissed her forehead, then guided her to the Bronco.

She managed to keep silent for all of fifteen minutes; then she faced him. "Why does she want to see me? I told Mr. Harris and Mr. McNally and all those cops everything I know. Why can't she simply read their reports?"

"No prosecutor would go into court, especially on a case this important, with witnesses he's never talked to before. She just wants to meet you, see how you come across, judge how well you'll stand up in court. She'll ask you all the questions the others have asked, help you rephrase your answers if it's necessary. It's nothing to worry about, Tess. She's thorough, and she's good. She goes into court very well prepared, and she generally wins."

She fell silent for another fifteen minutes, then spoke again. "If this case is so important, and if she's so good, why didn't she take it in the first place? Why did she give it to her assistant?"

Deke shrugged. "Maybe her caseload was too heavy. Maybe she couldn't give it the time and attention it deserved. But Frank Harris is good, too. If Julia is the best prosecutor I've met, Frank is second-best."

"But—"

"Tess." The strain was starting to show in his voice. "I know you're not happy about meeting Julia. I know you weren't ready to leave the cabin yet. I know you're edgy. I understand all that. Under the circumstances, it's perfectly normal. But don't go looking for trouble. Don't make a major issue out of this. Trust me, please.''

''All right,'' she agreed grudgingly. She settled back in her seat and turned to watch the scenery out the window. He was right, she admitted. She didn't want to meet Julia Billings. She didn't want to spend the next nine days wondering why Deke wanted *her* when he could have had the other woman. And she didn't want to leave the cabin. She didn't want to test the strength of the fragile bonds that had been woven between them, didn't want to find out if their relationship could withstand exposure to other places, other situations and, especially, other people.

And she certainly didn't want the first other person they exposed it to to be one of Deke's former lovers.

But she had no choice. Trust me, he'd said, and she did—with her life, her heart and her soul.

The farmhouse was located twenty miles due west of the city, sitting at the top of a gently climbing hill, several miles distant from the closest neighbor. In its isolation, it reminded Tess of her earlier impression of safe houses—a seedy motel or a house surrounded by acres of nothing. The latter description certainly fit this place. The dirt drive started at a gate in the barbed wire fence half a mile away and snaked its way up the hill, twisting first to the left, then to the right. No one could approach without ample warning to the occupants.

Parked at the side of the house was a sleek, silver-gray sedan that Deke identified aloud as Julia's car. He parked in front, switched off the engine, then turned to Tess. ''Are you okay?''

She nodded.

''Nervous?''

She nodded again.

''Don't be. You'll like Julia.''

''I sincerely doubt that,'' she said dryly.

''Ready?''

She took a deep breath, nodded and opened the door. Deke met her a few feet from the truck, taking her arm. The action would appear completely impersonal to anyone watching, but it offered her much-needed confidence.

The boards on the porch creaked when they walked across them. The shiny, heavy-duty lock on the door looked out of place, Tess thought, with everything else worn and showing the signs of age. She wondered if Deke had a key, but the door wasn't locked. When he turned the knob, it swung open with a squeak.

The door led directly into the living room, a big square room filled with the shadowy shapes of unused furniture. It smelled musty, and little of the late-afternoon light could penetrate the heavy dust and grime on the windows. Deke paused just inside the door, Tess directly behind him, letting his eyes adjust to the dimness.

Something was wrong, he thought, feeling the hairs on the back of his neck stand on end. If Julia was here, she would have turned on the lights and, in spite of the day's chill, opened the windows to air out the room. She didn't like closed spaces.

But that was her car parked outside. He recognized it because he'd gone with her not six months ago to pick it out. So where was she?

He reached behind him with both hands, one to pull Tess close to his back, the other to draw his pistol from the holster. He always carried it with a round in the chamber, so all he had to do was slide the safety off and it would be ready to fire. He accomplished that with a soft click.

Moving soundlessly, he went farther into the living room, staying close to one wall, painfully aware that Tess was right behind him. Then suddenly he stopped. "My God," he whispered.

She saw the vague outline on the floor at the same time he did, but it took her a moment longer to identify it as a body. She pressed her hand to her mouth, but not quickly enough to mask the soft sound of shock she made.

"Wait here." Still moving cautiously, gun in hand, he went to the figure, knelt and turned it over. It was Anthony Giamo. There was no need to check for a pulse. The bullet hole in the center of his forehead made it quite clear that he was dead.

Who would kill Giamo? And where was Julia? he wondered frantically. What kind of mess had she stumbled into here? Had their leak learned of her meeting here today, notified Giamo, then followed them out? Had he shot Giamo, ensuring that his identity would never be discovered, then been forced to kill Julia, too?

Another chilling thought came over him then. What if the man was still around? What if he wanted to make certain there were no loose ends? Deke surged to his feet and started toward Tess. He had to get her out of here. Before he searched for Julia, before he did anything else, he had to get Tess in the truck and send her to safety.

He couldn't say what alerted him to the fact that they were no longer alone—the creak of a board, the shadow that fell across the floor or the stale scent of a cheap cigar. He looked up, though, and moved away from Tess just as a man—one of Giamo's men—stepped into the room. He was as tall as Deke and forty pounds heavier. He stopped, as they had done, to let his eyes adjust, but he spotted Giamo's body much more quickly than they had.

"What the hell . . . ?" In an awkward move, he pulled a gun from beneath his coat and fired at Deke, who dived behind the chair, at the same time pushing Tess out of the way, then fired his own gun. The pistol was steady, and his aim was perfect—two rapid shots placed within an inch of each other in the other man's chest.

His body hit the wall, then slowly sank to the floor in a motionless, lifeless heap. Ten feet away, her hands over her ears, tears stinging her eyes, sickness roiling in her stomach, Tess slid to the floor, too, huddling into a tight, trembling ball.

Slowly Deke got to his feet, dusting off his clothes, still gripping his gun. He crouched in front of her, lifting her chin. "Are you okay?"

All she could do was nod. If she opened her mouth to speak, she was afraid she would start screaming and never stop.

He left her and approached the man he'd just killed. Near the door, where he'd fallen, there was more light, and Deke could see his face clearly. He recognized him as Giamo's driver, knew he had worked for the old man even at the time *he* had, but he didn't remember his name.

For a moment he simply stood there, looking helplessly around the room. What the hell was going on here? Where was Julia? What had gone wrong?

Then a tiny sob drew him back to Tess. He lifted her to her feet, offering her the support her trembling legs couldn't give. "I want you to leave," he said, leading her toward the door. "Take the Bronco and get the hell out of here, understand? As soon as it's safe to stop, call Scott Rowan and tell him what happened here. Do you understand me, Tess?"

"No!" she cried, clutching his arm. "You have to come with me! Please, Deke!"

"I have to find out what happened to Julia. I'll be all right, sweetheart, but only if I know you're safe."

She tried to pull back, but he dragged her, her feet sliding over the wooden floor. When they neared the second body, he pressed her face against his chest, hiding the slack face and sightless eyes from her.

Desperately afraid of leaving him, Tess tried once again to convince him. "Please, Deke, you're supposed to stay with me all the time, remember? Please don't send me away without you!"

"It's all right, Deke. Let her stay."

The voice came from behind them, cool, cultured, calm. Deke stopped short and whirled around to find Julia Billings standing at the opposite end of the room. There was a door back there, he remembered, that connected to the kitchen. She must have come from there. "Thank God you're all—"

Then he saw the gun in her hand, pointed at his chest, and suddenly he understood. The tall, slim blonde at the scene of Walt Davis's murder whom Tess had never been able to identify. Julia's refusal to order protection for Tess and Donald Hopkins. Her decision to let her assistant prosecute such an important case. The leak of the safe house location. Dear God, even Frank Harris's hit-and-run accident that had allowed her to take over the government's case and coax Tess out of hiding.

She was the one who had almost gotten Tess killed. *She* was the one who had lured Giamo here, then murdered him. *She* was the one who had betrayed them.

And now she was going to kill them.

Like Deke, Tess was staring at the other woman. So this was Julia Billings, she thought numbly, her tears of shock and simple fear dried by the cold terror that spread through her. This was Deke's close friend and ex-lover, the best prosecutor he'd ever known, the woman he admired and respected. She was beautiful, as Tess had suspected she would be—at least five foot ten and model-slim, blond-haired and blue-eyed, elegant and self-assured and confident. She wore a creamy off-white suit with a pale rose handkerchief tucked in the breast pocket and a blouse of the same soft shade, and diamond earrings and pumps that matched the suit. The black gloves on her slim, long-fingered hands and the small, deadly, black gun they held didn't fit the picture.

She appeared composed, but closer inspection showed Tess the signs of strain: her too-bright blue eyes, the slight tremor in her hands, the stress lines bracketing her mouth. Maybe killing didn't come easily to the woman, she thought with a glimmer of hope, and maybe killing her close friend and ex-lover would be impossible. Maybe she would let Deke live, and maybe somehow he would find a way to keep Tess alive, too.

Deke moved slowly, taking one small step at a time, until he stood between Julia and Tess. The action didn't go unnoticed by either woman. It amused Julia. "Doing your duty until the end, Deke?" she asked casually, but her voice shook just a bit. "Or is it more than duty? Did you make the same mistake with Miss Marlowe that you made with Angela Wright? Did you fall in love with her?" She didn't wait for an answer. "It doesn't matter, though, does it? It's not as if you have a future to worry about."

"Why, Julia?"

She answered his question literally. "Because I have to kill you. Because you're too smart and too good at your job. You know I shot Giamo. You know I was with him the night he murdered Davis. You know I gave him the address of the safe house and almost got Miss Marlowe killed. You would turn me in, and I would end up in prison. I couldn't stand that, Deke."

His fingers tensed on the gun he held at his side. He could kill her. Even though she was pointing her gun at him, he knew his training and all those years of long hours at the firing range would pay off. He could raise the pistol and kill her before she could even think to pull the trigger.

Seeming to read his thoughts, she smiled coolly. "Put the gun down, Deke, and move away from Tess."

Move away from Tess? Leave her open, an easy target? Smiling bitterly, he shook his head. "No. It's not going to be as easy killing us as it was shooting Giamo, because you don't hate us, Julia. He was a bastard who deserved to die, but we don't. Tess doesn't."

Julia drew the hammer back on the revolver, then took a step toward them. "Miss Marlowe," she said tautly, "if you don't move away from him, I'm going to shoot him right now. You don't want his blood on your hands—and I mean that literally—now do you?"

"Don't, Tess," Deke commanded.

But she was already moving. She didn't know if Julia could bring herself to kill Deke, but how could she risk even the slightest possibility?

Her heart thudding impossibly fast, her breathing rapid and shallow, she stepped over the dead man's feet and inched her way along the wall until she was an equal distance from both of them. She stopped there, but at Julia's impatient gesture, she moved again, this time stopping only a few feet from the other woman.

Tess stared at Julia, her eyes shifting from the blonde's face to the gun and back again. She matched the description Tess had given the police, but Tess still didn't recognize her. She could have sat down across from her a dozen times and never placed her as the woman with Giamo the night of the first murder.

Immediately Julia turned the gun on Tess. "Put the gun down, Deke," she repeated.

He knew he could still kill her, but with her gun only inches from Tess's head, it was too risky. What if she didn't die instantly? What if she lived long enough to pull the trigger? At that range, Tess wouldn't stand a chance.

He put the safety on, then leaned forward and gently tossed the pistol onto the dust-covered sofa. "All right, Julia," he said, his voice as quiet and calm as he could make it, but still laced with fear. "I'm unarmed, okay?"

A little of the tension that sharpened her features seemed to drain away, but she didn't relax her stance.

"Why are you doing this? Why were you working for Giamo? When did you get involved with him?"

"Does it matter?"

Deke made an obvious effort to control his temper. "My good friend is threatening to kill me. I think I deserve to know why."

She considered it a moment, then shrugged. "I met him fifteen years ago. I had just started working for the U.S. Attorney's office. I was young, inexperienced and eager to get ahead. One day Giamo came to me and offered information on a case I was prosecuting. Because of his help, I won. It became a regular thing. He would always come up with that one piece of information that cinched a case for me. Within a few years I had developed a reputation as one of the toughest and most successful prosecutors. Without his tips, it would have taken—'' she broke off and sighed ''—Lord knows how long. And he never asked for anything in return.''

When she fell silent, Deke supplied the next part for her. ''For a time. Then he wanted . . . what? Warnings about investigations? Confidential information about your cases? A little inept handling of the cases against his people?''

Anger blazed in her blue eyes. ''I had to do it, Deke! He threatened to ruin me! Even though I'd done nothing wrong, nothing but use the information he voluntarily provided to me, he could have destroyed my career. And he was the only one. I never took anything from anyone else, never gave anything to anyone else. I knew it was wrong, that it was illegal, but protecting him seemed a small enough price to pay for sending all those other people to jail.''

''You're rationalizing,'' Deke said harshly. ''Providing justification for behavior that can't be justified. How many laws did you break, Julia? How many crimes did you commit?'' He shook his head in disgust. ''You should be in jail along with all those other people.''

''I am a good prosecutor!'' she insisted. ''My only problem was Giamo . . . and now he's dead.''

''But now you have another problem. Me.'' Deliberately he didn't mention Tess, didn't call Julia's attention to her. ''How are you going to cover this one up? How are you going to explain away three murders?'' He gestured to the bodies on the floor.

''Four,'' Julia corrected, tilting her head toward Tess. ''I'm sorry—God, you don't know how sorry—but you both have to die.'' The muscles in her arm were beginning to tremble from holding the gun fully extended for so long.

She lowered it, bracing her arm against her upper body but keeping the revolver pointed at Tess.

"Actually, after all the pain and trouble and complications that bastard has caused me in the last fifteen years, the solution was really quite simple," she continued. "After Giamo's men failed to kill Miss Marlowe at the safe house, he was pressuring me to find out where she'd been taken. I told him that all Scott would tell me was that she was with a marshal named Deke Ramsey. The name interested him. He told me a kid named Deacon Ramsey used to work for him years ago, and he wondered if they were the same. He told me enough that I knew it *was* you." She laughed softly. "Can you imagine how I felt? This man had been a thorn in my side for *years*. He'd had the power to destroy my career at any moment. He'd made me despise myself. And suddenly, in one casual conversation, he'd given me the means to rid myself of him forever."

Her plan *was* simple, Tess realized with a shudder—so simple that even she could figure it out without help. Julia Billings was going to frame Deke. She was going to make it look like *he* was the leak. She was going to use his past association with Giamo to make him look guilty—and he wouldn't be able to defend himself. He would be dead.

"This morning, after Scott arranged this meeting," Julia said, "I went to your house, Deke. I had to break the window in the laundry room to get inside, but I called Giamo from your phone and told him that you were bringing Miss Marlowe here at four o'clock. I suggested that he come an hour or so earlier. Then I took one of your guns." She saw his gaze drop once again to the revolver and shook her head. "Not this one. This is Giamo's. I took it from him after I killed him. No, I took that little one you kept in the closet. That's what I killed him with."

So the murder weapon belonged to him, Deke thought grimly, and his fingerprints would be all over it and the bullets inside it. And when the FBI and the Marshals Service investigated the killings, they would check the phone records and find that shortly before he was murdered, Giamo had received a call, apparently setting up this meeting, from Deke's house. Julia is thorough, he'd told Tess earlier. He was only now beginning to realize just how thorough.

He moved a step closer to the two women. If he got close enough, there was a slim chance that he could disarm Julia. Slim, but possibly the only chance they had. "So I called Giamo to arrange Tess's murder," he said slowly. "And when he showed up, something went wrong. Maybe he wanted to kill me, too, since I could tie him to it. So he killed Tess, then shot me, and before I died, I killed him. Is that your plan?"

She nodded, relieved that he understood. "That's it."

"And in the course of the investigation, they'll just happen to discover, with a little help from you if necessary, that I used to work for Giamo years ago, right? And I imagine you made a sizable deposit into my bank account to give added weight to this story."

She nodded again.

He muttered an oath beneath his breath. She had prosecuted too many complex cases in her career, and she had learned from them, because if there was a flaw in her scenario, he couldn't find it. "What about your decision to let Frank prosecute the case?" he asked, stalling. "A major case, lots of publicity, lots of glory for whoever won it. Why did you turn it down?"

"Because there were two witnesses who might possibly identify me as the woman with Giamo when he killed Davis. I had to avoid Miss Marlowe and Mr. Hopkins at all costs."

"And Frank's accident this morning?"

She looked genuinely regretful. "I didn't want to do that, but for my plan to succeed, I had to get to you and Miss Marlowe. I tried to think of another way, something not so dangerous to Frank, but I couldn't. So I asked Giamo to arrange it for me. I told them to try not to hurt him too badly."

Tess made a scornful sound that she couldn't stop. Sure, she thought cynically, run the man down in the street with a two-ton car, but try not to hurt him too badly. Deke's friend and former lover was crazy. But almost immediately she amended that thought. Julia Billings wasn't crazy. No, she was quite coldly sane. She was *desperate*, incredibly desperate to clean up her past and create a future for herself that she could live with.

How easy it must have been for her in the beginning, she imagined, to accept Anthony Giamo's help. She had seen a chance to go from being a good lawyer to an outstanding one, to do her job and send the bad guys to jail, and it hadn't cost her a thing—yet. But she had been foolish and gullible to think Giamo would never ask for payment. She had let her ambition blind her to the reality of the situation, and Giamo must have known that. He had played her carefully, letting her dig a hole so deep that she could never get out before he made his demands. How she must have hated what he'd done to her, what she'd done to herself. How desperate she must be to make amends, even if it meant murder. Even if it meant Deke's murder.

Tess looked at Deke. He was slowly closing the distance between himself and Julia, planning to do...what? To wrestle the gun away from her and maybe get himself shot in the process? She wanted to move forward herself, to block his way. She wanted to cry out to him to be careful, not to risk his life to save hers. She wanted to tell him that she loved him.

But she said nothing, did nothing but wait.

"What about the gunpowder residue?" he asked. "When the lab doesn't find any on Giamo's hands, your whole plan is going to fall apart."

"I thought about that, too." She swayed, unsteady on her feet for a moment, then seemed to get hold of herself. "It's on his hands. I had to get him to shoot at me just once before I killed him." Her smile was soft and strange and dreamy. "He missed by a yard. I think he was too surprised, too shaken by the realization that I was a threat to him. He always had such an old-fashioned attitude when it came to women. He always believed he controlled me so totally that he was stunned to find out I had the strength to kill him.''

She realized he had come closer, and she took a few steps back to compensate, finding an unsteady table to lean against. ''Don't underestimate me the way he did, Deke. I spent days planning this. I thought of nothing else. It's truly a perfect crime, a once-in-a-lifetime chance to make things right. As soon as you and Miss Marlowe are dead—'' she paused over the word, seeming both repelled and drawn by it ''—I promise, I will never let anything like that happen again. At last I can be the tough, honest, upstanding prosecutor that I've always pretended to be. I won't have to hate myself for the lie I'm living. I won't have to lie awake at night, so eaten up by shame and guilt that I can't sleep. I won't have to spend the first hour after every trial in the bathroom throwing up because what I've done sickens me so.''

''It's not a perfect crime, Julia,'' Deke gently disagreed. ''You got involved in something that got out of control, something that was destroying you, and you took care of it by killing Giamo. But now you have to kill me, because I know, and then you'll have to kill Tess, because she knows, too, and soon you'll have to kill yourself, because you know. You think what you did for Giamo was shameful and sickening? Try living with what you plan to do to Tess and me. Try sleeping at night knowing that you killed a friend. Try facing the fact every single day for the rest of your life that you killed an innocent woman for nothing more than being in the wrong place at the wrong time.''

''I have no choice,'' she whispered mournfully. ''But I'll make it right, Deke, I swear I will.''

''How can you make her death right?'' he demanded. ''You're planning to murder a witness—a *witness*, for God's sake! Julia, she stands for everything you believe in. The law. Justice. Right. If you kill her, the hell that Giamo put you through will be nothing compared to the hell you'll be creating for yourself.''

"But I have to do it. Don't you see?'' When his expression remained unyielding, she turned her pleading gaze on Tess. ''I'm sorry, Miss Marlowe. God help me, if there was another way out, I would take it, but I can't find it. I know you don't deserve this. I know that killing you is going to cost me dearly, but I have to...." Her voice faltered, and bleakness crept over her face. Unmindful of the gun, she raised both hands to awkwardly cover her face, and a silent sob shook her body.

Swiftly, Deke moved forward, but the creak of the ancient wood floor betrayed him. Julia dropped her hands and pointed the gun at him. ''No heroic attempts, Deke, okay?'' she asked wearily. ''Don't you know this is hard enough as it is?'' Although her eyes remained on him, she directed her next words once more to Tess. ''It may not be much comfort, Miss Marlowe, but...your deaths will free me to do my job the best way I know how. I will be the best damn prosecutor, the most aggressive and the toughest, that I can possibly be.''

"What? Killing her is a small enough price to pay to save yourself, to get your career back on track?'' Deke asked derisively. ''That's the same kind of reasoning that got you into this mess in the first place, Julia.''

"Shut up, Deke,'' she ordered. ''We've talked enough.''

"You'll never be free of this, Julia. You'll never be honest and upright. You'll never be the best. Knowing that you murdered your own witness is going to destroy you more surely than anything Anthony Giamo could have done.''

"Shut up!'' Tears filled and overflowed her blue eyes, and her hands, locked tightly around the gun, trembled uncontrollably. ''I have no other choice! Damn you, don't you understand that? This is the only way out!''

Tess watched in horror as Julia placed her finger on the trigger. ''No,'' she whispered, then tried to scream, but her throat was constricted, locking her helpless cry inside. She took a step away from the wall, then another; then the sound of a gunshot echoed through the room. The scream forced its way out, full of terror and sorrow and grief, and she sank to her knees on the dusty floor.

Deke rushed to Julia, catching her slender body as it fell, lowering her to the floor. Blood soaked her blond hair and splattered obscenely on her off-white jacket. He checked for and found her pulse and whispered a silent prayer, then cursed her. "Damn you, Julia!" He looked around, saw that Tess was all right, then pulled the small square of rose-colored cloth from Julia's jacket pocket and pressed it gently over the wound.

Then he got to his feet, scooped Tess into his arms and carried her out of the house to the Bronco, stepping over the body of Giamo's driver on the way. He set her in the passenger seat and kept one arm around her while he flipped open the glove compartment and removed the radio inside. He got hold of Scott and gave him a terse rundown on the last half hour's events, then requested that an ambulance be dispatched and Thad McNally and the medical examiner's office be notified.

Next he shrugged out of his jacket and wrapped it, along with his arms, around Tess's trembling body. "God, I'm sorry," he whispered, resting his cheek against her hair. "I'm so sorry, sweetheart."

She lay limply against him, still shivering in spite of his warmth. Maybe she would never get warm again, she thought numbly, her mind detached from the horror of the last few minutes. Maybe she would never feel safe again.

She would definitely never forget.

Deke tilted her face back and kissed her, not the deep, hungry, thankful-she-was-alive kiss he wanted to give her, but a gentle brush of his lips. There was no color in her face, no warmth in her skin, and her eyes were big and shaded with fear, shock, terror, revulsion and tears. He cupped his hands to her cheeks, his thumbs tenderly stroking. "I have to go back inside, sweetheart,'' he whispered. "I can't leave her like that.''

There was no change in her expression. "Go on,'' she whispered almost soundlessly, barely moving her lips.

But he couldn't walk away. He couldn't leave her sitting there so helplessly. So hopelessly. "Sweetheart . . .''

A sudden shudder rocked through her, seeming to snap her out of her shock. She pulled his jacket closer, huddling into it, seeking its warmth. "I'm all right, Deke,'' she said, making a supreme effort to sound so. "Go check on Julia.''

She watched him go back inside the farmhouse, then drew her knees to her chest, nestled against the cool leather of the seat and silently cried—for Deke and for Julia Billings, but mostly for herself.

Julia had spoken of freedom, Deke thought several hours later as he stood at the front window in the farmhouse. Killing them was supposed to set her free from the nightmare her life had become. But in the end, the one who had been freed was Tess. With Giamo dead and Julia not expected to live through the night, there would be no trial. With no one to pay for the hit, the contract on her life would be forgotten. With no threats against her, entering the relocation program was no longer necessary. Protection was no longer necessary. And maybe neither was he.

She was still wearing his jacket, still sitting in the Bronco, even though the sun had long since set and the temperature had dropped to the mid-thirties. She had been interviewed at length by Scott Rowan and Thad McNally and yet another lawyer from Julia's office. She had remained calm, quiet, although still pale, and she had patiently answered each of their questions, even though it had been clear to him even from the distance of the house that repeatedly reliving this afternoon's nightmare had been difficult and painful.

He hadn't spoken to her since those few moments after he'd radioed Scott. First he'd needed to stay with Julia—no one should die as utterly alone as she had been. Then the ambulance had arrived, followed by what seemed like half the city of Atlanta. Now... He'd finished the last of his own interviews and was free to go at any time—free to go to Tess. Yet he remained in the house, torn between wanting to see her and hold her, and wanting to keep his distance.

He could think of plenty of reasons why he should stay away. She'd seen him kill a man this afternoon, had seen Julia shoot herself. She had put her trust in him, and he had very nearly cost her her life with his bad judgment. She was safe now, free to put this entire episode behind her and get on with her life.

And he could think of only one reason why he should go to her: he loved her. Was that enough to make her forget this gruesome afternoon? Was it enough to make her forgive the carelessness that had almost gotten her killed? Was it enough to make her love him back?

He didn't know the answers, so he stayed where he was, staring out the window.

While he watched, Thad McNally opened the door of the Bronco and extended his hand to help Tess out. She slid to the ground, paused long enough to remove Deke's jacket and hand it to Thad, then went alone to the car he'd pointed out several hundred feet away.

She was leaving without saying goodbye, Deke realized. Regret welled bitter and cold in his throat and twisted in his belly. Maybe the answer to those questions was no. Maybe she couldn't forget. Maybe she couldn't forgive him. Maybe she couldn't love him.

Thad came into the house, pausing briefly to glance around the room, then joined Deke at the window. "Here's your coat. I'm taking Tess to her parents' house now."

He accepted the jacket and realized as he pulled it on that he was cold. From the night air? he wondered. Or from the sight of Tess walking away without so much as a backward glance for him?

"You have any messages for her?"

He spoke mechanically without looking at his friend. "Tell her someone will get her things from the cabin and bring them to her as soon as possible."

Thad rolled his eyes upward and sighed. "That wasn't exactly the kind of message I was referring to. Do you want to talk to her before we go? Do *you* want to take her home? Do you want to tell her you'll be in touch?"

So Thad had figured out that there had been more between them than a simple marshal-witness relationship. Deke wasn't surprised. The FBI agent was perceptive.

He opened his mouth to say no—no message, no conversation, no future contact—but he couldn't force the word out. He loved her, and he knew that before this afternoon she had felt *something* for him—maybe not love, maybe just affection, but something important. Something precious. On top of that, there was the chance—slim, but there all the same—that she was pregnant with his child. How could he walk away from that? How could he let *her* walk away from it?

"Tell her I'll call her."

"When?"

"Soon."

"How soon?"

He scowled at Thad. "I have a case to wind up, reports to make, forms to file, more questions to answer, and I have a very good friend in the hospital who tried to kill herself because she didn't have it in her to kill us. I'll call her soon."

"*I* have a case to wind up, reports, forms, questions, et cetera, and Julia was a good friend of mine, too," Thad said bluntly. "But I could still make time to talk to Tess instead of leaving her waiting indefinitely. Are you afraid to commit yourself?"

Deke thought of the various meanings that could be attached to Thad's question and smiled faintly. Was he afraid to commit himself to a definite time to contact Tess, to find out if she wanted him out of her life? Yes. Uncertainty was better than the heartache of rejection. But was he afraid to commit himself to her, to spending the rest of his life with her, loving her, needing her? He would do it in a heartbeat. "Tell her I'll call her in a couple of days, as soon as everything is settled."

Thad nodded. "Are you going home soon?"

Home to an empty house? To a bed that didn't have Tess in it? Deke shook his head. "I'm going to check on Julia."

"I'll be in touch with you tomorrow."

Tess thought she'd kept the pain and disappointment off her face when Thad McNally delivered Deke's message, but the agent saw it. He carefully backed out, maneuvering around the other cars, then started down the long drive. "It's been a tough day for both of you," he remarked.

"Yes," she agreed, staring dry-eyed out the side window.

"Well, it's over now. The danger, the threats, the risk— it's all over."

That was what she was afraid of—that everything had ended, including her relationship with Deke. Until the ambulance had arrived, he had stayed inside with Julia. After she'd been taken away, he had remained there, talking to everyone but her. She'd tried to tell herself that he was busy, doing his job, but practically everyone else had found a few minutes for her. Then she had tried to convince herself that he'd been trying to protect both of them by hiding their relationship, but surely he could have managed a few words, a private touch, even just a look, without giving away everything.

A couple of days. That was when he'd said he would call her. If he did, that was when she would know if his feelings for her had been temporary or the basis of something permanent. If he called, that was when she would know if she had a future to look forward to...or merely a lonely, empty existence.

And if he didn't call, she would know, too—would know that he hadn't cared enough to even tell her goodbye. She would know that all he had offered her was a steamy, passionate affair—not caring, not a relationship, and certainly not love. She would know that, indeed, it was all over.

A couple of days. It was a lifetime away.

Chapter 11

Deke stood beside the hospital bed as he'd done for the last seven days and watched Julia. She looked peaceful, as if she were merely sleeping and would awaken at any moment, smile and tell him that it had all been a terrible mistake, nothing more than a bad dream.

But according to her doctors, she might never wake up, and if she did, she might never tell him anything. The bullet had entered her brain, damaging and destroying fragile tissue. Julia Billings, as he had known her, had ceased to exist the moment she'd pulled the trigger.

Then honesty forced him to admit that the Julia he had known had never really existed. He had known an honorable, admirable, hardworking, trustworthy, dedicated attorney when, in reality, she'd been no better than the people she'd sent to prison. She had been as guilty as they were—more so, because she had been one of the good guys. She had misused and abused her authority for her own gain—not for money, but for self-protection. She had made a mockery of everything she claimed to believe in—everything that *he* believed in.

No, he corrected that. There was one thing he believed in that Julia couldn't touch. Tess.

He hadn't called her yet. He'd told himself that wrapping up the case took all his time, but that wasn't true. He'd told himself that she needed more than a few days to deal with the shock of what had happened, to adjust to being back in her own home and living her normal life again, but that wasn't true, either.

The truth was that he was a coward. He'd been afraid to talk to her, afraid to see her and not see the warmth and the desire, the need and the hunger, in her eyes. He'd been afraid to learn that there was no room for him in her life. He'd been afraid to find out that she didn't, couldn't, wouldn't, love him.

Then he'd remembered one of her reasons for refusing to consider relocating. *I would worry about you,* she'd told him. *I couldn't cut you out of my life unless that was what you wanted.* So far she had taken most of the risks in their relationship—opening herself to him, setting herself up for possible rejection, trusting him, believing in him, giving herself freely to him.

Now it was time *he* took a risk.

He touched his hand to Julia's, his fingertips brushing across her cool skin in a gentle, silent goodbye. For all practical purposes, her life was over, but his still lay ahead. With Tess.

In the early-evening traffic, it took him nearly an hour to reach her apartment. The front door had been fortified with a sturdier double-key deadbolt, he noticed as he knocked. When there was no answer after his third knock, he walked to the end of the passageway and leaned against the wall. Just like old times, he thought with an uneasy smile.

He was restless and edgy, eager to see her, anxious to tell her that he loved her, fearful of how she might respond. He paced back and forth, checking his watch every fifteen minutes, shivering in the cold. If he could see her door from the parking lot . . .

The familiar thought made him smile faintly. It had been three weeks ago today since the first time he'd waited there. Three weeks, and so many lives had been changed. Donald Hopkins, Anthony Giamo and his driver were dead. Julia might as well be. Deke had lost an enemy and a friend, but he'd found something far more precious: the woman he'd waited a lifetime for. And Tess—how had her life changed? She had found strength and courage and determination, and a man who loved her. She'd been given a new appreciation of life, a better understanding of its fragile nature, and just possibly that baby she'd wanted for so long.

He looked once more at his watch. It was nearly eight o'clock. It was entirely possible, he admitted at last, that Tess wasn't spending the night here. She could be staying with her parents or her grandparents, or she could simply be visiting or shopping, like before. He would go home, he decided, and call until he reached her. Then he would meet her face-to-face and tell her that he loved her.

He had pushed himself away from the wall and started toward the stairs when he heard the soft thud of rubber soles climbing upward. Every muscle in his body tensing, he stood motionless and waited.

She came around the corner, a bag from a local department store in one hand, her keys in the other. She was going through the unfamiliar motions of unlocking the new lock when he stepped out of the shadows and softly spoke her name. She gasped, dropped her keys and stepped back all in a brief instant before recognizing him. When she did, she sagged against the doorjamb.

"I'm sorry. I should have realized you might still be a little jumpy."

"This is a wonderful job you have, Marshal, that keeps you hanging out in shadowy places late at night," she said dryly.

"Oh, there's more to it than that. Sometimes I get to protect beautiful women all by myself."

"And sometimes you have to kill terrible men."

Her words made his eyes darken and his voice lower. "I'm sorry you had to see that."

"I'm sorry you had to do it." She bent and picked up her keys, then just looked at him. He was so handsome, so dear, and she had missed him so much this past week. Hope—that he would call her, that he would want her, that someday he might love her—had carried her through the first few days, but slowly it had faded, leaving her with nothing but her own love and memories. And though she had assured herself at the cabin that memories would be enough, she had lied. They weren't enough. Nothing less than spending the rest of her life loving and living with Deke would ever be enough.

"So..." In spite of the emotions swirling inside her, she managed to make her voice sound close to normal. "How is Julia?"

"Alive, but in a coma. The doctors say she's suffered a lot of damage to the brain. She'll never be...Julia again."

"I'm sorry."

He studied her for a moment, then shook his head. "You are, aren't you?" Without waiting for an answer, he continued. "You should hate her for what she put you through. You should hate all of us."

"I pity her," Tess said softly. "Her ambition got her into something she couldn't handle, and eventually it destroyed her." Then she smiled wearily. "And how could I possibly hate you? You protected me. You saved my life. You gave me something very precious."

His gaze instantly dropped to her stomach while he did some swift calculations, then lifted to her face. "Are you...?"

She saw several things in his eyes—a little fear, a little dread, a lot of concern and...pleasure. She'd seen his pleasure too many times at the cabin to miss it. "No," she said gently. "At least, not that I know of. Deke..." She paused, words of love ready to spill out, then swallowed them and instead said, "I've missed you."

"I've missed you, too."

"Have you?" She gave a sad little shake of her head. "When you didn't call . . . well, I'm not naive. 'I'll call you' has to be one of the oldest brush-off lines in history. I thought you'd had a nice, pleasant fling, and now that the case was finished . . . so were we."

"Is that what you want?" he asked hesitantly, cautiously.

"I told myself it would be enough...but it isn't. I—" She stopped, blinking away the tears that filled her eyes, searching for a substitute for what she was about to say, for some word that he could accept without feeling bound by it. But the time for substitutes, for hiding behind words spoken and unspoken, was long past. "Deke, I—"

He touched his fingers to her mouth, silencing her. "You've made every first step in this relationship. You've taken every risk. It's my turn now. I love you, Tess. I don't know if there's room in your life for me now or if you want to forget me along with all the other unpleasantness of the last three weeks, but I need you, and I want you, and God help me, I love you."

The tears she had struggled to contain spilled over, sliding down her cheeks, tasting warm and salty on his lips as he kissed them away. He gathered her close, and she wrapped her arms around his neck.

Leaning back in his embrace so she could see his face more clearly, she smiled through the tears. "There will always be room for you in my life, because you *are* my life, and I could never forget you without forgetting myself. I need you, and I want you, and I love you, too. Always. Forever."

He kissed her then, with a gentleness that made her cry. With a tenderness that made her ache. And with a love that made her complete.

*   *   *   *   *

SILHOUETTE·INTIMATE·MOMENTS*

FEBRUARY FROLICS!

This February, we've got a special treat in store for you: four terrific books written by four brand-new authors! From sunny California to North Dakota's frozen plains, they'll whisk you away to a world of romance and adventure.

Look for

L.A. HEAT (IM #369) by Rebecca Daniels
AN OFFICER AND A GENTLEMAN (IM #370) by Rachel Lee
HUNTER'S WAY (IM #371) by Justine Davis
DANGEROUS BARGAIN (IM #372) by Kathryn Stewart

They're all part of February Frolics, coming to you from Silhouette Intimate Moments—where life is exciting and dreams do come true.

FF-1

 *Silhouette Books*®

proudly presents
the long-awaited "prequel" volume of

LOVE AND GLORY

by
LINDSAY McKENNA
Dawn of Valor

In the summer of '89, Silhouette Special Edition premiered three novels celebrating America's men and women in uniform: LOVE AND GLORY, by bestselling author Lindsay McKenna. Featured were the proud Trayherns, a military family as bold and patriotic as the American flag—three siblings valiantly battling the threat of dishonor, determined to triumph... in love and glory.

Now, discover the roots of the Trayhern brand of courage, as parents Chase and Rachel relive their earliest heartstopping experiences of survival and indomitable love, in

Dawn of Valor, Silhouette Special Edition #649.

This February, experience the thrill of LOVE AND GLORY—from the very beginning!

DV-1

You'll flip . . . your pages won't!
Read paperbacks *hands-free* with

Book Mate • I

The perfect "mate" for all your romance paperbacks

**Traveling • Vacationing • At Work • In Bed • Studying
• Cooking • Eating**

Perfect size for all standard paperbacks, this wonderful invention makes reading a pure pleasure! Ingenious design holds paperback books OPEN and FLAT so even wind can t ruffle pages – leaves your hands free to do other things. Reinforced, wipe-clean vinyl-covered holder flexes to let you turn pages without undoing the strap supports paperbacks so well, they have the strength of hardcovers!

Pages turn WITHOUT opening the strap

SEE-THROUGH STRAP

Reinforced back stays flat

Built in bookmark

BOOK MARK

BACK COVER HOLDING STRIP

10 x 7¼ opened
Snaps closed for easy carrying too

SILHOUETTE·INTIMATE·MOMENTS®

PAULA DETMER RIGGS
Forgotten Dream

AMNESIA!

Mat Cruz had come back to Santa Ysabel Pueblo to be healed. A car bomb had left him a widower with two young children—and no memory of the first twenty-six years of his life.

Susanna Spencer remembered Mat all too well. He had broken her heart once, and now she swore he would never do so again. He might be staying right next door, but that didn't mean she had to be neighborly—no matter how much she longed to relive the past.

Look for their story this month in FORGOTTEN DREAM (IM #364), by Paula Detmer Riggs. And if you enjoy your visit to Santa Ysabel, order these earlier books—TENDER OFFER (IM #314) and A LASTING PROMISE (IM #344)—by sending your name, address, zip or postal code, along with a check or money order (please do not send cash) for $2.95 each, plus 75¢ postage and handling, payable to Silhouette Reader Service to:

In the U.S.
3010 Walden Ave.
P.O. Box 1396
Buffalo, NY 14269-1396

In Canada
P.O. Box 609
Fort Erie, Ontario
L2A 5X3

Please specify book title(s) with your order.

FD-1

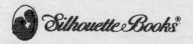
Silhouette Books®